BEAUTY AND THE BEACH

GRACIE RUTH MITCHELL

For my daughter, who said she wanted me to dedicate a book to her. Here you go, baby girl. Grow and flourish and be everything you want to be. I'll help you unfurl your wings so you can fly.

Contents

WELCOME TO SUNSET HARBOR

Sunset Harbor is a fictional island set off the west coast of Florida. Each book in the Falling for Summer series is set in this dreamy town and uses crossover characters and events, creating fun connections throughout the series. Be sure to read all seven books so you can fully experience the magic of Sunset Harbor!

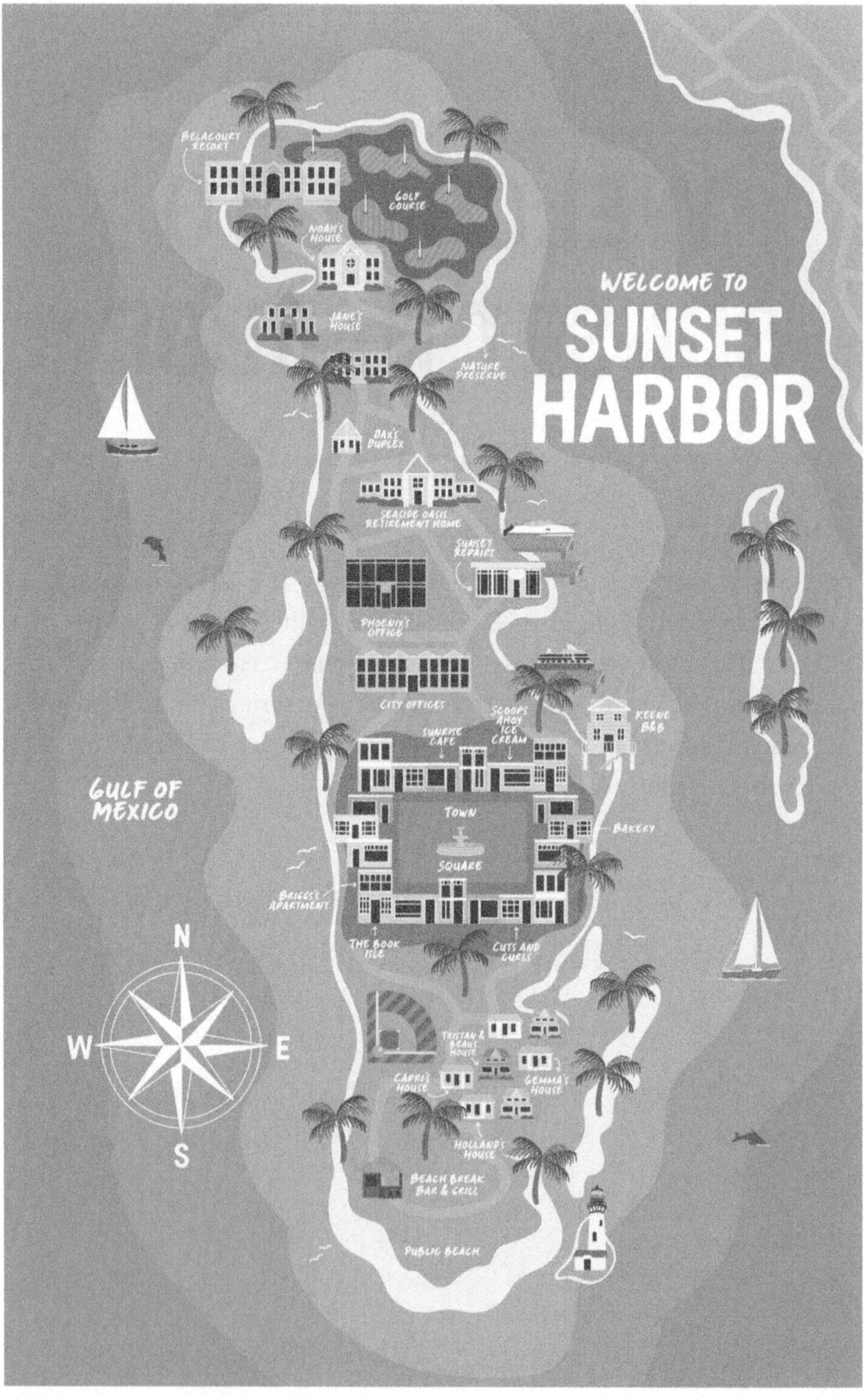

PROLOGUE

Phoenix

AT APPROXIMATELY SIX-THIRTY on the morning of May the second, Mavis Butterfield, the terminally ill matriarch and chairwoman of the Butterfield business dynasty, sent an email to all four of her children and all six of her grandchildren.

The subject line: *READ IT AND WEEP, PROGENY,* written in all caps and followed by one skull emoji and one poop emoji, the latter of which her secretary and her assistant both failed to talk her out of.

The contents: a link to a live document containing Mavis's last will and testament.

My mother, the eldest of the aforementioned Butterfield progeny, did indeed read the will. She read it before I even saw the email, because it was a Sunday, and I was still fast asleep in my California king after a sixty-hour work week. Then she called me—you guessed it—weeping.

It should be noted that my mother was not weeping because Mavis was terminally ill. Mavis might be my grandmother and my boss, but she is widely regarded as the most wicked human being alive, so most of us had eagerly made our peace with her impending death. The doctors had given her three months to live, much to the dismay of her children and grandchildren; I think I'm one of the few that wouldn't have preferred to hear three weeks instead. My dislike stops just short of wishing her dead.

"I've been staring at the doc for forty-five minutes, baby boy," my mother said in a blubbering voice that, over the phone, was nearly unintelligible. "She keeps changing things, right in front of my eyes."

"I'm thirty," I told her, sitting up and rubbing my eyes. "Stop calling me that." Then, despite knowing perfectly well that Mavis Butterfield has not one single humorous bone in her decrepit old body, I added, "And don't worry about it. It's probably a prank."

It was not a prank.

It was perfectly real—and perfectly brutal. Mavis continued to change things in the will at her questionable discretion, developments my family followed more closely than the stock market in the weeks that followed. Usually the changes were minor and petty—altered percentages or bequeathments. Sometimes the changes were less minor, though equally as petty—like when Mavis got drunk and removed entire sections.

Perfectly real. Perfectly brutal. And perfectly legally binding, according to the company's lawyer when I ferried over to the mainland to see him several days after the first instance of intoxicated deletions. Since Mavis kept her drunk changes after she'd sobered up and reviewed them, they were considered valid. I went into that meeting expecting a lengthy discussion full of explanations and technical jargon. But the lawyer just collapsed into his ergonomic chair, pinched the bridge of his nose like he had a headache, and then told me he needed a better benefits package so he could afford to see his therapist more often. "Insurance only covers once a week," he said.

"I'll see what I can do," I told him, my eyes lingering on

his shiny, sweat-beaded cue ball head. Anyone who works closely with Mavis should have access to mental health care and as many coping mechanisms as possible.

It was my most tried and true coping mechanism—denial, firm and absolute—that allowed me to handle these developments as the month wore on. I suffered through phone calls with tearful aunts and disgusted uncles, texts from cousins, and even a series of formal meetings with the matriarch herself, all by telling myself over and over again that these changes were not going to last. No matter what Mavis put in that document today or tomorrow or three weeks from now, when all was said and done, I would inherit Butterfield. I knew I was the best candidate. Mavis knew that too.

But at the end of the month, one tiny little text changed everything.

It was from my personal assistant, Wyatt, one of the few people in this world I actually trust, and it was only five words: *She added a new paragraph.*

Despite the fact that it was the middle of my day and I was neck deep in paperwork, meetings, and phone conferences, I pulled up the live doc on my desktop and began to search for the change, skimming the contents until I finally found the new section at the very end. I read it once, then twice, then three times. Then I picked up my phone, asked Wyatt to cancel my one o'clock, and hung up again, leaning back in my chair with just as much exhaustion as the lawyer had collapsed into his.

Married.

Married.

Mavis Butterfield was now requiring that her inheritor be legally and lawfully wed.

So I did the only thing I could do: I set out to find a wife...until Mavis's death do us part.

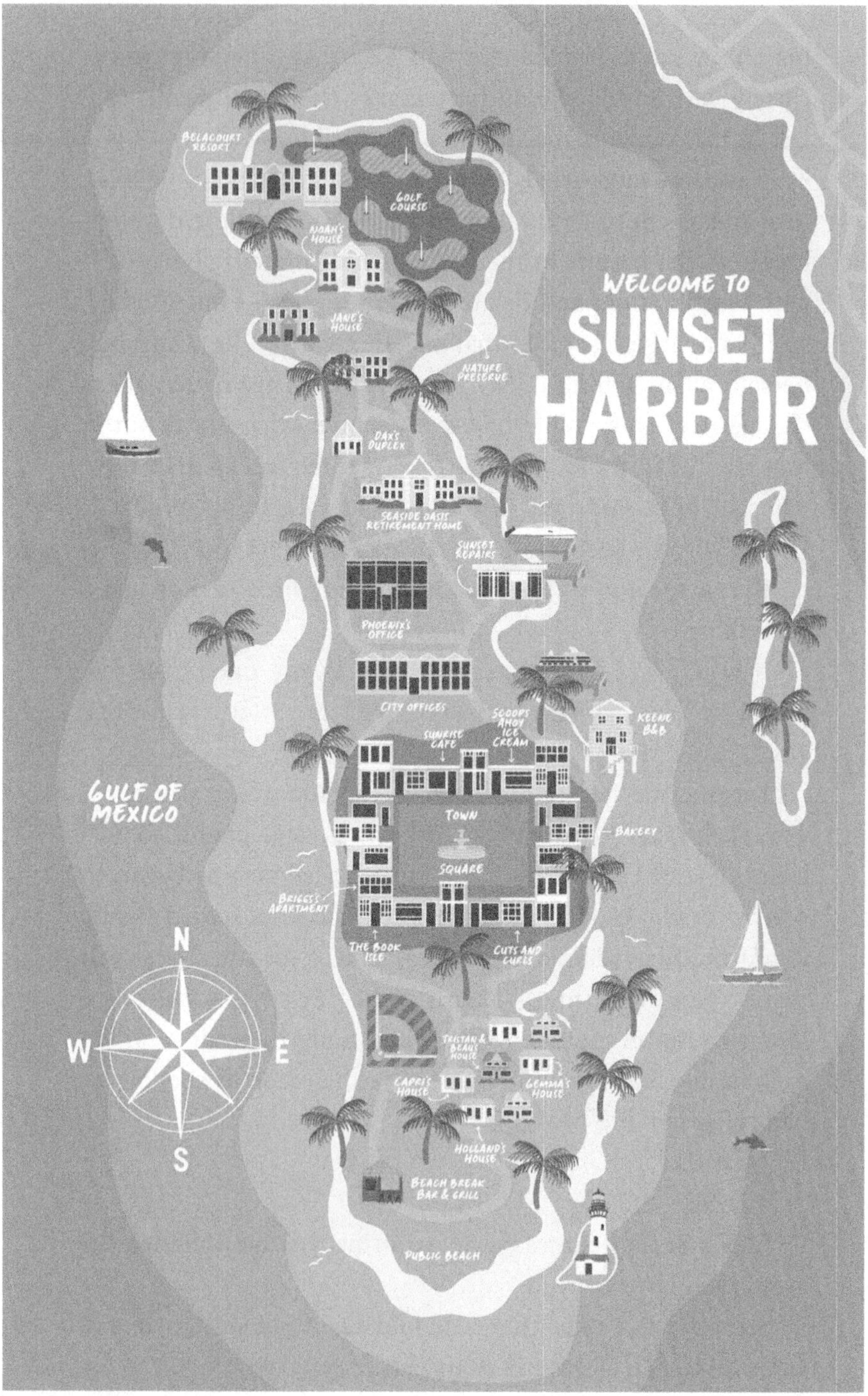

CHAPTER 1

Phoenix

I MAY BE A SINGLE MAN, and I may be in possession of a good fortune. No matter what universal acknowledgment says, however, I have never been in want of a wife.

I spent most of my life happily focusing on topics other than marriage. I figured it would happen when it happened, if at all. There are plenty of other things to occupy my time.

Leave it to Mavis to throw a wrench in my plans—or my lack of plans.

After receiving the unwelcome news that my grandmother expects me to marry if I want to inherit the family company, I spend the first two weeks of June trying to figure out how to find a wife. And as it turns out, there are a lot of people who have a lot of opinions about who I should marry and when.

My mother would love for me to choose someone beautiful from a wealthy background, someone who can be her informant on the inner life of her son—someone who'll be happy to provide for my mother financially. A trophy wife, devoted to me but equally devoted to my mother; that's what she wants for me. The number of women she's tried to put on my radar exceeds the number of women I have the mental space to keep track of.

My uncle Clarence and his son Lawrence, on the other

hand, would prefer for me not to get married at all. I've seen them a handful of times since Mavis's marriage decree, and they both look a little meaner than usual now that a new stipulation is in the works. Lawrence has an on-again, off-again woman—I don't think I can accurately call her a girl-friend, because that implies a degree of monogamy I know Lawrence to be incapable of—that he'll probably end up marrying so he can try to inherit instead of me. Neither he nor Clarence are above scare tactics and dirty hands to get what they want, so I have to keep an eye out for them.

Honestly, I'm not sure I'm much different. As callous as it may sound, right now I care more about inheriting Butter-field Paper and Sanitary than I do about finding a wife I love. Because I'll have time for romance later—but this is likely the only chance I'll get to take over the company. Mavis has been in and out of the hospital for months; I just visited her there, as a matter of fact. She was sleeping, thank goodness, but at least I can say I've done my duty as her grandson.

Once again, it may sound callous, but any moment could be her last.

So I need to get married quickly. Now. *Yesterday.*

Love can wait.

Unfortunately, this tagline is not inspiring to the women in my life—what few of them there are. Fewer still are the ones I'm not related to, and I can't imagine marrying any of them. I have a date lined up to go boating with a woman, but I think I'm going to cancel, because I don't really have feel-ings for her; and if I can't manage a date, how am I supposed to propose? I also refuse to get entangled with any of the women my mother tries to foist upon me, which leaves me with limited options.

I need someone I can be straight with, someone who will understand. Someone who will expect nothing from me and who won't think less of me for treating matrimony like a business transaction.

My assistant has ideas about this, and he keeps trying to bring them up.

He clears his throat, his glasses glinting as he looks at me in the rearview mirror. "If I may...you might consider Miss Blake—"

"No," I say, cutting him off before he can finish saying her name. Then I turn my head to stare pointedly out the window, watching the city zoom by as we head to the harbor where the ferry is docked. It's always strange to ride in cars when I visit the mainland, now that I've moved to Sunset Harbor—a little island off the coast where no cars are permitted.

"I really think she—"

"*No.*"

"Who do you suggest, then? Who else is there?" he says. I can hear the exasperation he's trying to conceal.

Wyatt is in his fifties, and his hair is graying more slowly now that we've left the high-powered corporate environment and switched over to an office on the island. Sometimes, though, I get the distinct impression that he blames me for any obvious display of aging.

"I don't know," I say, squeezing my lids shut and trying to banish *that woman* from my mind. "Just—not her."

"She wouldn't think less of you," Wyatt says.

"Only because her opinion of me can sink no lower," I retort, and he nods.

"Precisely."

Speaking of which...

"I wonder if she's gotten my gift yet," I say, pulling out my phone to check for any missed calls or messages.

"Your gift?" Wyatt says. He sounds skeptical—very wise.

"Mmm." I drop my phone on the leather seat next to me. I don't have anything from her, which means she hasn't found it yet. I'll hear from her when she does—loudly, possibly violently. She'll be furious.

A little smile twitches over my lips.

My smile grows when my phone begins buzzing. I look at the name on the screen, expecting it to be her, but it's not; it's my uncle Clarence. My expression vanishes abruptly, and I roll my eyes. Then I put the phone back down on the seat.

Thirty seconds later, it buzzes again.

I sigh and then answer the call. "It's well past end of day, Clarence," I say. "Any questions regarding the company will need to wait until morning."

"You little—"

I hold the phone away from my ear while Clarence curses; that prominent vein in his forehead is probably popping purple in his ruddy, pockmarked face.

I give him a few seconds, and then I return. "Are you done?" I say coldly.

"My sister spoils you," he says, his bitterness and resentment seeping from every word. "Just because you're the COO doesn't mean you can treat me like garbage. I'm your uncle, no matter what position you hold."

"My mother has never been present enough in my life to spoil me," I say. "And you and I have never had a familial relationship. Don't pretend otherwise. Why are you calling me outside of business hours?"

He's silent for a second; I can feel his dilemma. He called me for a reason, but now that I'm demanding an answer, he's feeling obstinate.

Finally he spits the words out. "To tell you to reconsider," he says. "Whatever you're scheming—"

8

"I'm wounded," I cut him off. "I would hardly call myself a schemer."

More creative cursing, and this time I can't help but smile a little. He's so easily provoked. I shouldn't enjoy that, but I do.

"Lawrence is going to get married soon," he says, "and he'll be ready to take over once your grandmother dies. He won't remove you from your position; he won't interfere in your plans. So give it up, all right?"

He's probably right; Lawrence wouldn't fire me or demote me. He's too much of a coward. But he would find the pettiest ways to make my life miserable, and he would run the company straight into the ground.

There are so many things I'd like to say to Clarence, frustrations to vent and accusations to level. Ultimately, though, they wouldn't matter, because they wouldn't change a thing. So I keep it brief.

"No," I say.

Then I hang up.

"Drive a bit faster, if you can," I say to Wyatt. I let my head drop back against the seat. "We'll miss the last ferry of the day if we don't hurry."

WE MAKE THE FERRY, but only just. It's a twelve-minute ride we spend in silence, for which I'm grateful; there's too much going on in my head right now, a chaotic whirlwind of family and work and my marriage dilemma. When we reach the island, I drop Wyatt off at home—using a golf cart, because that's the only kind of vehicle Sunset Harbor allows—and then I head to my office.

I've just finished unlocking the door when my phone buzzes again, and I check it with a sigh. I don't think I can stomach another conversation with my family right now. I straighten, though, when I see who's calling, and my exhaustion gives way to a burst of energy.

"What do you want?" I say when I answer.

The voice that speaks is clear, matter-of-fact, but simmering with anger. "I'm going to run you over with my car," Holland Blakely says.

"Don't be stupid," I say. "You don't have a car."

"Did you put a dead fish in my mailbox?" she demands.

I let out an obviously fake gasp, flipping the office lights on; the fluorescent buzz fills the room as I answer. "I would never."

"Yes, you would. This is disgusting. You better watch your back—"

"I think you'll find," I interrupt her smoothly, "that we could now be considered even, and that if you retaliate, I will have no choice but to do the same."

"What do you mean, we're even? I did nothing to provoke—"

"Did you or did you not mix Skittles and M&Ms into my giant bowl of Reese's Pieces?" I say, passing the empty row of cubicles as I head to my office.

Silence.

"And did you or did you not replace the cream in every single Oreo in the package with toothpaste?" I go on.

Another silence, and I nod. "I keep exactly two sources of sugar in my home, both of which are sacred to me, and you know this. You *know* that's the only sugar I eat. And you tampered with—"

But I break off as Holland begins to laugh. It's not a fun, joking laugh; it's merciless, evil.

10

"Are those the only two you've found?" she says through her witch's cackle.

My eyes widen as I step into my office. "The only two—wait. Are there more? What did you do?"

"Nothing you didn't deserve," she says, and her laughter dies abruptly. When she speaks again, I can *hear* her facial expression in her voice—casual, nonchalant, eyes gleaming with triumph. "Because you changed the name of every *S* contact in my phone to *Salvador* and every *D* contact to *Dalí*."

My anger dissipates as an evil smile of my own unfurls over my lips. Dalí's art has always freaked her out. "I did do that," I say, grinning. "I have no regrets."

"I loathe you with the fire of a thousand suns."

"I'm heartbroken," I say flatly.

"And I'm hanging up now."

I roll my eyes. "So soon?"

"Don't forget to visit Nana Lu," Holland says. "She, unlike me, has poor taste in men, so she's very excited to play bingo with you."

"I never forget about your grandmother," I say.

"Good," she says. She pauses for just a moment and then speaks again. "Also—"

"What?" I say impatiently.

"Buy some fresh vegetables or something," she says. "I poked around while I was over there tampering with your sugar supply. You have a billion protein supplements, but all that's in your vegetable crisper is one wilted head of lettuce. There's no way you're getting enough vitamins and minerals."

"I'll determine my own diet, thanks."

"Fine," she says with a snort. "Get scurvy." She starts to say something else, but I don't care to listen; I hang up instead, relishing how angry it will make her. Then I call my assistant.

"When you get a moment, log in and change the passcode for my front door," I tell him.

"Mmm," he says; I can imagine him bobbing his head and making note of it in the leather folder he always carries. "And the garage?"

I hesitate only a moment. There's no reason Holland Blakely should ever *need* to get into my house. But in case she does...

"Leave the garage," I say.

I'll set the alarm so that if she enters through that door, the police will show up. The thought fills me with joy, and by the time I go home for the day, I'm in a significantly better mood.

CHAPTER 2

Holland

A GIRL'S gotta do what a girl's gotta do, and sometimes a girl's gotta lie through her teeth.

For the record, I don't consider myself a liar, pathological or otherwise. But Nana Lu would be absolutely horrified to hear the real reason I'm picking up more shifts and odd jobs everywhere I can. Her dentures would fall right out of her mouth. I can't do that to her; I don't think her soft, ancient heart could take it.

So I lie.

"I just want some extra spending money," I say in a voice loud enough for her to hear, but not so loud she feels like I'm patronizing her in her old age. It's a fine line. I sandwich the phone between my cheek and my shoulder, freeing my hands to straighten the stack of papers on the table in front of me before the morning breeze can ruffle them further. "So I can take myself out to dinner and get a new pair of shoes. That kind of thing."

It's a low blow, playing on her desire for her granddaughters to treat themselves, but I need her to buy my story.

And it seems to do the trick. "Oh, good," she says in a bubblegum-sweet voice, feeble and trembling and full of love. "You deserve some new shoes."

I actually deserve a swift kick in the rear for being such an idiot, but I force myself to respond. "Thanks, Nana," I say, and despite the slither of guilt low in my gut, my smile is genuine. Somehow that makes me feel even worse. "I need to go, but I'll talk to you later, okay?"

"That's just fine," she says. "Come by soon and show me your new shoes."

"I will," I say, swallowing and wondering where I'm going to get new shoes now that I'm officially living paycheck to paycheck. "Love you, Nana."

"You too. Don't forget to treat yourself to something nice, sweetie. Bye bye."

My own farewell comes out as nothing more than a miserable whisper. Once I hang up and shove my phone into my back pocket, I have to take several deep breaths to dispel my discomfort. I lift one hand to shield my eyes from the sun, already feeling the prickle of sweat on the back of my neck despite the early hour.

I hate lying to Nana. To anyone, actually, but especially to Nana.

But lying is really my only option here. I can't tell my sweet, precious, feeble old grandmother that I was scammed out of every last cent in my checking account. I *definitely* can't tell her what I was trying to buy. I haven't told anybody but Cat, and I'll die before anyone else hears.

There's embarrassing, and then there's *embarrassing*. Unfortunately for me, my attempted purchase is the latter.

It's my own fault. Buying things in the middle of the night is never a good idea, for one, and especially not when you've arrived there via a social media ad.

But I was lying there on the cramped sofa in Nana's living room—or my living room, I guess, now that Nana has moved permanently to the senior living center—debating whether to go back to the bedroom or stay on the couch, and I was just so *uncomfortable*. I don't sleep well on that couch, but I sleep even worse in my bed after I've had a nightmare, so I stayed. I got a drink of water from the ever-dripping faucet, ran into the kitchen table and fell on my bad knee hard enough that I shed actual tears, and then I collapsed on the sofa. I knew I would wake up with a crick in my neck.

So I looked up affordable alternative seating. And bean-bags, as it turns out, are expensive. I gave up and scrolled social media for a while—another unwise decision, I'm aware —and not two minutes after I started, the algorithm fed me an ad I couldn't pass up. I forked over my money *so* fast...and my checking account turned up empty twenty-four hours later.

I called the bank first, but they said they'd need to do an investigation. Then I called Beau Palmer over at the police station, but he said there's not a lot they can do at this point. So here I am, scrimping and scrounging and lying to my grandmother.

I square my shoulders and take another deep breath, reminding myself that I'm just trying to preserve Nana's health and peace of mind. Then I force myself to think about something else—anything else, as long as I'm not dwelling on my newly broke status. The summer weather, the adoption fair I'm currently helping set up in the town square, my job at the salon—I'd even be happy to think about Phoenix right now, that dead-fish-vandalizing bane of my existence whose voice I keep hearing in my head, telling me to put my savings in a designated savings account instead of just keeping it all in checking.

I hate when he's right. He gets this smug look on his face, like he loves nothing more than proving me wrong, the corners of his lips curling up—

And on second thought, maybe I'd better not think about him either. I'll only end up feeling irritated and annoyed.

So I'm grateful when Jane Hayes appears in front of me, popping into my field of vision from out of nowhere. Maybe some of her lightheartedness will rub off on me, and I'll be able to get my mind onto happier things.

"Hi," she says, smiling cheerfully. She's dressed similar to me in denim cutoffs and a t-shirt, and her brown hair is pulled back into a cute ponytail. "How's it going?" She casts a quick glance at me and then at the table I'm supposed to be setting up. "Anything else you need over here?"

I look down at my table too. "I don't think so," I say. "I'm really just going to be keeping the till and handing out pamphlets."

Jane nods, her ponytail swaying slightly. "It's nice of you to help," she says. "Patrice seemed worried they wouldn't have enough staff when she came to talk to me about the permit."

"Well, I'll be here until noon," I say. "Staring at all the cute animals from afar."

"But you're allergic, right?" Jane says. I'm not even surprised she knows this, though I don't remember telling her; Jane knows everything about everybody.

"I am," I say. "To dogs. But I'll stay over here." I smile at her. "Hey, how was your date the other night?"

Jane grimaces but doesn't answer, and I laugh.

"That expression doesn't look too promising."

"I know," she says with a sigh. "We'll see." Then she tucks one hand into her pocket. "Well, I've got to head out. Have fun here!"

"I will," I tell her. "See you later!"

She hurries off, waving over her shoulder again with one last smile, and I turn back to my table. I pull the rest of the brochures and pamphlets out of the paper bag Patrice gave me—fliers from local businesses, mostly, that we're promoting as thanks for the donations they made to this event—and arrange them neatly around the cash register. Then I plop myself down in the metal folding chair behind me.

I will be glued to this spot for the next three hours, and when the adoption fair is over, I will have fifty more dollars in my bank account. It's not a ton, but it's better than nothing. It's nice of Patrice to pay me at all; realistically, if she'd asked me to help for free, I would have been tempted. Pets are family, after all, and my family is what makes my life worth living, even if sometimes I have to lie to them about things I've been buying in the middle of the night. I already lost my brother, and the grief that followed tore my family apart; without my little sister and Nana, I'd be lost.

A sudden, painful twinge in my knee pulls me out of my thoughts; I grimace, rubbing it. I try to massage around the knee cap, but the bruising from the other night makes this difficult, and I'm just about to stand and hunt down some ibuprofen when I hear the sound of a throat clearing above me.

I don't even have to look—I know who it is. He's blocking the sun, but a hot wave of irritation settles over my skin anyway. I don't attempt a neutral expression; I let my dislike show clearly and blatantly when I finally give him my attention, turning to see what he wants.

And sure enough, looming right over my chair is my least favorite person on this entire island. He's got on his usual custom-fitted suit, briefcase in hand, and he's staring at me with a mixture of irritation and exasperation.

"What are you doing here?" I say, blinking up at him.

"I could ask you the same question," Phoenix says. He

casts a glance around the square, the breeze playing in his classic businessman-styled hair. "Is this the adoption fair?"

"Maybe," I say. "But the farmer's market is setting up too." I point at the stalls and carts on the other side of the square, their owners arranging things neatly. Dill O'Donnell and his wife Mildred seem to be arguing over where their watermelons should go, and Mildred's already got her table of homemade jewelry out.

"You're here for the adoption fair," Phoenix says in a flat voice, pointing at the sign on my table that says *Sunset Harbor Animal Haven*. "You cry at adoption videos on YouTube, Amsterdam."

"So?" I say, willing myself not to be embarrassed and ignoring the nickname.

"And you're allergic to dogs."

"That's why I'm all the way over here," I say slowly, gesturing to my table, "and the dogs are all the way over there." I point to the dog enclosures—which, yes, I specifically set myself up far away from.

But he exhales and rubs his temples. "And here I thought your decision-making skills couldn't be any worse. Come on." He leans down and wraps firm fingers around my wrist, tugging me to my feet. "We're leaving."

He's like this; he thinks he can barge in and tell me how to live my life, like I haven't been doing just fine for the last twenty-seven years. He says it's because he made a promise to my older brother before he died, but I know the truth: he just really loves making people miserable, and he especially loves making *me* miserable.

I yank my arm out of his grasp and sit resolutely back in my metal folding chair. "No," I say, and I look directly at him so I can enjoy that expression he makes when he's trying not to get annoyed. It's a little crease in his forehead, one that pushes his black brows to shadow his eyes like storm clouds.

"I'm not going anywhere," I go on. Goodness knows I need the money. "Patrice is paying me to be here, Emu. I'm staying."

He looks around quickly, undoubtedly checking if anyone is in earshot, and then he leans closer, caging me in with one hand on the back of my chair and the other on the table in front of me. He smells like leather and mahogany, and I want to punch him in his stupid face.

I want to never look at him again. I want to forget everything that's happened to us, every nightmare that keeps me awake, every painful memory.

But he's never seemed to want the same thing, regardless of how poorly we get along. "Give me one more ridiculous bird name," he breathes, his eyes flashing, "and see what happens—"

"Emu," I repeat loudly, snickering even though I know it will annoy him. But why call him Phoenix—an *imaginary* bird —when there are so many *real* bird names available? "Be grateful it wasn't *Titmouse*"—a nickname I've used before and will absolutely use again—"or *Rooster* or *American Woodcock* —" But I break off as he moves, my grin dying as he reaches for me. "Wait," I say. His hands find my waist; my eyes widen. "What are you—wait. Hey. *Hey!*"

He's not listening; he's too busy hauling me out of my chair.

"Let go right—now—" I say, trying to land hits on whatever bits of him I can find. His grip tightens as I continue to squirm. "Put—me—*down*—"

But my words turn into a yelp of surprise as he hoists me over his shoulder right there—in the middle of the town square, in front of Patrice and the rest of the shelter employees and the poor animals who just want to find homes —he slings me up like a freaking sack of potatoes.

I call him a name that Nana Lu would make me gargle with soapy water for using.

"Tsk, tsk," he says, sounding smugger than I've ever heard him before. "Language, Amsterdam." I can hear that curl in his lips and the flash of triumph in his eyes. "I'm sorry"—he grips me tighter around the thighs, sounding not at all sorry—"but I promised your brother I'd keep an eye on you, which means I can't let you die of anaphylaxis."

"Yeah, right," I say with a scoff as all the blood rushes to my head, my blonde hair falling around me and obscuring my vision. "This is about the bird name." I pound my fists on his back. "Put me down!"

"No," he says. "Now smile nice and big for all the people who are watching you flail around like an idiot."

The square is surrounded by shops and businesses on all four sides—including Cuts and Curls, where I work—so I have no doubt there are a lot of people seeing this. I don't smile, though. I pinch him as hard as I can in the side instead.

He doesn't say anything; he doesn't even flinch. He just says one thing: "You smell like dead fish."

CHAPTER 3

Holland

THERE ARE a few things you need to understand about Phoenix Park.

Phoenix Fact #1: He's hot. Like, stupidly hot. And he knows it. Taller than is frankly necessary; gorgeous tanned skin; thick blue-black hair that is absolutely wasted on him. If I had hair like that, I would grow it down to my butt and flip it around in people's faces all day, and they would thank me for it. "Thank you, Holland, for blessing us with the existence of your hair. Thank you for poking us in the eyes with your luscious locks." That's what they would say.

Phoenix Fact #2: He's rich—and at the risk of sounding like a broken record—I would even say *stupidly* rich. He's the eldest grandson of the Butterfield corporation or company or whatever it's called, and the only grandchild who was deemed competent enough to hold an executive position.

I will grudgingly admit that while his hair is wasted on him, his wealth is mostly not. He lives in a nice-but-not-exorbitant home on the west side of the island, and he doesn't throw money around. He also works a billion hours a week, so it's not like he's lazy. This might be the only positive thing I can say about him.

Phoenix Fact #3: Our relationship is nothing short of overtly hostile. We didn't get along when we met years ago, and we don't get along now—especially since we knew each other mainly through my brother, and Trev has passed. There are no thinly veiled barbs, no passive aggressive snipes; we go to war whenever we're together, and we don't waste time pretending otherwise. *Time is a precious commodity,* after all, which is what Phoenix says and happens to be one of the only things we agree on.

This sort of relationship would be tragic if I were pining after him, but I am decidedly not. He's a dream turned nightmare, the kind of man who's sexy on paper but less sexy when you're the one who has to put up with him day in and day out. Bossy, arrogant, overbearing—everything I would expect from Butterfield's youngest-ever chief operating officer.

And don't let the idea of some giant, successful company seduce you. In romance novels I read about thirty-year-old executives working at any number of cool, suave, urban corporations; there is none of that here. Yes, Butterfield is one of the most profitable companies in its sector, and yes, it's a household name, but it's not doing vaguely defined tech work or app development or financial advising. Butterfield is not a shiny, sexy, Fortune 500 company.

Butterfield is a tampon company.

Or, rather, they started out as a tampon company. Tampons made from eco-friendly, nontoxic, biodegradable materials. They then moved on to incorporate other sanitary products—pads, mostly, along with wipes, toilet paper, and diapers for babies and senior citizens alike. And though I will never, ever, *ever* tell Phoenix this...Butterfield's tampons are pretty great. As far as tampons go, anyway.

I'm not really a pads girl. They give me wedgies.

"I talked to your grandmother last night," Phoenix says as

he walks, pulling me back to the present. My fist stops mid-punch where I'm hitting his lower back.

"So?" It's something he's done for years, ever since Trevor died. Nana Lu adores him. She showers him with love, and they trade stories about Trev, and he's a total gentleman to her.

I guess if he's going to be a gentleman to someone, it should be Nana.

"She said she was going to ask you why you've been taking extra shifts at the salon," he says. "Hold your breath; we're passing the dogs."

I inhale shallowly and wait; Phoenix's stride lengthens as he picks up his pace, and I hold my hair aside with one hand so I can wave my apology to Patrice with the other. She watches with a look of bemusement as I disappear out of sight over the shoulder of this caveman. When the dog enclosures are no longer visible, I let go of my breath.

"Don't use Nana Lu to pry into my business," I tell him. "You have your own grandma. And put me down or I'm going to spray paint every nickname I've ever given you all over the outside of your office."

"My grandmother is psycho, and Nana would be very disappointed to learn you'd done something like that," he replies, and I grit my teeth.

He's enjoying this thoroughly; I can hear it in his voice. And my hair might be swinging around me again, but I don't need to see to know people are staring. I look like an idiot.

"Put me down," I say, the words clipped. "Immediately."

"I will," he says, "just as soon as you tell me what's going on."

"Nothing's going on!" I pound my fist against his back again.

A faint snort of disbelief reaches me. "You're clearly lying. Nana says you're working more shifts even though you're dead tired as it is, and now you're trying to work at the adoption fair. Plus," he adds reasonably, "your voice is going high-pitched."

Dang it. He's right.

I clear my throat. "Nothing is going on," I repeat. "Nothing is wrong. It's just work. You work all the time; why can't I?"

"You can," he says, "but you usually don't. Tell me and I'll put you down. Do you need money? Did something happen?"

I could scream right now, and Phoenix's shoulder is digging into my hips, and I can feel my pulse in my ears.

"Fine!" The word explodes out of me, loud and abrupt, but I don't quiet myself. I just keep talking to the middle of his back. "Good grief. You couldn't possibly be more invasive, could you?" Heat is rising in my cheeks, and it's only partly because I'm hanging upside down. "I need money, okay? Yes. That's it. That's all. Can we drop it now?"

"See?" he says as I feel his hands around my waist once more, and three seconds later, my world is righting itself. "That wasn't hard."

I stumble for a second, finding my footing and looking around to see where we've stopped. The back of the salon, I realize as I spot the glass door that leads to the small lot—unnecessary, since there are no cars on the island. Even from here I swear I can smell the scent of hair product wafting from the little red-brick building.

"You're the worst," I say, turning to Phoenix and forcing myself not to smack him. "Did you know that?"

"I've heard," he says with a little smirk. "Now tell me why you need money, Amsterdam."

"It's none of your business," I say with a scowl. It's true; Phoenix doesn't need to know my embarrassing story.

He doesn't need to know what I tried to buy: a dog bed.

A *human-sized* dog bed, for twenty-four-ninety-nine. That's the product that got me to enter my card information on a website I'd never heard of at two in the morning: a human-sized dog bed, about four feet long with poofy edges and a built-in pillow.

It looked plush. It looked soft. It looked *comfortable*. I was sold.

"None of your business," I say again, muttered this time.

But he just hums, his dark brows quirking skeptically. The sun overhead loves the angles of his face, his sharp cheekbones, his straight nose. "I disagree," he says. His mouth twists into a grimace as he stares at me, and for a moment, it seems as though he's debating with himself. He looks torn, reluctant, like he's about to do something he doesn't want to do.

"All right," he says, a muscle twitching in his jaw. "Fine. It's possible—I might be able to help you. *Might*," he adds quickly, like coming to my aid is hurting him.

But it always pains him to offer me help, and he always offers anyway. He's constantly in my space, offering his unasked-for advice, trying to take care of me in his weird, overbearing way.

"I don't need help," I say automatically.

This claim is a little less true; I do need help. But I want to help myself. Is that really so bad? Is it really so wrong, trying to stand on my own two feet instead of turning to him for everything?

Because here's the thing: he doesn't actually *want* to help me. If it weren't for Trevor, he would have nothing to do with me. But because he and my brother were as close as brothers themselves—and because the three of us were together when Trevor died—he clings to that misplaced sense of duty.

It's nice in theory, I guess, but he's not sincere, and he dislikes me as much as I dislike him. Why would I put myself in his debt?

"You need help," Phoenix says, like he can hear everything I'm thinking.

I shake my head, still feeling the blood pound in my ears.

He rolls his eyes. "You need to see a doctor about your knee—"

"My knee will be fine, not that your little caveman show did any good there—"

"And I know you've been helping your sister—"

"Maggie is fine too—"

"And you're paying for Nana to stay in the senior center," he finishes. His hands clench into fists, and that little muscle jumps in his jaw again. "So stop being stupid and let me help you."

"I'm not going to just take your money!" I say, stomping my foot—and regretting it instantly when another twinge of pain ricochets through my knee.

"I never said you'd be taking my money," he snaps. "It's a job, idiot. I'm offering you a job."

The words I was ready to spit out die instead; I narrow my eyes at him, and he crosses his arms, looking expectantly at me.

"A job?" I say.

He gives a little jerk of his head. "A job." Then, pausing just briefly, he goes on, "Or—I guess—maybe an arrangement."

That feels ominous, especially since his face has gone oddly blank, devoid of any expressive hints. I shake my head again, swallowing my sudden spike of nervousness.

"No," I say, and before he can respond, I'm turning around. "Thanks, but no thanks. You mind your business, and I'll mind mine. Okay?" It's little more than a wish, because Phoenix has never once minded his own business— not even when we first met, before we knew each others' names, before I learned he was Trev's roommate. He was invasive even then.

He says something under his breath as I walk away, but I don't hear what it is.

WELCOME TO
SUNSET
HARBOR

BELACOURT RESORT

GOLF COURSE

NOAH'S HOUSE

JANE'S HOUSE

NATURE PRESERVE

DAX'S DUPLEX

SEASIDE OASIS RETIREMENT HOME

SUNSET REPAIRS

PHOENIX'S OFFICE

CITY OFFICES

SUNRISE CAFE

SCOOPS AHOY ICE CREAM

KEENE B&B

TOWN SQUARE

BAKERY

BRIGGS'S APARTMENT

THE BOOK ISLE

CUTS AND CURLS

GULF OF MEXICO

TRISTAN & BEAU'S HOUSE

CAPRI'S HOUSE

GEMMA'S HOUSE

HOLLAND'S HOUSE

BEACH BREAK BAR & GRILL

PUBLIC BEACH

N
W   E
S

CHAPTER 4

Nine Years Ago

Holland

"MY BEAUTIFUL BLOSSOMING BUTTERFLY," I say, my face pressed up against the closed bathroom door, the white wood probably leaving imprints in my skin. "You're turning into a *woman!*"

"Holl," my baby sister whines. The sound echoes through the little bathroom and then out into the tiny third-floor walk-up I share with two other girls. "Can you please just go get me some pads or tampons or something instead of being all dramatic?"

I roll my eyes, placing my hands on my hips. "Fine. Yes," I say to the bathroom door. "So sassy. But are you sure there aren't any under the sink? There used to be a box there, I'm pretty sure—"

"I already checked!" Maggie says, her voice muffled. I hear the sound of a cupboard door opening and then closing. "The box is empty. How is that possible? Three girls live here."

"All right, all right." I bustle over to the front door, slipping my sandals on, and then move back to the bathroom door. "I'm hurrying," I say. "And when I get back I'll instruct

29

you in the noble female art of blood removal from clothing—"

"Holland!" Maggie wails.

I grin, giving the bathroom door a little pat. "I'll be back ASAP. If anyone tries to break in, kick them in the teeth."

Maggie's flat voice returns through the bathroom door. "You have to know that's not part of my skill set."

I just laugh.

The campus corner market is one block away, a distance I cover more quickly than I normally would. September in Florida is still warm, but the wind is stronger today, blowing my hair around my face. I don't stop to wrangle it into submission; I just keep going, tucking it behind my ears as I move.

I don't remember when I got my first period, but I do know that my mother wasn't particularly helpful; I'm glad this is happening while Maggie is here visiting me and Trev rather than at home. I've been showing her around town, and Trev has been showing her around the university. I wanted her to come to some of my cosmetology classes at the beauty school, but she was decidedly more interested in Trev's engineering courses. It's probably for the best; our parents would flip if she, too, decided to eschew a traditional college education in favor of *hair and makeup nonsense that you'll never earn a living with, Holland, so don't think for a second we're going to pay for something like that.*

I sigh, shake my head, and pull the heavy glass door open, stepping into the corner mart. Mariah Carey sings a Christmas song three months too early over the tinny speakers as I grab a shopping basket and hurry to the pharmacy and health section. I choose the cheapest packet of pads, the cheapest box of tampons, and then I swerve past the candy aisle for some chocolate—a necessity.

There's a long enough line when I reach the checkout that my heart sinks, but I queue up anyway and wait the ten minutes it takes for my turn to come. I load everything from my basket onto the conveyor belt as quickly as possible, glancing over my shoulder at the person behind me to make sure they're not looking too impatient—and holy *crap*, he's hot. Tall with black hair and black eyes, dressed in a suit that looks totally out of place in this little corner market—he looks young enough to be a university student, but he should be in a board room somewhere.

I clear my throat, jerking my attention back to my order before the guy notices me staring at him. I swipe my card, my toes tapping anxiously in my thrifted sneakers. I've been here too long already. I'm just tucking my card back in my wallet when the card reader lets out a sound—not a cute little blip or a bird-like chirrup, but a loud, angry beep that's accompanied by a flashing red light. That beep reverberates through my skull, the soundtrack to my sinking heart.

Denied.

"Uh," the cashier says, looking suddenly awkward. She can't be more than a few years older than Maggie—sixteen, maybe—and her forehead is shiny, her eyes rimmed with eyeliner that's much too dark for her natural coloring. "Do you want to try again, or…?"

"I have cash," I say quickly, fumbling to open the cash flap of my wallet.

It's fine. This is fine. Everything is fine. Tuition must have gone through at the same time as insurance. It could happen to anybody. I'll get paid on Friday; I can manage until then.

I pull out the wad of neatly tucked bills, my hands trembling as I flip through them, my horror growing with every millisecond that passes.

No—no—*no.*

Ones. These are all *ones*.

"Excuse me," a clipped voice says from somewhere behind me. His voice is smooth and deep and slightly impatient, which is how I know it must be the hot guy in the suit. Hot guys in suits have beautiful voices, and they're always in a hurry.

"Yeah," I say, trying to keep my composure as I do some rapid math in my head. If I get rid of the chocolate bars and keep the tampons—

But my train of thought comes to a screeching halt when I'm nudged sideways, the suit guy stepping into my field of vision.

"Allow me, please," he says, giving me only the briefest of glances before extending his arm, a shiny black card in his hand.

"No," I say, grabbing his arm and pushing it away. "That's kind, but I'm really—"

"Please don't mistake this for kindness," he says, pulling out of my grip. "I'm in a hurry, and I frankly don't have time to stand around waiting while you figure this out." Then he turns his gaze to the cashier, who's watching with wide eyes. He points to the bags on the counter. "Is this all?"

I gape at him as a twinge of irritation plucks at my insides. It seems his personality is not nearly as pretty as his exterior.

"Um," the cashier says, looking back and forth between me and the man. "Yes?"

"What's that?" the man says, pointing to one of the bags —out of which is poking the large box of tampons. He frowns, moving forward and pushing the bag down, revealing more of the box. "No," he says, shaking his head. "Absolutely not."

That twinge of irritation grows stronger. What the heck is even going on right now?

"Excuse me," I say faintly. "What exactly do you think you're doing?" There's blood boiling under my skin, a furious blush arising because this man has just revealed to the entire line waiting behind us—and it is *quite* the line—that I can't even afford tampons right now.

"I'm not paying for that junk," he says, pointing at the tampons.

"They're not *junk*," I say, my voice heated. "A woman's menstrual cycle is a normal biological function—"

"I *mean*," the man says, cutting me off with a roll of his dark eyes, "I'm not paying for that brand. Calm down, please." Then he turns to the bag boy, whose pimply face has gone pale. "You." He points at the box of tampons. "Take these back and grab a box of Butterfield instead." Then he glances at me, frowns, and says, "Better make it two boxes. The kind for normal flow, please."

The *audacity*.

"Heavy flow," I manage to say. I think my brain has short-circuited. I can't think of any other explanation for what's happening right now. Sadly, I also can't think of a way out. Maggie is waiting for me at my place, probably scared and nervous, and I'm wasting time here. I'll figure out how to pay the stranger back later; right now I just need to swallow my pride and get home to my little sister. "Heavy flow."

The hot suit guy cocks his dark brow at me. "Do you really insist upon that?"

Unbelievable.

"What—who—who do you think you are?" I say instead of answering him. "Are you going to be picky about what kind of tampon I use? The heavy flow ones are more cost-efficient. You can keep them in for like twenty-four hours—"

"I strongly recommend against that," he says, another frown creasing his forehead. "The maximum I would recommend is eight hours—"

"What kind of psycho are you?" I say, stomping my foot. My already fraying patience is wearing thinner by the second. "Do you get off on this kind of thing? If you're going to buy my groceries for me, just buy them! If not, stop talking. I thought you said you were in a hurry?"

The man's lips twist at this, but he just grunts, and I feel a petty stab of satisfaction.

Got you there, you weirdo.

"I'm sure there was a 'thank you' in there somewhere," he says after a second of glaring at me. "But fine. Just so you're aware, those"—he points to the box of tampons—"are full of synthetic junk that's horrible for disposal. They will sit in a landfill for a hundred years and remain in pristine condition. Butterfield are biodegradable with organic cotton—"

"I. Do. Not. *Care,*" I hiss at him, turning on my heel and poking him hard in the chest.

Ooh, muscular.

"I am broke," I say, seething, "and my little sister just got her first period, and I need supplies for her, and I need her to believe that I've got my crap together so that she doesn't worry. All right? So I am buying the cheapest tampons and the cheapest pads, and I would very much like for you to take your commentary and shove it up your—"

But I break off and stumble out of the way as the man bumps me to the side—not at all gently—and swipes his card. The little light that flashed red at me turns green for him, accompanied by the kind of blip I was denied in favor of my angry beep.

I swallow, relief and humiliation warring for control of my mind and my body. "Thank you," I say stiffly, grabbing the plastic bags and hurrying out of the way. "I would be happy to pay you back on Friday."

"Please don't bother," he says, like I expected he would.

I just jerk my head in a nod. "In that case, thank you. I sincerely hope we never meet again."

"Likewise," the man says, his voice flat. "Have a lovely day."

I leave so quickly I almost trip, but I don't turn back or look at him again. I book it back to my little sister, and I forget all about the man in the suit.

WELCOME TO
SUNSET HARBOR

GULF OF MEXICO

BELACOURT RESORT

NOAH'S HOUSE

JANE'S HOUSE

GOLF COURSE

NATURE PRESERVE

OAK'S DUPLEX

SEASIDE OASIS RETIREMENT HOME

SUNSET REPAIRS

PHOENIX'S OFFICE

CITY OFFICES

SCOOPS AHOY ICE CREAM

SUNRISE CAFE

KEENE B&B

TOWN SQUARE

BAKERY

BRIGGS'S APARTMENT

THE BOOK ISLE

CUTS AND CURLS

TRISTAN & BEAU'S HOUSE

CAPRI'S HOUSE

GEMMA'S HOUSE

HOLLAND'S HOUSE

BEACH BREAK BAR & GRILL

PUBLIC BEACH

N
W   E
S

CHAPTER 5

Phoenix

"She's impossible."

They're the first words that burst out of my mouth when I storm into my office, followed closely by my assistant. Wyatt closes the door behind us and then moves wordlessly to one of the leather chairs by the bookshelf while I begin pacing in front of the window.

"Mm-hmm," he says once he's seated. His hum is absent-minded, even bored, and when I glance over, I find his attention not on me but on the leather folder open in his lap.

"She does the stupidest things," I go on. "She's stubborn on purpose."

Another droning hum from Wyatt. I shake my head and resume my pacing, passing back and forth in front of the large window.

The view from my Sunset Harbor office is nothing like the view from my office on the mainland. When I first set up here five years ago, I wasn't sure how it would feel; I'd been visiting and then working at headquarters since my senior year of high school. Not as an executive, of course—I did a little of everything, though not necessarily well. I was horrible at product development; generating ideas isn't my strong suit. I'm not particularly creative, so design and ergonomics weren't great either.

37

Implementation and logistics, though? Organizing all the moving pieces and making sure they do what they're supposed to do? That's where I found my niche. Now I oversee teams of people putting plans into action, taking care of the tedious details—and I do it from my office here on Sunset Harbor. I traded in the city skyline for a distant view of the ocean and the faint jingle of bicycle bells as people pass.

Never thought I'd live on an island where no cars are allowed, but here we are. Wyatt came with me, of course, because I'm one of those unfortunate workaholics who would not function without someone keeping track of all the little details in my own life.

He jots something down in his folder; the leather chair dwarfs his slight frame, but the seat still squeaks as he leans forward and continues to write. Since it doesn't appear he's going to respond, I speak again.

"And half of my time is spent chasing along after her, making sure she doesn't catapult right over the edge of a cliff."

"I think it's possible you're underestimating her ability to avoid cliffs," Wyatt says, finally looking up at me.

"She was trying to work at the adoption fair, Wyatt," I say as I continue to pace. I can hear the incredulous note in my voice, and just the memory of her sitting at that table makes me want to roll my eyes again. "She's *allergic to dogs.*"

"Mmm," Wyatt says, returning to his folder.

I shove my fingers through my hair and then turn to him, stopping in place so I don't wear tracks in the carpet. "Can you please say something more helpful than that?"

"If you tell me what you'd like to hear," he says, distracted once more as he flips through the pages of his legal pad, "I'd be happy to oblige."

I narrow my eyes at him, and even though he's not looking at me, I still catch the ghost of a smile in response.

"Am I being unreasonable?" I say stiffly. I have to force the question out, because I doubt I'll like his answer.

"It's unreasonable to think you can control another human being," he says without hesitation. His glasses glint in the light as he glances briefly at me. "Especially one like Miss Blakely."

"I don't want to control her," I say. "I just want her to stop doing dumb things." Then, pausing, I add, "And what do you mean, especially someone like her?"

Wyatt shrugs mildly. "She's shown herself quite averse to your suggestions."

"She has, hasn't she," I say in a grim voice. It's not a question.

"And you must admit," he goes on, pushing his glasses up the bridge of his nose, "that her frustrations are somewhat warranted."

"If she doesn't want to be treated like a child, she shouldn't act like one." But even as the words leave my mouth, I know they're not quite right. I let out a tired breath. "No. I just—want her to make smart decisions. I want her to take care of herself so that *I* don't have to take care of her. And then someday when I've died, probably of a Holland-induced heart attack, I can look Trev in the eye and tell him his little sister grew up well. And then"—my voice is louder now—"I can tell him not to dump responsibilities like this on his best friend who's already stressed enough as it is, dealing with succession wars and insane family members."

"Speaking of insane family members," Wyatt says, "your mother called."

"I bet she did." I rub my temples as a wave of exhaustion hits me.

"Indeed," he says, and one corner of his mouth quirks as he looks at me again. "She asked me to pass along her message."

"Let's hear it, then," I say with a sigh.

He ducks his chin. "She wishes you to stop ignoring her calls, and she would like you to know that she's hurt you're avoiding her. She would also like to tell you that she knows many young women—"

"There it is," I mutter.

"Any of whom would make excellent partners in matrimony," Wyatt continues. "She would like to remind you that your grandmother is very serious about the company being inherited by someone who's married, and she would also like to remind you that your cousin Lawrence has been dating someone for the last year, so you can feel reasonably assured that he'll propose to her soon in hopes of inheriting."

I pity the woman who shackles herself to Lawrence.

"Anything else?" I say.

"Yes," Wyatt says, and I'm not surprised, because Marshana Butterfield-Park is neither brief nor succinct. "She made a rather tearful plea for you to remember that she loves you and wants you to be happy, and for that, you need to get married and inherit the company."

What she actually wants is to be supported financially and never work another day in her life. She doesn't need to convince me to do whatever I can to succeed Mavis; that's always been my plan.

I'm not sure she'd agree with the *rest* of my plans if she knew what they were, though.

Butterfield is doing well. We're creating products that do their job for consumers as well as for the environment. But we could be doing so much more, and that's the direction I'd love to take the company. I want to set up a humanitarian branch of operations, one that provides sanitary paper products to communities in need. Shelters, homes, entire cities—whatever it is, I want to help. I want to do something good. I *need* to do something good.

"Mmm," I say, narrowing my eyes as I turn my attention back to Wyatt. "A tearful plea?"

He nods.

"Fake tears or real tears?"

"Very definitely fake."

"Right. Well," I say, taking a deep breath and then letting it out, "I'm going to ignore all of that for now. I'll call her"—I wave my hand—"I don't know. Sometime. I can't really focus on her right now."

"Well, as for Miss Blakely—the only person responsible for her future is herself," Wyatt says firmly, closing his folder with a *snap*. He hesitates; then, in a gentler voice, he says, "However, I understand your feelings, and I understand why you feel you need to watch out for her."

Something faintly warm tries to blossom in my chest; I push it down and clear my throat. "I don't need someone to understand my feelings," I say. My family has never understood me or even tried—only Wyatt. "I just need to figure out what to do. She wouldn't hear me out when I offered her a job."

"I think that may have something to do with the tone in which you offered it." He pauses briefly and then says, "Which job might this be? I wasn't aware you were hiring."

"I'm not," I say, rubbing my hand down my face. "But I could. She could work for me. I'd pay her well. Plus insurance and benefits—she needs those."

"And...the marriage?"

The word I would use to describe my vague noise of response is *disgruntled*. "I suppose—it's possible," I say, because while the personal side of me abhors the idea, the business side of me can grudgingly acknowledge the merits. "I refuse to wed a perfect stranger, and I refuse to pretend to love someone in order to marry. That leaves few options."

Wyatt ducks his head slowly.

"Except if she wouldn't listen about a job, there's no way she'd listen about—" But I break off, because no matter how I try, I can't make myself say the words.

Would I really ask Holland Blakely to *marry* me?

"Maybe I could still find someone else," I say. The thought of marrying Amsterdam fills me with roiling, churning dread.

Wyatt snorts with uncharacteristic sarcasm. "I think you know perfectly well that there is no one else," he says, and I raise my brow at him. "Sir," he adds mildly.

I roll my eyes. "I have other friends," I say. It's true, more or less. I know other women. But...

"If you'll accept my humble opinion, sir—"

"Sarcasm doesn't suit you, Wyatt," I say.

Another ghost of a smile flits over his face. "As long as you maintain your current relationship with Miss Blakely, there will not be room for another woman in your life."

I blink. "What? What relationship?"

"The relationship between you and Miss Blakely," he says. "Though not romantic in nature, perhaps, it does leave little room for anyone else in your life."

"That's ridiculous," I say, biting the words out.

He shrugs. "You're not close enough to anyone else to propose marriage, anyway."

I frown. "I'm not close to Holland, either. If anything, I would call us the opposite of close."

"I disagree."

My eyebrows shoot up. "You're not serious."

His chin dips. "You're not close friends, perhaps," he concedes. "But opponents, rivals, maybe enemies—whatever you are, you're close ones." He falls silent, watching me as I grit my teeth and try to hold back my retort. I'm not one to hold my tongue in most situations, but Wyatt has earned my respect, no matter how much I disagree with him.

He was the one who helped me stand and brushed the dirt from my little black suit at my father's funeral, when my mother had forgotten about me in her hysterics. He's the one who made sure I was fed and clothed and taken care of when she confined herself to her room for days at a time.

In many ways, he raised me.

So I keep my thoughts to myself—that Holland and I are not close, not as friends or enemies or anything else. I give her my time and attention because I promised Trev I would. I made a promise to my best friend, and I owe him everything, because he's dead and it's partially my fault.

He's dead, and it's partially my fault, and—I realize with horror—I think I might actually ask his sister to marry me.

"Let's finish here for the day," I say, because there's a weight pressing down on my chest, one I can't dispel. Thinking about Trevor and the past always makes me feel heavy and tired and hopeless. "We can pick up on Monday."

Wyatt just nods. And when he looks more closely at me, his wiry, brown-gray brows pulling low with concern, I turn away.

Long gone are the days when I unburdened my soul with anyone; I wouldn't know what to say.

I wouldn't even know where to start.

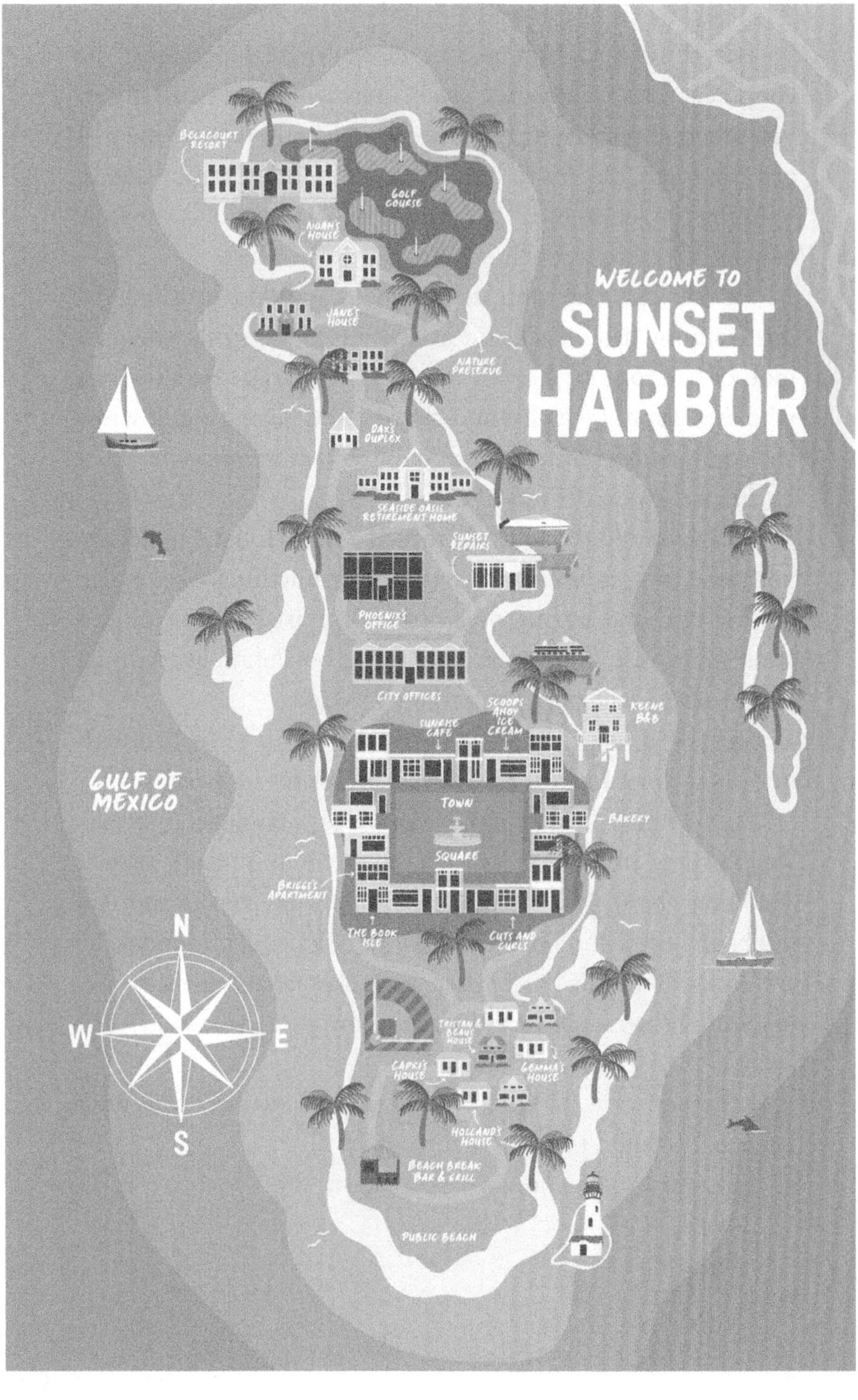

CHAPTER 6

Holland

WHEN I MEET up with Cat later that afternoon, I'm still thinking about Phoenix's face as he offered me a job—or more specifically, when he corrected himself and used the word *arrangement*.

I don't usually see such a lack of expression from him, especially when I know he's annoyed. It reminds me of a Lifetime documentary I saw about this serial killer, and the lady who was his neighbor for years and never knew. She said he was grumpy and rude but otherwise normal—except that his expression sometimes sent chills down her spine.

That's kind of what's going on with my spine right now: chills, because I can't get that blank look out of my head.

"So, wait," Cat says, frowning at me. She sets down the menu in her hands. "An arrangement?"

I nod. "That's what he said. He called it a job first, and then an arrangement."

Sunrise Cafe is packed for the afternoon rush, and Cat and I have leaned gradually closer across our little table— orange, chipped paint, the exact same color as the surfboard on the wall behind us—so we can hear each other over the hum of conversation and clinking silverware and laughter. Cat's platinum blonde hair, lighter than mine, is pulled back into a braid, and even her freckles seem confused as she looks at me.

"That's weird phrasing. Did you ask him any more about it?" She pauses and then answers her own question before I can say anything. "Of course you didn't. But Holls"—she leans in further—"do you think you should?" She wrinkles her nose and then sits back in her chair. "I know he's a snob—"

"The *biggest* snob."

"But you're not in a great situation," Cat says with a little bob of her shoulders. "If he wants to hire you, it might not be so bad."

"I already have a job." I point to her blonde hair. "That. That's my job. I love working at the salon."

"I need my roots done soon," she says, touching the top of her head.

I've been experimenting on Cat's hair the entire time we've known each other—since five years ago, when I moved to Sunset Harbor to live with Nana Lu. Nana was struggling to get around, her mobility growing more and more limited, and I was just struggling, *period*. The owner of the wellness spa where I worked gave shifts to her friends and her favorites, and the rest of us were left to fight over the scraps. I didn't feel safe in the complex where I lived. I struggled to get out and make friends, especially because in my free time I wanted to sleep after being awoken by nightmares at night.

It was a bad set of circumstances. So when Nana started talking about moving to Seaside Oasis—the retirement home on the island—I left my apartment and my job and came to stay with her. We managed to make things work in her house until last year, when she finally started needing more help than I was able to give.

It was the best move I've ever made. I met Cat at book

club, and we bonded over books and our shared dislike of the ocean—despite living on an island. We've been friends ever since, and I've seen her hair through varying shades of blonde, brunette, and even a stint of auburn.

"Come over sometime and I'll do them," I tell her. I cross my legs for all of one second before remembering the pain in my knee; I grimace and uncross them again.

"Thanks," she says, picking her menu back up. "And you know, you might not have to quit at the salon, even if you worked with Phoenix."

"*For* Phoenix," I say. "I'm pretty sure he would be my boss." And then I'd have to do whatever he told me. Which is fine, I can be professional—except his whole face just makes me so *stabby*.

"Well, maybe it's a side job type of thing," Cat says.

"Mmm," I say slowly. "Maybe he needs a drug mule."

She nods, grinning. "Or maybe it's an MLM."

"Can you imagine?" I say with a laugh.

"Or maybe—" she begins again, but then she breaks off as her eyes catch on something. "Oh, here's Ivy."

I look up just in time to see Ivy approaching our table, her mass of curls pulled back in a bun and a stressed expression on her face. Her waitress's apron has a splotch of what might be mustard on the bottom hem, and her order pad is clutched in tight fingers.

"So many people," Ivy says with wide eyes when she's reached our table. She gestures at the diner around us. "This is my first Saturday since moving back, and I was not prepared."

I laugh. "It's a lot." I look back and forth between her and Cat. "Was it like this when you guys were growing up?"

"Yes," Ivy says immediately. "I even worked here in high

47

school. I just forgot how busy it gets." She sighs and shakes her head. "Well, what can I get you?"

"A cheeseburger," Cat says. She gives the menu a little waggle. "I don't know why I bothered looking through this; I knew I wanted a cheeseburger." She passes the menu to Ivy, who tucks it under her arm.

"And I'd like a hot chocolate, please." Normally I'd get the stack of three pancakes with whipped cream and bananas, but my budget has decreased drastically for the time being.

"One of these days," Ivy says as she jots down our orders, "I'm going to have to resample everything on this menu." She gives a satisfied bob of her head and then looks back at us. "Give me a few and I'll bring it out!"

"Thank you," Cat calls at her retreating back as she hurries off. Then she turns to me. "I think you should at least ask Phoenix what the job is. Or the arrangement—whatever. It won't hurt to ask, will it?"

"No," I say, stretching the word out. "But it would offend my pride a little bit. I know, I know"—I cut her off as she opens her mouth to speak—"that's a bad reason not to ask."

"Because you're helping Maggie with her tuition, aren't you?" Cat says.

I shrug and take a sip of my water. My little sister sort of fell through the cracks when my parents split. They love her, and if she asks for help they'll give it, but she usually won't ask. She's working to put herself through college, just like I did, and it's hard.

"Plus *that* doesn't look good," Cat says, pointing to my knee. "You might have messed it up again."

"You're saying all the same things Phoenix did," I grumble. But as I look down at my leg, I can't help worrying she's right. The bruise is bigger than it probably should be, the mottled purplish-bluish color of a mushy blueberry, and it's been painful ever since I came down on it wrong. The surgery I had after the crash seven years ago went fine, but my knee never really returned to how it was before; what if I've reinjured something in there?

"All right, fine. I'll ask," I say with a sigh. "Now let's change the subject."

NANA LU'S place is a little yellow house with white trim and a white door. There's a tall fence around what would technically be called her front yard, except it's really more of a courtyard; there's no grass, just gravel and green-felt-covered concrete separated by a few old railroad ties. She has a little table on the side with the green felt, but the chairs are too uncomfortable to spend much time there. So when I step outside the next night, I sit down for about three minutes before standing again.

As much as I dislike going into the ocean, living on a little island has its weather benefits. Most people don't like humidity, but I personally don't mind how balmy every day feels. A warm breeze tugs at my hair as I stare up at the night sky, watching the few stars I can see past the porch light.

I'm stalling.

I haven't reached out to Phoenix yet, even though I told Cat yesterday at the diner that I would. It's taken me this long to convince myself I need to hear him out and then to work up the nerve to call.

His contact info isn't saved in my phone. I refused to give him his own place—petty, undoubtedly. But it doesn't matter; I have his number memorized, because he texts me once a week, sometimes more. After he goes to visit Nana Lu, he always lets me know how she seems.

I don't love hearing from him in general, but I do appreciate the thought. Whenever I visit Nana, she does her best to seem strong and healthy and well, because she doesn't want me to worry. She doesn't pretend as much in front of Phoenix.

I go back inside, the screen door slamming shut behind me as I make my way into the little living room. My hands are steady as I dial Phoenix's number, and when he answers after three rings, I find myself both relieved and disappointed that he picked up at all.

"Yes?" That's all he says. His phone voice is always clipped, slightly impatient, like he has a million other things he needs to be doing. It's the same way he talked when we first met at that corner mart.

I stop pacing the living room and settle myself on the uncomfortable couch. It's an ugly old thing from the eighties, dark cream velour with brownish-orange damask. I sink into the cushion; then I take a deep breath and speak.

"You said you might have a job for me."

He's quiet for a second. "I might."

"What is it?" I say, leaning back into the squashy couch. "How's the pay?"

There's another beat of silence before he answers. "The pay is negotiable," he says slowly, and another chill runs down my spine at how *blank* he sounds, his voice devoid of taunting or smugness. "But…I think you would find it competitive."

He's talking to me in a way he usually doesn't. Why is he acting strange? He doesn't *actually* need a drug mule, does he? A little squirm of nervousness pinches at my insides.

Competitive pay, though; that could be helpful, much as I hate to admit it.

"All right," I say. I trace my fingers over the pattern in the couch, ornate leaves and haughty curlicues. "And what is it, exactly? What would I be doing?"

For one long moment, he doesn't say anything. I can feel his reluctance filtering down the line, and that squiggle of nervousness inside intensifies.

"Rooster," I say loudly, my fingers digging into worn velour. "What's the job?"

"This is something we should discuss in person," he says finally. "Let's meet up."

"What?" I say, looking down at my pajamas. "No. It's already ten. Why are you being weird about this? It's making me really anxious." I hesitate and then add, "I'm not doing anything illegal."

He snorts. "Would I ask you to do anything illegal?"

No. He wouldn't.

But I don't answer.

"We can meet up tonight or tomorrow," he says, and with relief I hear that his voice is back to normal; businesslike, slightly impatient. "Take your pick. But we really have to talk about this in person."

"I—you—" I break off and then release my breath in a gust. "Tonight is fine." I won't want to meet tomorrow any more than I do now, and I'll stay awake dreading it.

Because the truth is, every time I see Phoenix Park, one thing and one thing only flashes through my mind—one image conjured up from the darkest recesses of my memory.

The two of us, shaking and bleeding and soaked to the bone, watching as Trev's lifeless body is rolled away on a sheet-covered stretcher.

That's what I see. Every single time I see him, I'm hit

with that memory. Talking to him hurts; looking at him hurts. It physically *hurts*, like a blow to the chest—like all the water I swallowed when we went over that bridge seven years ago is still in my lungs, festering, rotting.

It hurts to be near him. But he keeps inserting himself in my life anyway, and part of me hates him for it. The other part of me, smaller, feels sorry for him—or sorry *to* him, maybe. Sorry that I hate him for something he has no control over.

Because he won't back out of my life. He won't let me be. He's never said as much, but I know he won't. If Phoenix Park is one thing, it's loyal—loyal to the people he deems worthy.

He promised Trev he would look out for me, take care of me. So that's what he's going to try to do. I'm not even sure I can fault him for it.

"My bike chain is broken, and I'm not walking all the way to your neighborhood by myself in the dark," I tell him, running my hand down my face.

"Absolutely not," he says immediately. "I'll come to you." Then he coughs, a harsh, barking sound.

"Are you sick?" I pause. Then, grudgingly, I add, "Do you need tea?"

"Why?" he says. "Looking for new ways to poison me now that I spotted your Skittles scheme from a mile off?"

My lips twitch; he hates Skittles. "Scald you, actually," I say, keeping my voice light. "I thought maybe if I could burn your tongue, I might finally get a few days free from your nagging."

"You wish, Hamster Slam."

My grip on the phone tightens.

I put up with him calling me *Amsterdam*. I call him bird names instead of *Phoenix*; he can call me *Amsterdam* instead of

Holland. But every now and then he tries to get really obnoxious; that's when he pulls out names like *Hamster Slam,* or *Gangster Glam,* or—the worst—*Dumpster Ma'am.*

"Just come over if you're going to come over," I say. "But don't expect me to change out of my pajamas for you—"

Except he's already hung up.

I toss the phone to the opposite side of the couch and scowl at it for a good ten seconds. Then I stand and go into the kitchen to brew myself a cup of peppermint tea.

There's something relaxing about the sounds of brewing tea in a quiet house; the *clink-clink-clink* of the stirring spoon, the light *chink* of porcelain on the countertop. I immerse myself in that peace for as long as possible, brewing and stirring and sipping and savoring, until fifteen minutes later there's a knock at the door.

I debate making him wait—the idea has real merit—but ultimately I'm too impatient. Something's off with him and this job he claims to have for me, and all I can think about are those women who cross the border with balloons full of cocaine in their stomachs.

So when I fling the door open, I don't waste any time.

"Tell me what the job is," I say.

Phoenix raises his brows slowly at me as his black-brown gaze runs from the top of my head to the tips of my toes and then back again; heat gathers beneath my skin, simmering just below the surface until I can feel the flush in my cheeks.

I snap my fingers in front of his nose to get his attention. "Don't ogle. It's rude."

He snorts and brings his eyes back to mine. "Nothing you have"—he gestures to my body—"is appealing enough to ogle, Amsterdam. I'm simply surprised you're willing to show yourself like this."

"The job," I say through gritted teeth. "Tell me what the job is."

He doesn't answer; he just steps forward and pushes past me, entering Nana's house and leaving me in a lingering cloud of his leather-mahogany scent.

I force myself to take a few deep breaths, staring vaguely out into the night and listening as his footsteps travel down the hall behind me. Then, without another word, I turn and follow.

CHAPTER 7

Phoenix

SOMETIMES I WISH Holland looked more like her brother.

Trevor would never be caught dead wearing tiny silk pajama shorts and a matching silk button-down top. If he were, however, he would look absurd. Not like—*her*.

I squeeze my eyes shut and shake my head.

"Hurry up and tell me," she calls from down the hall as I settle onto the ancient sofa in Nana Lu's living room.

Trevor and Holland's grandmother Lu is one of my favorite people on earth. She's everything a grandmother should be—everything my grandmother isn't.

Mavis Butterfield barks half-deranged orders at me and delights in inciting succession battles in her family; Nana Lu just tells me how handsome I am and that I need to eat more. I always leave our visits with a variety of hard candies tucked in my pockets, because she insists, pressing them into my palms with her shaky, age-spotted hands. I eat every last one, even though the only kind I really like are the strawberry ones with the gooey centers.

Lovely though she is as a grandmother, however, Luella Blakely is not a gifted interior decorator. There are tacky seashell displays everywhere—very Florida—and the walls are all different summer colors; pastel lime, sky blue, bright yellow, and sunset orange create a spectrum that's over-whelming to the eye. It's awful.

This couch might be the worst part. It's still on the cinderblocks Holland put beneath when Nana could no longer get up on her own from such a low surface. It should have been burned decades ago.

I sink back into the orange-brown cushion anyway, turning my gaze to Holland as she emerges into the room. She comes to a stop in front of the couch, her arms crossed once more, her foot tapping impatiently.

"Come on, Peacock," she says, shooting me an irritated look. "Tell me what the job is."

"It's not quite a job," I say. Then, weighing my words carefully, I go on, "It's more of an arrangement."

Her brown eyes narrow, and she steps closer to the sofa, all five-feet-six-inches of her towering over me. "So you mentioned," she says. She couldn't look more suspicious if she tried. "Explain."

I keep my expression passive, blank, but my mind is working furiously as I try to figure out what to say. I've never had a conversation like this before, and I've certainly never had it with someone as explosive as Holland.

"All right," I finally say. There's nothing to do but spit it out. "I'm interested in entering a contract-based matrimonial agreement with you." And I'm playing a game called *How can I make this marriage proposal sound unlike a marriage proposal?*

"A contract-based—what?" she says, and she's confused enough to stop glaring. Lines furrow her brow instead as she blinks at me. "Did you say *matrimonial?*"

"I did, yes," I say with a slow nod. "Have you heard of contractual marriages?"

"Yeah," she says, fainter now. "It's a whole genre."

I blink at her. "Sorry?"

"Never mind," she says. "Forgot you don't know how to read. But—you're obviously not proposing *marriage.*"

When she says it like *that*—

"I think you'll find semantics very important moving forward," I say quickly. "But—technically—I suppose I am proposing that we get married."

The words have barely left my mouth, and I already know they're going to be received poorly.

"I'm not marrying you," she says, and I can read every emotion playing over her face—her confusion, her shock, her utter bewilderment. "You're not—you can't possibly be serious."

Once again, I nod. "Sadly, I am."

"You're not." She shakes her head, her blonde hair brushing against the silky fabric of her pajamas. "I can't believe I actually thought you'd be helpful."

"I'm not messing around," I tell her firmly. Can she hear how uncomfortable I am with this entire conversation? "Our usual pranks aside, I'm very serious about this."

"You can't possibly—"

"I can," I cut her off. "And I am. I'm asking you to become my legal wife—in name only," I stress.

"I'm obviously not marrying you," she says. "Get out. Get out of my house." Her eyes are deer-in-the-headlights wide, darting back and forth; she's on the precipice of losing it completely.

I'm right there with her.

I sigh. "You might *have* to marry me."

She scoffs, an unhinged sound. "That has never been true, and it's certainly not true today." She turns away from me and folds her arms. "I'm not marrying you." I can't see her now that her back is to me, but I can hear her facial expression—brows set, mouth pinched into a tight line.

There might even be a muscle twitching in her jaw—left side only.

I stand up and lean sideways, just a bit, and sure enough, there it is: that little muscle that ticks only when she's *really* pissed off.

I roll my eyes. "Look, Amsterdam. I don't want to marry you any more than you want to marry me. But they're making me get married. Do you understand? My grandmother is forcing me to get married, or I can't inherit the company—not all of us have a Nana Lu, you know? If I don't get married, the company will go to my cousin Lawrence instead." I glare at the back of her head. "That's the one who found your number on my phone and called you to ask if we were sleeping together. A few years ago. You remember Lawrence, don't you?"

"Lawrence can swan dive off the nearest cliff," she says icily.

I sweep my arms in exasperation. "Wonderful. It's settled, then. You and me, one week from today."

"I'm not marrying you!" she says, finally turning back around. She stomps her foot and then winces; my gaze darts to her bruised knee.

"I'm not doing it!" she goes on. "What would I be getting out of this arrangement?"

"I'll pay you," I say coolly.

"You'll—what?" she says, freezing. Then, like a prairie dog standing at alert, she turns all her focus on me.

Some interest at last.

"You would pay me?" she says, and I duck my chin in a nod.

She clears her throat, her gaze darting away and then back to mine. She'll probably start fidgeting with her hair soon; she does that when she's overwhelmed.

"How—how much?" she says.

"Like I told you before—I'm flexible, but it would be competitive." I pause. "As part of your compensation, I would cover any treatment you needed for that." I gesture to her knee. Then, taking a deep breath, I bring out the big guns and aim them directly at her weak spot: "*And* I would cover Maggie's tuition for the remainder of her degree. Grad school too, if she wants."

It's this, finally, that seems to get through to Holland; her jaw drops. "You're serious," she whispers, and one hand comes up to play with the ends of her hair. "You're actually serious. You really think we—you and I—that we could—"

"Get married," I say. "Yes. That's my hope. I would compensate you well; we would both sign a contract listing acceptable terms. We would remain married until I'm able to inherit Butterfield and until my grandmother dies; after that, we would go our separate ways."

She mouths wordlessly for a second, repeating the things I say, and then she speaks. "Insane," she says faintly. "You're insane." She shakes her head. "No. I'm not marrying you. You're rude, you're arrogant—"

"I'm hardly arrogant," I say, bristling.

"And you snore like a wild sow birthing a full litter—"

"Like a wild—" I stutter, outraged. "A wild *sow?*"

"And you're incredibly overbearing—" She breaks off, chest heaving, nostrils flaring. "No," she says. "No way. Find someone else."

My eyes narrow on her. "Find someone else?" I say, my voice quiet now. "Really? You think I can just *find someone else?*" I take a deep breath and then go on. "It's a small island; not many women. I'll just marry one of your friends, then, I guess? Cat? Should I marry Cat? Or Jane?"

Her gaze darts away from mine, just barely—just a fraction of a fraction of an inch—but enough that I'm taking it as a win. I pounce.

"Or should I ask a stranger? Should I make some woman fall in love with me so she'll be willing to get married?"

Her jaw drops. "No," she says, sounding offended. "You can't trick someone—"

"See?" I say with a jut of my chin. "There's no one else, Amsterdam. There's no one else for me to marry. No one who will understand, no one suitable."

"Oh, please," she says, but her scoff is less convincing than it was a moment ago. "There are dozens of women who would quite literally kill to marry you, all of them *suitable*." She spits the word out. "Your mother has been parading them in front of you for years. Choose one of them."

"No."

"A blonde, or maybe a brunette, or a nice redhead—"

"Don't be stupid," I say curtly. "I clearly will not marry anyone but you."

A faint pink flush rises in her cheeks. "I don't want to be the wife of a CEO, *Titmouse*," she says angrily—and this bodes ill, because that's the bird name she pulls out when she really wants to annoy me. "I'll have to smile all the time—"

"Only sometimes—"

"And I'll have to be in charge of things—"

"I'll be in charge of all the things—"

"And I'll probably have to speak in public—"

"I'll find you a body double!"

"Stop trying to be nice!" she says. "It's creepy!"

"Fine," I snap; the word bounces angrily around Nana Lu's living room. "Would you prefer me to be rude or arrogant or overbearing?"

By now her eyes are spitting fire. "We can't get married,"

she says. The yellow overhead light catches the gold in her hair and taunts me with it as she shakes her head. She's had friends who assumed she used dye, but that hair is all natural, long and silky and easily one of her best features.

"Don't you see that?" she goes on, and I pull my gaze back to her face. "We don't like each other. You tried to *blackmail* me—"

"We tried to blackmail each other," I reply hotly, "and that was a long time ago, and it was barely even a threat. It doesn't count." I can hear the faint note of desperation in my voice, and it sends a flush of anger over my skin. I stare at her for a second, seething, until finally I can't take it anymore.

"Gah!" I throw my hands up in the air. "Every time I look at you I just get so—I get so—"

"Angry," she says with a nod. "I know. Me too." She tilts her head and waves one vague hand at me. "It's something... hmm." She breaks off, looking thoughtful as she smirks. "It's something about your face."

I clench my jaw so hard my entire skull might crack. And this—this is the real reason I didn't want to ask Holland. Because I knew this was how we would end up: with me *begging* her to marry me, and her still refusing.

My pride trampled into dust.

But I grit my teeth and force out the words I know I need to say. "You can come work for me, then. At the office. Think about it."

"No," she says with one final shake of her head. "Get out. Leave." She points down the hallway to the front door. "Now. Go."

Deep breath in; deep breath out. "If you're reluctant because of what happened..." I begin. It's a step onto a minefield.

"I'm not!" she says quickly.

But I hear it then: fear, real fear. Her eyes have widened, and the flush in her cheeks burns brighter. For a second, the tiniest second, I think I might catch a glimpse of her truest self—soft, hurt, and desperately trying to pretend she doesn't care—but I must be imagining things, because before I can look closer, she's just normal Holland again.

"Fine," I say, because she pretends, and I play along. "Just asking—"

"Leave." And, when I don't move—*"Now!"* she shouts.

I storm out of the room without another word, down the hallway, and out the front, wishing I didn't care about Nana Lu so much, because I would really love to slam a door right about now.

When I get outside, I glare up at the star-strewn sky. "Your sister is a brat," I tell Trev, breathing deeply. "Forget about marrying me—she'll be lucky to find anyone at all."

"Hey!" she shouts from behind me, and I startle—I didn't even hear her open the door. I don't turn around, though; I'm too angry. I'll say something I regret. I just walk faster, out through the gate, holding my tongue the whole time.

All of my pent-up retorts play through my mind on my way home, and when I fall asleep, it's to the sound of her shouts ringing through my memory.

CHAPTER 8

Holland

THE GIRLS at the salon can tell something's wrong.

When I say *girls*, I actually mean *ladies*. Felicia and I are the youngest ones there, both of us in our late twenties, and everyone else is in their fifties, sixties, and even seventies. Betsy Barnes, the owner of Cuts and Curls, is fifty-something, and she has more energy than I do; she waltzes around with her pixie cut, her skin tan from spending so much time in the sun.

That energy is infectious, though, and it fills the inside of Cuts and Curls, turning the little salon into a cheerful, lively place to be. She painted the walls a pale lavender last year, and the year before that she changed out the black product shelves on the wall for pink ones. I don't know how she has time to do everything she does; her husband is Mayor Barnes, but she's still here five days a week.

Maybe I could ask her what it's like being married to someone in the spotlight.

No, I tell myself firmly, shaking my head as I wipe down my station and my tools at the end of the day. It doesn't matter what it would be like being married to a mayor or a CEO or anyone else, for that matter. Because I'm not getting married—not now, anyway, and definitely not to Phoenix Park.

I wasn't the kind of girl who dreamed about her future husband as a child or even a teenager. I focused more on the day-in, day-out present, even when I had boyfriends. I knew they weren't marriage material; we were in high school. I never expected otherwise.

But things have changed very drastically in the last twenty-four hours, because right now, marriage is all I can think about. I tossed and turned all night, and today hasn't been any better.

How desperate must Phoenix be to come to me? Because asking *me*, of all people, to marry him—it's insane.

I would cover Maggie's tuition for the remainder of her degree. Grad school too, if she wants.

I shake my head again and try to get his offer to stop bouncing around in there. It's ridiculous—absurd. It would never work, not in a million years.

"You're a little off today," Felicia says as she appears in my peripheral vision, and I jump, glancing over at her. Our stations are right next to each other, but they look vastly different; while I keep my counter mostly bare, preferring to store my tools in the drawers, Felicia keeps her things out. We spend most afternoons with clients, chatting in between and bonding over lungs full of hairspray.

"I guess I am," I say vaguely, smiling even though I don't feel like it. "Is it obvious?"

"You've been wiping down that same spot for ten minutes," she says, pointing at my counter. "So, yeah. It's kind of obvious. What's up?"

My brother's best friend asked me to marry him.

"Nothing much," I say. "I didn't sleep well last night. And it was a rough weekend." All true. "But I'll be fine. My clients were all good today."

"So were mine," Felicia says with a bob of her head that

causes her curly ponytail to bounce. "Let's hope tomorrow is the same."

I give her another smile and put down my rag—because Felicia is right, I've been cleaning the counter for way too long. "I'm sure it will be. I'll see you then, okay?"

Her answering nod and smile are half hearted, her brows furrowed with concern, but I can't bring myself to talk about what's going on. I sweep the floor quickly and quietly, wipe down my chair, and then head out before anyone can ask any more questions. My parting wave as I hurry out the door is too exuberant, my smile too cheerful, and I cringe internally.

By the time I've made it out of the salon, my mind is a million miles away from Sunset Harbor. The warm, early-evening breeze tugs at my hair and cools my skin; I inhale deeply, savoring the fresh air as I trudge through the town square, my thoughts racing.

Why is Phoenix asking me to marry him? I don't get it. Yes, he wants to inherit the company, and I can admit that his cousin is the worst—he really did call me and ask if Phoenix and I were sleeping together, completely out of the blue. It's understandable that Phoenix wouldn't want Butter-field to go to him.

But is that important enough for Phoenix to ask me—someone he hates—to marry him?

He must know other women. Him marrying one of my friends would be weird, but there's a whole world out there, full of other people.

So why me? Why does he want to marry me instead of someone else, when he dislikes me so much?

Unless…

I gasp, slapping my hand over my mouth. The faint scent of hair product left on my skin stings my nose, but I ignore it.

He doesn't like me, does he? Phoenix Park doesn't *like* me.

"No way," I mutter. A shaky little laugh escapes. "No." I'm not likable—not to him, at least. We're not nice to each other. "There's no way."

I look ridiculous, I realize, talking to myself, but I need to talk to somebody. So I pull out my phone and call Cat.

"Hey," I say when she picks up. "I have a hypothetical question for you."

"Is this one of those hypothetical questions that's not actually hypothetical?"

I don't want to lie to her, so I don't answer. I just go ahead and speak. "Is there any reason a man would propose to a woman he doesn't have feelings for?"

There's a split second of silence, and then Cat's voice explodes down the line. "Did Phoenix *propose* to you?!"

"Shh!" I hush her. "Don't just shout that! He—not really —kind of—" I sigh and force out the word. "Yes? But it wouldn't be a proper marriage, to have and to hold and all that," I say quickly, because it feels very important to clarify. "There would be no having or holding. He basically just needs to be married to inherit the family company. And I could use some extra cash, so he would compensate me in return."

"Okay..." Cat says, and I can hear her struggling to keep up. "So a marriage of convenience thing? I didn't realize people actually did that in real life."

"Me neither," I say. "I just finished reading a good one the other day, though. By Sunny Palmer." I pause. "Her fictional man was much more tolerable as a fake husband than Phoenix would be."

"I don't doubt it," Cat says grimly. "So Phoenix asked you specifically because...?"

"That's my question," I say. Then, though I feel stupid thinking it, much less saying it: "There's no way he likes me, right?"

"I mean, I don't know," Cat says, sounding uncomfortable now. "I obviously can't say for sure. But I think you're very lovable"—I snort— "and you guys do pay a lot of attention to each other."

"Not good attention."

"I know," she says. "I really have no idea. I can say this, though: if I were an ultra-rich hot guy who could feasibly get any woman I wanted—"

"Hey," I say.

"I wouldn't propose to the woman who hates me. But hey, I have to go, Holls," she says. "I need to go strip a few beds and get the linens washed." Cat runs a bed and breakfast, located on the other side of the town square; I send a little wave in the direction of the pale-yellow house with a white porch and white shutters.

"I'm sending my love from over by the salon," I tell her. "Talk to you later."

"Later!" she says, and we hang up.

I take a deep breath and begin walking again, turning her words over in my head. Despite the breeze that was so pleasant before, I find myself feeling too warm now, the prickle of sweat on my scalp and clammy hands still clasped around my phone.

"Another deep breath," I say. It takes more than one to steady myself, however.

Because the thought of Phoenix Park having *feelings* for me—it's laughable. Unfathomable. And even if he doesn't...if we got married, we would have to pretend to like each other. I would have to look at him every single day. Could I handle that? For much-needed income and health care and Maggie's tuition…could I handle that?

No.

Right?

Maybe. I don't know. But if he does have feelings for me —there's no way.

The oxygen feels heavy in my lungs as I breathe, and I can't seem to swallow properly. So with clammy fingers, I dial Phoenix's number before I can think better of it. He answers after the first ring, and I don't even let him say anything before I speak.

"We need to talk."

"Do we really, though?" he says, sounding distracted.

I roll my eyes. "Yes."

"In person?"

I swallow. I need to see his face to know if he's telling the truth. "Yes."

"I'm at the office," he says. "So if you insist, you'll need to come to me. Preferably before it gets dark, as I don't trust your self-defense skills, should you be ambushed."

Relief floods through me as the tightness in my chest eases. This Phoenix is familiar—this, I can handle. "Our crime rate is famously low," I say. "Beau said so."

When Phoenix responds, his voice is less absent. "When did he say that?"

Oops. "I don't know. I just—remember him saying something." Very recently, in fact, when I reported that I'd been scammed. Now that I think about it, I should have made sure he wouldn't tell Phoenix; they're good friends.

Thankfully, Phoenix doesn't ask anything else; he just hums. "Well, come over, if you must." Then he hangs up, and I'm left glaring at my phone. I hope he can feel it from here.

It's a fifteen minute walk from the salon to Phoenix's

office building, and I make it just as the sun is starting to sink in the sky. It's a small, two-story building, with neatly maintained rock beds and palm trees. There's nothing beachy or island-like inside, though; the temperature drops as soon as you enter, and it looks like I'd imagine all big city corporate offices look. An overall sense of gray, mostly, with fluorescent lighting and neatly arranged cubicles. The windows save the whole place; the sunlight streaming in during the day makes the environment bearable.

I look decidedly out of place in my sundress and white sneakers as I stroll past the nearest row of cubicles, but the people smile at me anyway; I blink in surprise when a guy at the water cooler actually greets me by name.

"Hi, Miss Blakely!" he says, sounding more chipper than I would sound if I worked here.

"Hi," I say, but the greeting trails off in my confusion. How does he know me?

I clear my throat and tuck my hair behind my ear—nervous habit—before hurrying to the stairwell in the back. I take a direct left when I reach the top floor, passing more cubicles and listening to the sound of *click-clacking* keyboards and pleasant, professional phone calls.

When I finally reach the floor-to-ceiling windows of Phoenix's office, I slow down. I can't see what he's doing in there, since the windows are lined with blinds, but it's probably something stuffy and bossy. I hesitate briefly at his door, and then I knock.

If I wait too long, I'll lose my nerve.

"Come in." His voice, clear and professional and authoritative, filters out to me, and I enter, closing the door behind me again—rustling blinds and a little *click*.

"Hi, Wyatt," I say to Phoenix's assistant, a middle-aged man who's way nicer than Phoenix deserves. He dips his chin at me from his leather chair, a large folder open in his lap, and Phoenix speaks from behind his giant executive desk.

"What do you want, Amsterdam?" he says, not looking away from his desktop. There's a furrow of concentration between his brows, a little frown bracketing his lips.

"There was a man downstairs who said hi to me," I say, dropping into the armchair across from Wyatt's. My pulse is jittering at the conversation I'm about to have, and while I normally enjoy looking around Phoenix's office, today I'm too nervous.

"I prefer to employ pleasant people," he says, eyes still on his computer. "Part of why I only reluctantly offered you work here."

I ignore this barb in favor of the point I'm trying to make. "No, he greeted me *by name.*"

"I don't understand the question," Phoenix says. He clicks the mouse with an air of finality and then leans back in his chair, finally looking at me. "How does he know your name, you mean?"

"Yes," I say. "He called me Miss Blakely."

Phoenix shrugs his broad shoulders. "You visit the office relatively frequently."

I blink at him, frowning. "No, I don't."

He snorts and swivels his chair, standing up. "Yes, you do. Wyatt, I'm done on here," he says to Wyatt, gesturing to the computer. "You can get in there and organize those accounts now."

Wyatt nods while I think back, mentally examining my calendar of the last month. I came once to pick up the window locks Phoenix insisted I use; another time I dropped by to return the suit coat I had to have dry cleaned after I (mostly accidentally) sprayed hairspray on it.

I guess I come here sometimes.

I shake my head. "Fine. Whatever. It doesn't matter." Taking a deep breath, I stand up. "We need to discuss something." My gaze darts to Wyatt, but I don't say anything; I'm not his boss, and he's under no obligation to listen to me.

He seems to understand, though, because he inclines his head again and rises from his chair. "I'll be in my office," he says tactfully, and some of the tension leaks out of my shoulders.

I don't really want anyone else to hear this conversation.

Phoenix rounds his desk slowly, eyes on Wyatt as he exits. Only when the door has clicked shut behind him does he turn his gaze on me.

"Have you reconsidered my offer?" he says, strolling casually toward where I'm standing. His hands are in his pockets, and one dark brow is raised at me—he fills this role so easily, with an arrogant elegance that comes from a lifetime of privilege and power.

It's a look he wears well.

I swallow and don't let myself shrink away, standing taller instead. "No. Or—I don't know." *Admitting you need help is its own form of bravery,* I remind myself. "Maybe." And here comes the heat creeping up my neck; I ignore it. "We need to clarify something first."

His eyes narrow on me, but he nods slowly and takes another casual step in my direction. "All right. I'm listening."

Say it. Just say it. It will sound stupid, but it would be more stupid not to clarify.

So I take one last breath, so deep my lungs hurt, and then I blurt it out:

"I'm worried you might have feelings for me."

CHAPTER 9

Phoenix

"I'm worried you might have feelings for me."

I hear those words come out of Holland's mouth—I definitely hear them, but they don't register very well. I stop dead in my tracks, because walking and processing are too much for my brain to handle at once.

"Feelings," I say dumbly. "For you?"

She tucks a few strands of that blonde hair behind her ears, shifting her weight. Her eyes dart away before meeting mine again, like she's forcing herself to hold my gaze. "Yes," she says. She raises her chin defiantly. "I'm concerned that you might feel romantically toward me."

She's a vivid spot of color in this office, bright hair and blue fingernails and a little yellow dress that shows off more tan skin than I need to see. I take pride in my space—brown leather chairs and dark wood bookshelves; a large, comfortable desk; lots of natural light—but when she's here, she makes the place look dull.

Even when she's spitting nonsense.

"I seem to remember telling you," I say, "that nothing you have appeals to me. Personality was included in there." I take another step toward her, until only a couple feet separate us.

"I also remember that," she says, glaring at me. "But you asked me to marry you, Flamingo."

"Haven't heard that one before," I mutter, clenching my jaw.

"And even though you said it would just be a contract marriage," she goes on as though I haven't spoken, "people don't propose to people they don't like. That's not something that happens in real life. You only propose when you have feelings for someone."

I roll my eyes. "Grudgingly asking for your help and having feelings for you are two very different things. Don't give yourself so much credit." I let out an exhausted breath. "I don't like you, Amsterdam. I'm not even attracted to you." Is she objectively beautiful? Sure. Blonde hair, gorgeous body, dimples I never see because she never smiles in my direction. But her personality usually kills any pull she might have on me, so I don't feel dishonest right now.

Her cheeks, already pink, darken slightly; that muscle in her jaw jumps. "You need to tell me if you're lying," she says, stepping closer.

I scoff, and she goes on.

"Do you think I would be saying this if I were just trying to be annoying? These are embarrassing claims for me to make," she says, angrier now. "They're presumptuous and conceited. I know that. But I *cannot* marry you if you have feelings for me."

Unbelievable. I shake my head as a dull pain begins to throb in my temples. Is this what will kill my dreams for Butterfield? Her misplaced, unfounded belief that I *like* her?

"I don't have feelings for you!" I burst out, throwing my hands in the air. My mind races, searching, hunting, until it lands on a half-developed solution. "Look," I say. "Watch." I close the distance between us, grab her roughly by the cheeks, and kiss her—hard. Two uncomfortable seconds of our mouths slammed together, and then I push her away, my chest heaving with frustration. "I feel nothing right now, Amsterdam," I say, pointing at my heart. "Nothing. At *all.*"

For a second, she just gapes at me; her arms hang motionless at her sides, and even the swishing skirt of her dress seems frozen. I'm frozen, too, because I just did something terrible and horrible and who knows how she'll react?

I'm not surprised when her wide eyes narrow, or when she lets out a disbelieving laugh. When she steps toward me, though, eliminating the space I just established—that, I'm unprepared for. And when she saunters closer, closer, closer, lifting up onto her tiptoes?

I'm not ready for that, either.

I hold my breath and quiet every fight-or-flight instinct in my body, waiting. She leans slowly toward me, every centimeter excruciating; her nose brushes mine before our mouths ever touch, and her breath is soft on my lips.

I refuse to give her what she wants; I refuse to back away, and I refuse to move nearer.

I refuse to be the one who breaks.

But she *lingers*. This insufferable woman lingers, and when her lips finally touch mine, I barely feel them; they're soft, gentle, her hands light on my shoulders as she steadies herself, and my vision is beginning to swim from lack of oxygen—

She leans back, and I inhale as quickly but discreetly as possible. She doesn't go back down from her tiptoes; she doesn't even remove her hands from my shoulders.

"I don't feel anything," she says, and the mere sight of her inches from my face is enough to make my blood simmer and my jaw clench. "But you," she goes on, challenge in her eyes, "your face is red, Hummingbird."

"Because I've been holding my breath so I don't have to smell you," I snap, though I know for a fact that she always

75

smells like peppermint and vanilla, somehow sweet and sharp at the same time. "Get over yourself." In one swift motion I slide my arm around her waist, tangling the other hand in her hair, and then I yank her body to mine. The last expression I see on her face is one of daring and taunting, and I can't stand it. I can't stand *her*.

My lips crash down on hers.

I kiss her with every emotion she stirs in me—frustration and exasperation and wild, red-hot anger—except it's not a kiss; this is a battle. We're holding onto each other too tightly, breathing too hard, and none of it is romantic. I nip at her bottom lip, and she gasps, her fingers digging painfully into my sides.

"You think you can just—"

"Watch me," I snarl against her lips, a surge of triumph rising in my chest as I steal the rest of her words, swallow them. I tangle my hand further in her hair, tilt my head; this is still a fight for dominance, and I'm not going to let her win.

But when she slides her hand into my suit coat, something heats behind my sternum—a tiny, flickering flame that jumps and flares as her touch travels sharply from my waist to my back, fingers curled and grasping.

And when her other hand slides up my chest, finds my tie, and *tugs*, that flame grows brighter.

No, I tell myself desperately as I'm forced even closer to her. I can barely hear my own thoughts over the sounds of our harsh breathing. *You are not enjoying this. You're proving a point.*

She scrapes her teeth against my lip, a bite of pain that heats my blood, and I hate it, I *hate* it—I hate that she can have this effect on me. I hate how well she knows me.

In fact, at this very second, I hate everything about her.

I deepen the kiss, taste her, the strokes of my mouth punishing. She gasps and then retaliates; she pushes me, hard, but not away from herself—she stumbles after me, our mouths still slanted together as my back collides with the bookshelf, and I wince. I can feel the shape of her lips as she grins, and she breaks away just enough that I can see that same challenge in her eyes.

"You can't claim you're not attracted to me and then kiss me like this—"

"Like what? You're kissing me the same way," I say breathlessly. I yank her body back to mine and spin us around, pressing her none too gently against my shelf of classics. Her hair spills around her shoulders, mussed and staticky against the spines of Tolstoy and Dickens and Twain. "This is fueled by spite, Amsterdam. Not love, not attraction," I go on, trying desperately not to notice the rapid rise and fall of her chest or the flush of her skin.

"No one said anything about *love*." She spits the word out, her hands fisting angrily into the fabric of my shirt.

I keep my eyes firmly on hers, don't let them pull away like they want to when I hear that word coming from her lips —because it's too intimate, and I know her too well, and I've seen too much of her deepest soul to trifle with subjects like that.

"It doesn't matter," I say. "I don't love you, I don't like you, and I'm not attracted to you. Can you say the same, Holl?"

I let it slip without thinking, the name I take care never to call her. Her eyes widen infinitesimally; she's still pressed so close that I can feel her breath hitch.

She inhales, shallow, brief, and then speaks as her gaze shutters closed once more, blank brown eyes framed in long, dark lashes. "Don't call me that, *Phoenix*."

My pulse stutters with an odd mixture of nostalgia and regret.

See this? her expression tells me. *This is the line we don't cross. Do you understand?*

I swallow and then duck my head in agreement, the sole concession I can make, because those names belong to a different time, different versions of ourselves. I move my hands from her waist to her shoulders and push gently away, stepping backward—because she's too close, and I don't want her near me. I don't even want her in my line of sight right now.

So I turn my back to her, just as she speaks.

"I'll do it," she says, her voice empty of emotion. "I'll marry you. Once you've legally inherited the company and once your grandmother passes, we separate. As compensation, I want a salary. I also want Maggie's tuition paid for in full, and I want to be added to your insurance." She pauses just briefly. "I think I did something to my knee."

Her knee. Crap.

I jerk my head to glance over my shoulder. "Did I hurt it?" I say, my voice gruff.

"No."

I give a jerk of my head and turn away again. "Fine. Come back tomorrow and we'll discuss terms. I'll have the contract drawn up after that."

"Here?" she says. "In your office?"

"Do you have a problem with that?"

"No." I can picture her chin jutting, her jaw clenching. "I'll be here at five."

I hear her move, and she brushes past me, heading straight for the door. She stops just as one hand comes to rest on the handle; then, without looking back at me, she adds one more thing. "This never happened."

"Obviously," I say coolly.

"There will be no romantic feelings between the two of us."

My eyes narrow. "Not a problem."

"And people would misunderstand, so don't tell anyone."

I roll my eyes. "Go home, Amsterdam." I hesitate. "And fix your hair before you go out there."

She leaves without another word.

THE NICE THING about being your own boss is that you don't need permission to take a day off. So when I leave the next morning, driving my ridiculous little golf cart because I refuse to walk everywhere on this island, I don't go in the direction of my office building. I head over to Dax's place instead.

Some might say I'm avoiding the office—"some" being Wyatt, and he *did* say that—but really I just need a break. I slept horribly last night, plagued by dark, murky dreams of vague foreboding, pulled directly from my memories of the crash—the darkness, the car filling with water, the other-worldly horror that comes from knowing your life is about to end. I woke up drenched in sweat and in a foul mood, made worse by the memory of what happened between Holland and me.

I should have known better. Never kiss the enemy, even if you're doing it to win an argument.

I shake my head and take a deep breath, savoring the crisp ocean air as I pull around to the side of Sunset Repairs. My eyes scan the docks to see if Dax is there, since he's the island's go-to boat mechanic, but I don't see him. I turn to the large, open car bay instead, where a few golf carts are stationed, as well as an ambulance—the island's sole emergency vehicle, and one that gets very little use.

"Dax," I call, killing the engine of my golf cart and hopping out.

From beneath the ambulance, one tanned, grimy arm pokes out; it waves and then disappears again. I approach the vehicle and then crouch down.

"Hey," I say, speaking loudly so I'll be heard over whatever tinkering he's doing under there. "Do you have any spare bike chains lying around?"

The noises coming from under the ambulance stop, and a second later, Dax rolls himself out, his head, arms, and upper torso appearing.

"Maybe," he says, a frown wrinkling his grease-smudged forehead. "Check over in the bin by the cabinets."

I stand up, looking toward the back of the car bay. "The big blue one?" I say, pointing.

"Yep," he says, and his dark head of hair disappears under the ambulance again.

"Thanks," I say, thumping the side. I let him get back to work, dusting off my suit to make sure it's not getting dirty and then heading toward the back. There's a row of black metal cabinets against the wall, next to which I see a giant blue tub; I lean over and peer inside.

"Spare parts," I mutter. I'm going to have to dig.

So I take off my suit coat, hanging it lightly on the cleanest-looking cabinet corner I see, and then I roll up my sleeves.

"Getting ready to fight, Park?" a voice calls from behind me, and I turn to see Beau Palmer emerging from indoors. He's got on a short-sleeved button down and tan shorts, which means this must be his day off.

"I wish," I say. I gesture to the blue tub. "Instead I'm hunting for a bike chain in all this."

He stops next to me and peers into the tub too, then lets out a low whistle. "Good luck," he says with a grin.

I just snort and get started, moving aside metal pieces and parts.

"Hey, how's your girl doing?" Beau adds from behind me, and I freeze. Then, scowling, I turn to glare at him.

"What?" he says from where he's just seated himself on top of a small table. His voice is too innocent, as is his smile.

"She's not my girl," I say. I resume digging.

"But you knew exactly who I was talking about," he says, and I can still hear the grin in his voice. "Either way—is she doing okay after what happened?"

I freeze again; this time, though, I don't scowl or glare when I turn around. "What do you mean?" I say, a metal handlebar still dangling in my grip. I straighten up. "What happened?"

Beau's grin vanishes, giving place to surprise. "Did she not tell you?" he says.

I shake my head.

"Huh." He eyes me skeptically, like he's deciding whether to share, and then he ducks his chin. "She called me. A week ago? Maybe a week and a half? She fell for some internet scheme. She said they wiped out her account."

"They wiped out—"

"Her entire account, yeah," Beau says, nodding. He's serious Beau now, the police officer instead of my friend. "I had her file a report, but there's not a ton we can do. We're not sitting on a world-class cybercrimes division or anything."

I scrub my free hand down my face, exhaling heavily. "Amsterdam," I mutter, suddenly hit with a wave of exhaustion. This is why she needed money, I guess. "What internet scheme?"

"She was trying to buy something off some sketchy site," he says. "I don't remember what it was called; it's in the report."

"What was she trying to buy?"

Beau's lips twist into a reluctant smile. "A dog bed."

Am I hearing him right? "A *dog bed?*" I repeat.

"Yeah—a human-sized dog bed. She seemed super embarrassed, so don't give her a hard time," he adds sternly. "I didn't ask for details, but she said it just looked comfortable."

A human-sized dog bed—good grief, Holland.

I sigh. "Well, I'm going to hire her, so I think she'll be okay."

"You're giving her a job?" Beau says, looking surprised once more.

I jerk my shoulders and turn back to the bucket of spare parts. "Something like that." Then, without looking back, I add, "Come help me dig."

CHAPTER 10

Holland

I KNOCK on Phoenix's office door at four-fifty-nine.

I've actually been here since four-fifty, but I didn't want to seem too eager, and I wanted to give myself a few more minutes before I officially committed to marry him. This whole shindig probably won't include a bachelorette party; it felt right to take a moment and commemorate my singledom.

It has, on the whole, been unremarkable.

I smooth my hand down my shirt, checking to make sure everything looks okay; I'm dressed out of character in tight jeans, a white v-neck, and a fitted tan blazer. Thankfully I own a pair of tan ankle boots, because my knee keeps giving me trouble, and I don't want to deal with heels today.

I brush away one last wrinkle as Wyatt opens the door to the office, and the smile I give him is genuine and full of relief.

I'm being stupid, obviously. I can face Phoenix just fine. I can face this room just fine. Nothing is different today from yesterday. Still, it's nice to have two extra seconds before I'm forced to see him.

Usually when I see Wyatt, though—which admittedly is not often—he's wearing an expression of vague politeness. Something about him is different today. He's dressed the same, but he looks more alert—more present, maybe, his eyes quick and sharp and focused.

He steps back and gestures for me to enter the office, and then he returns to the same leather chair he was sitting in yesterday. He doesn't open the large leather folder he always seems to carry; he just waits, his hands folded in his lap, his eyes on Phoenix.

Phoenix, meanwhile, doesn't even look up from the papers he's signing at his desk; he just waves one absent hand and says "Close the door, please."

I do as he says, mostly because even though the office staff are all filtering out for the day, I don't want to risk anyone hearing about this arrangement. The door clicks shut just as Phoenix speaks again.

"Glad to see you're taking this seriously," he says, and I turn to find him gazing with reluctant approval at my outfit. I smooth my hands over my blazer once more.

"Money is changing hands," I say. "We're signing a contract. This is a business meeting."

"I agree," he says. He stands up, straightening his tie.

His tie, which is similar in color to the tie I yanked on yesterday, in this very office.

I can't believe I did that.

"Are you ready?" Phoenix says, and I jump, pressing the back of my hand to my warm cheeks.

But he's not talking to me. "Whenever you are," Wyatt says promptly—and out comes the leather folder, which he flips open to reveal a legal pad.

I'm glad he didn't ask me the same question, because I don't know what my answer would be. I don't think I'm ready; I don't think it's possible to be truly ready for some-thing like a contractual marriage to a man whose mere face makes you angry.

But ready or not, this is what needs to happen. I need his financial support, as much as I absolutely hate to admit it. So I clear my throat and then dive in anyway.

"If we're going to do this," I say, "I have some conditions."

"I'm sure you do," Phoenix says under his breath. Then, louder, he goes on, "But that's why we're meeting today. Give me a moment, please, and we can discuss everything."

I stare at him for a second, frowning. That sentence he just said was so...*nice*. Polite and professional. Is this what business-meeting Phoenix is like? Why can't he be like this all the time? Is that too much to ask?

He would probably be nicer to you if you were nicer to him, a little voice chimes in my brain.

I ignore that voice.

Phoenix rounds his giant desk and takes a seat in the chair between mine and Wyatt's. He looks back and forth between us for a second and then begins. "All right," he says, folding his arms across his chest. "Let's start. First things first: duration. This contract would be for the remaining length of my grandmother's life. She's been given several more months to live, so realistically, we're looking at the rest of the summer. Is that agreeable?"

I nod slowly, thinking it through as Wyatt's pen scribbles furiously on his legal pad. "Yes," I say. Then, more decisively, "Yes. That's agreeable."

Phoenix gives a brisk bob of his chin and speaks again. "Excellent. I propose the following, then: you and I marry quickly and quietly at Town Hall. We'll take official wedding portraits, however, because my family will already be suspicious as is. For the duration of the contract, we will live together—"

"Is that necessary?" I cut in, my stomach flipping at the

thought of actually living with Phoenix. I tuck a few strands of hair behind my ear. "We're over here on the island. Your family's not going to know if we're not cohabitating."

Phoenix's only response is a dry, humorless laugh.

"It will be necessary," Wyatt says, putting down his pen and looking apologetically at me. "The Butterfields will be very suspicious about the timing of these nuptials, and more than one of them will want to prove that your marriage is fake. I think it's safe to assume that people will be watching you."

I blink at him. "I—are you serious?"

"Very much so," Wyatt says.

"My family is insane," Phoenix says. The words are short, clipped.

"I mean, everyone's family is a little weird—"

"No," he says, shaking his head. "*Weird* is not the correct term. My aunt Rita once tried to hit my uncle Clarence with her car because he set her living room on fire. My mother is deeply in debt but continues to expand her fascinator collection using my money. Barbara is just the same, and the cousins are all crazy, too. I'm glad to be alive, but my grandparents had no business procreating."

"Okay," I say, my eyes wide. "We'll live together. Fine. But I get my own room," I add.

He dips his head. "Yes. We will live together, but we will use separate rooms and separate beds. We will tell no one on the island—none of your friends or mine," he says with a severe look, and I nod quickly in assent.

"Cat already sort of knows a little bit," I admit, ignoring his glare. "But agreed for the rest." I don't want anyone knowing my shame. "Maggie…"

His expression softens the tiniest bit. "Maggie should be

fine, as long as she doesn't tell the rest of your family. The fewer people who know about this, the better."

Amen.

"As for public expectations," he goes on, "when we are with my family, we will behave as a loving couple. We will hold hands and touch and all the normal things couples do." The look he shoots me is cool, assessing. "Is this going to be a problem?"

I swallow. "No," I say, because he's talking about this in such a detached, businesslike manner that he must be totally fine with it. If he's fine, I'll be fine, too. "It won't be a problem."

"Good." Another brisk nod. "For the sake of appearances, you will also need to conform to a certain look. Your normal attire is fine when we're here, but when we're in the presence of my grandmother or other family members, you'll need to take my direction on clothing and styling."

I grimace as images of pants suits and pearls fill my head. Three or four snarky replies dance on my tongue, but I hold them in, because I'm trying to be professional about this. "Fine," I say. "How's that going to work?"

Now Phoenix grimaces, looking even more put out than I do. "It may require a joint shopping trip, which will no doubt be painful for all involved."

Good grief. Is he going to *Princess Diaries* me? Is this going to be one of those things where he passes his black card to a sales associate and she returns with piles and piles of clothing and makes me try all of them on?

But he changes the subject before I can protest or ask more questions. "For compensation, this is my offer," he says. Wyatt slides a sheet of paper out of his folder and passes it to me, and Phoenix goes on. "One-third delivered upon signing, one-third delivered upon marriage, and the last third delivered upon dissolution."

I take the paper, look at the number, and feel my jaw drop. I stare at it for a second, just to make sure I'm not hallucinating. Then I look at Phoenix.

"You're stupidly rich," I say.

"Mmm." He doesn't look particularly happy about it. "Yes. I am."

I lean back in my chair. "Does this include Maggie's tuition?" I say, waving the paper.

"No," he says, businesslike once more. He leans back too, crossing one ankle over his knee. "Maggie's tuition will be added on top of that, as will any medical expenses you incur." He gestures at my bad knee. "You'll be added to my insurance as well, of course. Is this acceptable?"

"Yes," I say. I guess I'm a gold digger now.

"My family is going to be very suspicious, Amsterdam," he says, and it's weird hearing him speak so professionally but still calling me that. He pins me with a look so serious that a little twinge of anxiety pulses low in my gut, and then he goes on. "They will be watching for any sign that something is not right between us. Lawrence wants to inherit, as do several others. Ultimately I believe it will come down to either Lawrence or me, but I can't rule out other possibilities. So while we are with my family..." He exhales softly. "You need to look at me like I hang the sun, the moon, and the stars."

"I understand," I say, but my words are unsure.

"Do you?" he says, leaning forward. His black-brown eyes paralyze me, hold me so firmly in place that I can barely breathe. "You will need to behave, Miss Blakely"—he leans further, close enough that I can smell his leather-and-mahogany scent—"as though I'm the one you dream about."

His voice is soft but firm as he goes on, "We will need to convince them that we are deeply, deeply in love."

And I swear at this very moment, you could hear a pin drop in this office—he's staring at me so intently, so *seriously*. His black brows wing severely over his dark eyes, and his mouth is set in a grim, uncompromising line as he waits for my reply.

This is not my Phoenix, the one who puts fish in my mailbox and calls me rude names. This is executive Phoenix, get-stuff-done Phoenix—this is don't-mess-with-me Phoenix.

He's kind of...intimidating.

No, he's not, I tell myself. *There's nothing intimidating about him. Suck it up.* I look at the paper in my lap; I think about Maggie. Then, finally I nod.

"I'm in," I say.

Some of the tension leaks out of Phoenix's shoulders as he sits back in his leather chair once more. "Good," he says. "In that case, now is the time to list your conditions."

"I have two," I say. "The first one is that we're not going to sleep together."

"Agreed," he says immediately, his expression blank. "Next."

"The second is that you cannot fall in love with me, and vice versa. No feelings will enter into this arrangement."

I know it sounds stupid—I know. And the risk of us falling for each other is almost nonexistent. But I need to be thorough.

But Phoenix just smirks, and it's the first time this whole meeting that I've seen an expression I'm so familiar with— now that our business is coming to a close, it looks like he's back to his true colors. "You already said that," he says. "Yesterday. You're safe from me, Amsterdam."

"Fine," I say, relief coursing through me. "That's it for me, then."

"If that's all," Wyatt says, "I'll have a contract drawn up and ready for you to sign by end of day tomorrow."

I stand up, nodding. "Sounds good. Thanks, Wyatt."

Phoenix stands too, and I'm surprised when he holds out his hand. I stare at it.

"Shake, Gangster Glam," he says, the faintest hint of taunting in his voice. "It's what people do when they make business deals."

I put my hand in his and squeeze it as hard as I can.

He cocks one eyebrow at me and squeezes my hand in return, a quick, bone-crushing pulse of pain.

"Ow!" I say, kicking him in the shin.

He winces and gives my hand one last squeeze, and I kick him again.

"Get out of my office," he says, wrenching our hands apart and pointing at the door. "Wyatt will email you the DocuSign tomorrow evening. Start looking for a wedding dress; we're taking official wedding photos in three days."

My eyes widen as images of me in a frilly, floofy wedding monstrosity pop into my head. "That soon?" I say.

"Yes. I'll pay, so don't worry about price," he says briskly, straightening his suit coat. "And I don't care about the style, but choose something classy, please, and not too casual."

I scoff. "I'm a classy person, Toucan."

He just points to the door again. "Go. Wyatt will drive you home."

"In the golf cart?" I say with a groan.

"Yes. Don't complain."

"Do you always do the things he tells you to do?" I say to Wyatt, who's closing his folder and standing with a twinkle of humor in his eyes.

"He pays me well enough that I have no objections," Wyatt says with a little smile.

Phoenix snorts from behind us, and when I look over my shoulder, I see that he's returned to his desk. Is he going back to work?

"Leave your account information with Wyatt," he adds, his attention already on the computer screen. "He'll deposit enough funds for the dress."

I nod and leave the office, Wyatt following closely behind me.

My mind reels on the way home, and I'm grateful that Wyatt lets me stew in silence. He ducks his head politely when he drops me off at Nana Lu's, giving me another little smile, and I hop out after giving him my bank account info.

The gravel crunches under my feet as I enter the courtyard, but I barely hear. I nearly trip over the railroad tie, and it takes me several tries to get the door unlocked. When I finally get it open, I call Maggie.

Shopping for wedding dresses by myself is one of the most depressing things I can think of. I'm going to need reinforcements.

"You want me to do what with you?" she says. Her voice still hasn't completely lost its sweet, youthful quality. "Did you say _wedding dress?_"

"Yes," I tell her, toeing my ankle boots off as I step inside. Sometimes I come home still half-expecting Nana Lu to be here, seated on that awful couch with a large-print book or snacking on a vanilla cupcake at the kitchen table. I always deflate a little when I realize the house is empty now. "Wedding dress shopping. I'm getting married."

Maggie is silent for a moment. "I'm sorry," she says finally. "I'm confused."

"I know," I say, sighing as I trudge down the hall, past the living room, and to my bedroom. "It's complicated. Come hang out with me tomorrow and I'll explain."

"You haven't even been dating anyone, have you?" she says. "Why are you getting married? Who's the guy? Holland..." She trails off, and I hear her take a deep breath before speaking again. "Are you pregnant? You can tell me if you are—"

"*No!*" I say quickly. "No, definitely not pregnant. Come tomorrow and I'll tell you, okay?" I try to make my voice coaxing, but it sounds more like begging. "Please? It's only an hour's drive."

"I have statistics tomorrow, Holl," she says. "I can't—I don't—" She breaks off and then sighs, the sound staticky over the phone. "You're actually getting married?"

"Yeah," I say softly. Seriousness bleeds into my voice, a reality that I still can't quite believe myself. "I am. I promise I'll explain everything, okay? Just come help me, please." I swallow and then admit the truth: "I don't want to shop for wedding dresses by myself."

Without even changing clothes, I pull back my turquoise comforter and climb into bed, curling up on my side with the phone balanced on my cheek. I still have hours before I would normally go to sleep, but right now, I need to cocoon.

It's Maggie's soft, loving voice that plays in my ear as I close my eyes.

"In that case," she says, "of course I'll ditch statistics. I hate it anyway." I can hear her teasing smile, the one I know she's giving me because she can tell something's up. "I'll see you tomorrow morning, bride-to-be."

My eyes sting suspiciously, but I blink until they stop. "Thanks, Mag." I pause and then add, "You can't tell anyone about this."

"I figured," she says. "You're going to explain everything the second I get there."

"I promise," I say, pulling the covers up under my chin and tucking them tightly in place. "Drive safe, okay?"

"I will. And Holl?"

"Mmm."

"Start thinking about what kind of lingerie you want me to get you for your wedding gift."

I just laugh.

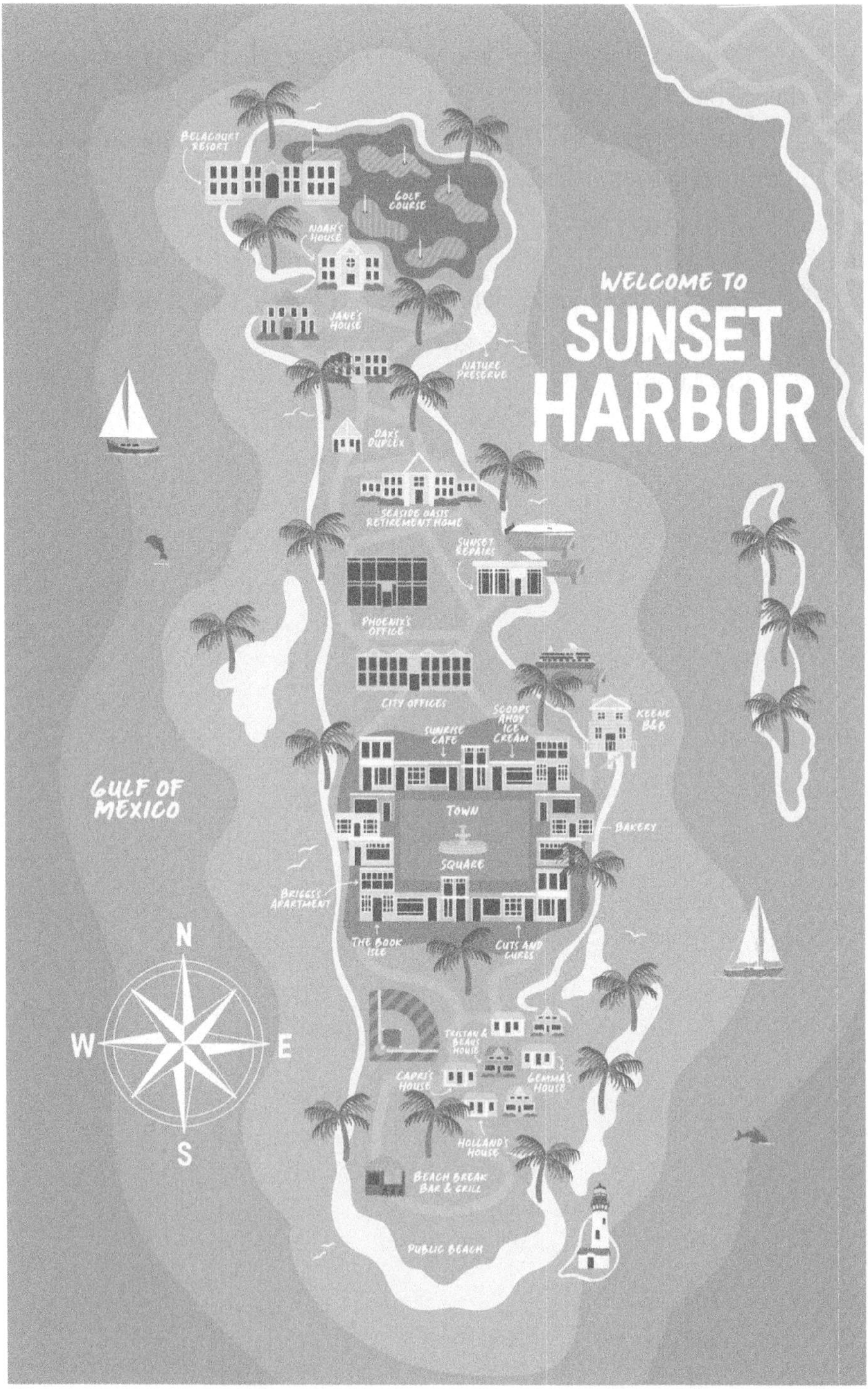

CHAPTER 11

Holland

MAGGIE IS the cutest person I know. Maybe I'm biased because she's my little sister, but I've always thought she's adorable. She doesn't appreciate when I tell her this, now that she's older, but I tell her anyway.

My smile blooms freely when I get off the ferry the next morning and find her waiting for me, a giant insulated tumbler of what I'm sure is Diet Coke clutched in her hand. She's leaning back against her little Toyota Corolla, her other hand shielding her eyes against the sun. She's got on jeans today, even though she's usually a t-shirt and joggers girl.

"Nine is too early to be anywhere," she says when I reach her.

"Don't be silly," I say, throwing my arms around her and squeezing extra hard. She lets out a little *oomph* and then laughs, hugging me back.

I breathe her in for a minute, the faint scent of shampoo in her honey-blonde hair, the smell of the lotion she uses every day because her hands and elbows are perpetually dry.

She feels like home.

"It's so good to see you," I tell her, my voice muffled by her hair. "You look so cute." I step back and hold her at arms' length. "Look at your freckles, Mags!"

"They're multiplying," she says with a scowl that wrinkles her button nose. It's an expression that looks a lot like the one I give Phoenix. "Because of the sun. And I'm not cute. I'm twenty."

"Just because you're twenty doesn't mean you're less cute," I say with a smile. "How was the drive?"

"It was fine," she says with a careless roll of her shoulders. "You know I'm not really a morning person, but I have my caffeine." She holds it out to me. "Want any?"

"Yes, actually," I say, taking the giant thermos from her. I take a few drinks and then pass it back. "Okay, let's go. I'm under strict orders from Nana to bring you over this afternoon. I figure we can do the dress this morning and then go over there, and you can still make the evening ferry back." I glance at her as I head around to the passenger side. "Does that work for you?"

"Yep!" she says. She pins me with a look. "So hop in and then start talking."

"I will!" I say. "I will." I wave my phone at her as I open the door. "Let me just pull up directions to the dress shop first. There are two of them around here."

It feels amazing to be back in a car; I love Sunset Harbor, but all the walking and biking and golf carts took some getting used to. I find the directions to the first place once I'm in my seat, and then I close the door.

"Basically," I say once Maggie is in, "I'm marrying Phoenix."

Her hand freezes in the process of turning the key in the ignition, and her head whips toward me. "Phoenix?" she says, her blue eyes wide. "*Trev's* Phoenix?"

He's not just Trev's Phoenix. It's the first thought that pops into my mind, but I don't say it. Maggie would misunderstand. So I clear my throat instead, looking pointedly down at my hands in my lap. "Yep. Trev's Phoenix."

I thought a lot last night about how much to tell Maggie. I don't want to lie to her or keep things from her. But I don't want her to worry needlessly, either. So sometime around one in the morning, I decided on the abridged truth.

"I could use some extra cash," I say, "and Phoenix needs someone to marry him." Thankfully the glossed-over truth doesn't come out high-pitched, which is what usually gives me away. "You remember he's part of Butterfield, right?"

"Yeah." Maggie pulls out of her parking spot.

I nod. "His grandmother recently changed things so that if he wants to inherit, he needs to be married. So I'm going to marry him, just for a few months, because his grandma doesn't have long left. He'll pay me—a salary, basically. Once he's inherited and she's passed, we'll separate."

"You make it sound like you're both waiting around for an old woman to die," Maggie says, keeping her eyes in front of her. She flicks the turn signal, and a little *click-click, click-click* fills the car.

"I know," I say, wrinkling my nose. "And as awful as it sounds, I actually think that's kind of what's going on. You know him; he's not cruel." Because whatever else Phoenix might be—rude, offensive, sometimes even mean—he's not cruel.

"Right."

"But it sounds like there's no love lost between his grandma and the rest of the family," I go on. "Or between Phoenix and the rest of them, either."

"Wow," she says in a low voice. "So you're doing the whole thing, then? Wedding dress, walk down the aisle?"

"Not quite," I say. "We're taking wedding photos, because he thinks his family is going to be suspicious that this is a fake marriage."

"Which…it is," Maggie points out.

"Yeah, it is." I nod. "I mean, we're legally getting married. But it will be at the Town Hall, and it's not going to last."

"Okay," she says, her eyes narrowed as she thinks. "I think I'm following. But you and Phoenix aren't—you guys don't—"

"No," I say quickly. "No. We don't get along. At all. But he doesn't have a lot of options, and the extra money for me won't hurt."

"Wow," she says again. She shoots me a look and then gives her attention back to the road. "Are you sure you know what you're doing?"

"No," I admit. "Not completely. But weighing the pros and cons, this course of action seems to be in my favor."

"All right," she says with a little shrug. Then she smiles. "In that case, let's get you a wedding dress. You'll be the most beautiful fake bride in the world."

Something eases inside of me at her acceptance, a tension I hadn't realized was there. "I don't know about *most beautiful*, but I'd like to at least look put together. Turn right at the next light," I add.

"You'll look more than put together," she says. "You'll be gorgeous. You're going to knock Phoenix's socks off."

"Oh, no—no no no," I say to her. "No. Phoenix's socks will stay on. We were very clear about that. Everyone's socks will remain on. Besides," I go on, scrunching up my nose, "Phoenix is—"

"Hot," she cuts me off. She turns into the large parking lot of our first bridal shop. "Phoenix is hot. He's dreamy. He looks better in a suit than anyone I know." She finds a spot to park and pulls in neatly; then she looks at me, her eyes sparkling. "Do you think you guys might—"

"No," I say again, more firmly. "Definitely not. Whatever you're going to say, the answer is no."

She pulls the keys out of the ignition and then gives me another little scowl, just like when I complimented her freckles. "Fine," she says. "But I'm going to hold out hope."

"You do that," I say, patting her on the arm. "Just know that you're wasting your time."

The inside of the bridal shop is immediately overwhelming; the door hasn't even closed all the way behind us before a little thread of panic shoots through me. Everything is either white or light blue, and there's nothing simple about the decor; I see lace and sparkles and fanciness all around.

The idea of getting married in a white sundress suddenly sounds ten times more appealing. Would that fly with Phoenix?

But Maggie must be able to sense how I'm feeling, because she puts one firm hand on my back and pushes me forward, further into the shop.

A smiling woman hurries over and greets us, enthusiasm positively dripping from her; I have to force my answering smile. She introduces herself as Marie and then asks what she can help with, and I stare at her for a good two seconds before I'm able to say anything.

"I'm getting married, Marie," I say. The words are still bizarre to me. "So I need a wedding dress. And I guess some shoes too, if you sell those."

Marie looks at me like *Of course we sell wedding shoes, who do you think we are?* Then she smiles again and whisks us further into the belly of the wedding beast, around several little displays topped with accessories, through racks and racks and racks of white lace and tulle and chiffon, past several brides trying on dresses in front of mirrors, and finally to a back corner of the shop.

"We don't have any appointments scheduled right now," she says, beaming as she gestures to two poofy chairs in front of a large, three-paneled mirror like the ones we just passed. "So why don't you tell me what you're looking for, and I'll pull some for you to try on."

"Simple," I say immediately, glancing at the tulle ball-gown a woman at the next mirror is wearing. It's lovely, but it's not my style. "Simple. And—classy, I guess."

Marie nods, tapping one long finger against her chin as she thinks. Then she nods again, and her blunt bob doesn't sway an inch. I think it must be hairsprayed solid. "Elegant and timeless; I love it. What about shape? Do you have any ideas there?"

"Not really," I admit. I settle into one of the chairs, and Maggie sits in the other. "Maybe just not a lot of volume."

And to her credit, Marie is great at her job. The first two dresses I try on aren't my favorites—too much tulle on one, a slit I don't like on the other—but the third...

"Holland," Maggie says, her hands on her cheeks as she smiles at me in the mirror. "It's *gorgeous*."

She's right; dress number three is gorgeous.

It's long and flowing, with a v-neck, fluttering chiffon sleeves, and a plunging back. There's light beading on the bust, but that's it; the rest is unadorned.

Simple but not boring; sexy but not cheap. It's perfect. And the woman staring back at me in the mirror looks like a *bride*. An actual, real-life bride.

"Maggie," I whisper as Marie looks rapturously on. "I'm getting *married*."

"I know," she says, her eyes wide, her smile tremulous. "You're getting married. How weird is that?"

For a second I debate with myself: Is this a dress I want to wear for a wedding that isn't real? Do I want to waste this gorgeous gown on a man who's not actually going to be a true, loving husband?

But my questions are brief. Because the truth is, I don't know if I'll ever wear another wedding dress after this. I hope to get married for real someday, but who knows?

So I stand up a little straighter. "Marie," I say to the woman. "I think this is the one."

Marie claps her hands loudly and shows every single one of her pearly whites as she smiles.

After giving in and allowing Maggie to buy me a set of jewelry—which she refuses to let me look at until the day of the photos—we head back to Sunset Harbor to see Nana Lu.

We look absurd carrying everything on the ferry. I've got the hanging bag with the dress draped over my arm so no one can see the name of the bridal shop emblazoned on the front—thankfully it's opaque—and we've transferred the shoes and jewelry into an old duffle from Maggie's trunk so no one will see the bridal shop logo there either.

"Remember," I say once we've dropped the enormous bags of shoes, jewelry, and dress back at the house, "not a word about this. Nana's heart would stop if she thought Phoenix and I were actually getting married."

"She would be so happy," Maggie says wistfully, and I let my breath gust out of me.

"She would. So don't say anything."

It's a little past noon when we get to Seaside Oasis, where the receptionist informs us that Nana's probably still eating lunch down in the cafeteria. We find her there, hunched over a meal of some sort of pasta dish with green beans and jello. She sets down her fork with trembling hands as soon as she sees us.

"My Maggie Moo," she says, trying to scoot her chair back.

We hurry the rest of the way to her before she can stand.

"Stay sitting, Nana," Maggie says quickly, wrapping her

arms around Nana's thin frame and hugging her. "We'll join you and you can finish eating, okay?"

"It's this pasta today," Nana mumbles when Maggie has let her go. She picks up her fork and pokes at the meal. "They overdo the noodles."

"So it's easier to chew," Maggie says, sitting in the chair to Nana's left.

"Hi, Nana," I say, swooping down and kissing her soft, age-spotted cheek.

"Hi, sweetheart," she says. She looks back and forth between us once I've settled on her right, her smile as wide as I've ever seen it. "Both my granddaughters," she says happily. "Isn't this a treat. How have you been, Maggie Moo?"

No one has called Maggie that since she was about eight, but Nana always will.

"I've been good," Maggie says, patting Nana's hand and smiling. "My classes are fine, and I've got really good professors."

Nana Lu blinks owlishly at Maggie from behind her round glasses. "It's summer, sweetheart. Do you do school in the summer now?"

Maggie bobs her head. "I'm doing the summer term this year. It's more condensed, so I have one class four days a week instead of two, and the other class I have five days a week."

"Is that too much?" Nana says, glancing at me and then back at Maggie. "A girl should have time for fun, shouldn't she?"

"I still have lots of fun," Maggie says, waving her hand. "I hang out with my friends and that kind of thing."

"Oh, good," Nana says with a wobbly nod. "Good. You

should play sometimes. And what about you, sweetie?" she says, looking at me now. "Did you buy your new shoes?"

I swallow my guilt and smile. "I bought some new shoes just today," I say. "Maggie came with me. They're very pretty."

Nana Lu positively beams.

It takes some prodding to get Nana to eat now that she's distracted, so we sit with her and remind her to keep taking bites until all her food is gone. My mother doesn't take after her much, but both she and Nana are picky eaters.

Nana Lu, thankfully, is much warmer than my mother— soft and friendly rather than standoffish and detached. My mom cares, and she loves, but she doesn't do it openly, and she doesn't express herself well, if at all. She's always been that way, even before Trev died.

These moments with Nana, then, are like a warm hug. She wants to know every detail about our lives, and she's overflowing with love and affection. The afternoon flies by, the three of us laughing and chatting in Nana's room, until it's time to get Maggie back to the ferry.

"I'll come see you again soon," she promises, giving Nana a hug.

"Oh, yes," Nana says, patting Maggie's back. "Please do."

"I heard a rumor that Presley James has been spotted around here, so I'll bring some binoculars for spying."

I turn to her, frowning. "Presley James? The actress?"

"Yep," Maggie says.

"She's such a cute girl," Nana says.

"Around here? Like, on the island?" That's ridiculous. A giant movie star would never come to Sunset Harbor.

"It's just what I heard," Maggie says. "Come on, Nana."

We tuck her into her bed and turn on Jeopardy—her favorite—and then I press one last kiss to her fluffy hair.

"Bye, Nana," I say, and with another wave, we leave.

By the time I get home after seeing Maggie off, it's evening, and I'm exhausted. I would love nothing more than to curl up in bed with a book. But I check my email first, and sure enough, the contract is ready and waiting for me to sign. I read it through, not once but twice, and then, after staring at the signature line for a solid two minutes, I sign it digitally.

The first payment from Phoenix hits my account the next morning.

CHAPTER 12

Holland

"I DON'T WANT to do this."

"I don't care."

We're standing in the hallway of a very nice hotel, bags in tow, staring at a fancy door with a gold *110* on it. It's a set of double doors, actually, and it's at the end of the hallway, so I assume it's a suite. I'm not surprised; this is Phoenix we're talking about. He probably doesn't use regular hotel rooms.

I have my wedding dress bag draped over my arm, and it's heavier than it should be. Wyatt, bless his heart, is carrying the bag that has my shoes, jewelry, and beauty supplies inside. That one isn't light either, but I don't notice any signs on his face that it's too much. Either way, I bet he'd love to put it down, and I'd like to hang my dress up somewhere too, instead of carrying it.

But to do that, I'd need to enter the hotel room.

I glower at Phoenix—who, by the way, is carrying exactly *nothing*—and then reiterate my point. "I brought my own makeup, Penguin. My own hair supplies too. I don't need a team of people to help me get ready for wedding pictures—"

But I'm forced into silence as Phoenix steps suddenly toward me; my jaw snaps shut as I shuffle back. The tan carpet is so thick and plush that our footsteps are silent.

"Did you or did you not sign the contract?" Phoenix says

quietly, his expression heartlessly impassive. He's already wearing his wedding clothes; a suit, thank goodness, rather than a tuxedo, navy blue and tailored to perfection. His hair is styled more carefully than normal, too, swept back in a way that somehow looks effortless. The hallway light above us casts shadows over his face, illuminating his sharp cheekbones.

He looks good. That's what I'm trying to say here; he looks really, really good.

I swallow and square my shoulders, trying not to think about my current velour tracksuit ensemble. "Yes," I say. "I signed it."

He takes another step toward me, and that faint leather-and-mahogany scent tickles my nose. "And did you or did you not receive your first payment?"

"I received it."

He nods slowly, raising one eyebrow. "Then you know that you're required to adhere to whatever style I believe is appropriate when interacting with my family. Since these portraits will be used as proof of our union, they fall under that umbrella." He looks down at me for another second before jerking his chin over my shoulder, in the direction of the door to the suite. "So let's go, Amsterdam. We don't have all day, and believe it or not, I'd like to get this over with just as much as you would."

"If you're so worried, why didn't you pick out the dress too?" I say. "Why stop at the makeup and hair?"

"Because I don't believe you incapable of choosing a nice wedding dress," he says. "You prefer casual clothing, but you're neither cheap nor trashy, and you know what looks good on you. You were better suited to choosing a gown than I would have been."

I blink at him in surprise—I'm pretty sure that was a compliment—but he keeps talking.

"Let's *go.*" And with that, he reaches around me and slides the card key through the reader; from behind me sounds a little beep. Phoenix steps past me and pushes the door open, disappearing into the suite. Wyatt follows him, and I'm left with no choice but to do the same.

I try to be classy about my amazement, but in truth, it's the biggest hotel room I've ever seen. It's not even just one room; it's multiple. The double doors open into a large, pristine living area, with a flat-screen TV and several stiff-looking couches. There's a little kitchenette off in one corner and a few rooms off the living area. Everything is very neat and very clean, which is intimidating; I hope there's no dirt or mud on my shoes.

Phoenix walks like he knows where he's going, so I just follow him. He passes through the TV area and into one of the rooms on the other side, which turns out to be a giant bedroom, complete with vanity, closet, and a jacuzzi in one corner. This is my stop, I can tell, judging by the three ladies pulling out cases of makeup and a box of styling tools. They're dressed all in black, and they work with a brisk efficiency that can only come from being hired by Phoenix.

"Do you have everything you need?" he says, looking around the room.

"I think so," I say with a sigh.

He cocks his brow at me. "I was talking to your stylists."

Of course he was. Heat rises in my face, but I ignore it.

"We have everything," one of the ladies says—the nicest-looking one, and the youngest. She gives Phoenix a little smile, and he jerks his head in satisfaction. Then he turns to me.

"Here," he says, reaching into his pocket. He hesitates for a second and then pulls something out. "Put this on."

There, in his open palm, is a ring—a diamond solitaire, winking and glistening in the light of the large windows, at least two carats, with a thin gold band.

"Is that *real?*"

It's the first thing that pops out of my mouth, because that stone is enormous. It will snag on my hair and my clothes. It will be the set of brass knuckles I've never had.

But Phoenix just looks at me, nonplussed. "Of course it's real."

I swallow, staring at the ring. "Are you sure you want to do that? That diamond is huge."

He sighs, looking tired. "I wish I didn't need to marry you, but..." He trails off, then shakes his head. "You're not a fake-diamond woman."

"What is that supposed to mean?"

"It means what it means," he says shortly. "Put it on. We can have the size adjusted later if necessary." Then he turns to the ladies setting up. "I've got quite the headache, so I need to excuse myself for a while. I'll be back in a bit. All right?"

They give him varying replies of assent, and he sweeps out of the room without a backward glance.

"Please sit down, Miss Blakely," the nice-looking one says. She gestures at the chair they've put in front of the vanity.

I slip Phoenix's ring on my finger—it fits, bizarrely enough—and then, taking a deep breath, I move to the chair and sit down.

The nice woman smiles at me in the mirror. "Let's make you beautiful," she says.

This is going to be a long morning.

IT'S a full hour before we hear from Phoenix again.

I have been moisturized and plucked and painted; my eyelashes look so long and so dark that I can see them in my peripheral vision, and my lips are a pink that they've never been before. I actually don't mind the color.

When Phoenix knocks on the door and asks how everything is going, I jump so violently that the lady working on my hair frowns at me in the mirror. She wields the curling wand like a weapon, so I still myself and then answer.

"We're fine," I say. "We're..." I glance at the lady in the mirror. "Almost done?"

She lifts broad shoulders and continues to curl my hair.

"Can I come in?" Phoenix calls, and the nice lady speaks before I can.

"Of course," she says.

I disagree, but I guess I have no say here, so I keep quiet.

"I meant to ask you, my beautiful bride," he says as he sweeps into the room, his eyes on his phone instead of on me. He heads straight for the bed and settles himself on the edge, then continues. "I heard from Beau that you were scammed."

I freeze, gaping at Phoenix in the mirror. When he finally glances up and finds my gaze, a little smirk forms on his stupid face.

"I—is he allowed to tell you that? Isn't there something about confidentiality?" I say, turning to look at him. The lady with the curling wand *tsks*, grabbing my head with an iron grip and forcing it back forward.

"I don't know," Phoenix says. "But he said you fell for an internet scam trying to buy something." He eyes me. "What, exactly, were you trying to purchase?" His smirk widens. "Something scandalous?"

You'd think so, wouldn't you? But…"No," I say. "Get your mind out of the gutter."

He stands up, tucking his phone into his suit coat and then sliding his hands casually in his pockets. He moves toward me until he's standing right behind me, looking down at me in the mirror from next to my hair-wand-wielding stylist.

And I can see the exact moment he spots the half-open zipper of my shirt; his eyebrows shoot up, and then his gaze swings to mine.

"They were contouring my collar bones," I mutter, giving him a look which clearly screams *You asked for this, don't complain.*

He grins like he knows exactly what I'm thinking.

I, meanwhile, daydream about what kind of imprint this ring would leave if I punched him in the nose.

He pulls his eyes away from my open zipper and then leans down so that his head hovers directly over my shoulder. "So what did you try to buy, Amsterdam?"

"Nothing."

"Was it maybe…" He turns his head until his lips are right at my ear. "A dog bed?" he whispers.

And once again, I find myself gaping at him in the mirror. "He told you?" I say, outraged.

"A *human-sized* dog bed, I heard."

"I was—it was—" But I'm too flustered to do anything but stutter, so I snap my mouth shut. "I don't have to justify my purchases to you," I say. Then I narrow my eyes at him. "I thought you had a headache."

"It's gone."

"Would you like me to bring it back?" I ask sweetly.

That grin of his widens. "How? Will you chatter inces-santly in my ear for five minutes? That would do the trick."

"Go away."

"It's almost time to get your dress on," the nice stylist says. I can't help but notice that all of them are ignoring Phoenix's presence, even though he's probably in the way. Does he get to do whatever he wants, just because he's footing the bill?

"I'm not getting dressed with you in the room," I tell him. "Go away."

He stands up, his eyes still glittering with amusement. "I'll be in the living room," he says as he turns and heads for the door. "Our session is supposed to start in fifteen minutes, so try to be ready by then." And with that he leaves, closing the door behind him.

The nice stylist offers to help me get into my dress, but I don't feel like showing off my underwear to a complete stranger, so I decline. When the woman with the curling wand finally proclaims her job done, the three of them pack everything up while I take my dress into the bathroom to change.

And while it actually might have been helpful to have someone else there with me, I do manage to get everything on okay. There's just some one-legged wobbling involved. But the dress is pretty much backless, so the zipper doesn't go up too high, and I don't step on or rip anything. When I'm in and zipped and tied and buttoned, that's when I finally turn to the mirror—and my breath catches.

Because I look like a freaking princess. Not a princess at a ball, but a princess from a fairy tale—out in the woods, maybe, or riding a pure white horse. I look elegant and graceful and ethereal, with the flowing skirt of the dress and the loose curls tumbling over my shoulder.

Plus my contoured collar bones look great.

I smile a little, because I can't help it. I know this marriage is going to be fake; I know we're not really in love. But right now, I look like a woman who's off to live her happily ever after, and it's a good look on me.

The stylists *ooh* and *ahh* when I come out of the bathroom, and I preen like a vain peacock. They hold me steady so I can step into my heels, and then we're off—I have to gather the skirts of the dress just slightly when I go through the door and into the living room, letting them fall again with a pleasant rustle.

Phoenix doesn't look up when I enter; he's on the couch, his phone pressed to his ear, and there's a little furrow between his brows as he speaks. "Let's move that to the thirtieth, then," he's saying, "and schedule the next shipment one week prior."

When Wyatt clears his throat, Phoenix glances at him; Wyatt gestures to me and the stylists spilling into the room, and Phoenix turns to look at us.

And at first, his gaze finds me for only the briefest second before jumping to the stylists; he gives me barely a glance, nothing more than noting my presence.

The double take doesn't come until one second later.

I watch with immense satisfaction and triumph as his eyes fly back to me, widening so slightly I might be imagining it; his dark brows twitch, and he stops speaking in the middle of his sentence.

His pause lasts only two seconds; that's how long he stares, his lips parted, his eyes blacker than ever. Then he looks away, clears his throat, and continues speaking. "And once those two go out," he says smoothly into the phone, "we can work on finding a different distributor if need be."

He sounds normal; he sounds the same. But there's a

little muscle twitching in his jaw that wasn't visible before, and the hand resting on the arm of the sofa is uncurling from a fist.

I smirk. Evoking this kind of reaction in him feels like winning the Superbowl. It shouldn't just be me who's secretly attracted to him.

"You look lovely, Miss Blakely," Wyatt says with a little smile.

"Thank you. I feel lovely," I admit as Phoenix says something about talking more next week. He hangs up a few seconds later and looks at me again. Then he turns to my stylists.

"Well done," he says, nodding at them.

They all smile, and the nice one says, "Do you need anything else?"

"Nothing," he says, standing up. "I'll be sure to recommend your services in the future."

"We appreciate it," the one who curled my hair says. The three of them smile once more, incline their heads at me, and then shuffle out of the room, leaving me alone with Phoenix and Wyatt.

"You think I look good," I say the second the door shuts.

"I think you look passable," Phoenix corrects me, straightening his suit coat and then turning to Wyatt. "Would you grab the rest of the bags from the bedroom, please, and follow us out to the gardens with them?"

"Passable?" I say, my jaw dropping as Wyatt hurries into the bedroom. "You did a double take, Rooster. Your jaw twitched."

"My jaw did nothing of the sort."

"And your eyes widened."

"You're delusional, Amsterdam," he says, rolling his eyes.

"Let's move things along, please. Exit and turn left out the doors to the gardens."

I grin as I head to the fancy double doors. I know I'm right on this one.

"What do you think of the dress from this angle?" I say over my shoulder as I walk. I pull my hair gently over my shoulders so he can see the plunging back.

"I think there's not enough fabric," he says. His voice is clipped, tense, and it feels like he's handing over a big gold trophy.

My smile just widens.

CHAPTER 13

Phoenix

OUR PHOTOGRAPHER IS SHORT, burgundy-haired, and more enthusiastic than I'm comfortable with.

"Ugh, this is *gorgeous*," she says as she snaps photo after photo of Holland. "Arm down a little—perfect, yes, *love* it. Love. You're fierce"—*click!*—"you're a goddess"—*click!*—"tilt the chin a little bit, down to the left, perfect"—*click!*—"I hate that you guys booked a mini session. I could shoot you all day."

I guess I have to thank my lucky stars that she's doing bridal portraits before I'm required to join in; I didn't realize that was part of the process, but I'm glad it is. I've parked myself and our bags on a smooth stone bench along the garden path while Holland poses awkwardly next to a tree further down, showing off the back of her dress.

And she looks beautiful. I hate that I have to admit it, but I do. She's so gorgeous, so sexy, that my brain keeps trying to forget what a pest she is, irritating and annoying. All I seem capable of processing is that bare expanse of skin—smooth gold against the white of the dress, the curved wings of her shoulder blades. If she were any other woman, I would be imagining trailing one finger down the delicate crease of her spine, just to see how she reacted—

But she isn't, and I'm not.

I will, however, need a minute before I have to go stand next to her and pretend to be in love.

"Oh," Holland says, speaking for the first time in over a minute, and I look up to see her craning her head toward me. "My jewelry!"

I look blankly at her.

"My jewelry," she says, rolling her eyes but not moving otherwise; her body is still in its look-over-the-shoulder pose. "In the paper bag. Can you reach in and grab it for me? It's a biggish velvet box."

I exhale and lean sideways, digging through the bag until I find the box, soft red velvet and the size of a large calculator. "This is giant," I say, holding it up.

"It's nice jewelry," she says. "Can you open it and bring me the stuff? It should just be a necklace and earrings—"

But she breaks off when I open the box and something flutters to the ground. "What's that—" she begins, letting go of her pose and turning to face me, frowning.

I lean down and pick it up. It's pure white, lacy, and at first I think it's a handkerchief—until I look closer.

Lingerie. This little scrap of fabric is unmistakably lingerie. In fact—I put the box down next to me on the bench —it's a *set* of lingerie, *two* little scraps of fabric, and I cannot touch these or look at them or even think about them. I turn my head pointedly, swallow, and set the clothes blindly to the side.

Seventeen times two is thirty-four. Seventeen times three is fifty-one. Seventeen times four is sixty-eight—

"Maggie," Holland groans, hurrying toward me, heels *click-clacking* against the paved stone path. "I'm going to *kill* her."

I keep my head turned the opposite direction until Holland reaches the bench, her cheeks pinker than they were thirty seconds ago. She mutters murderously under her breath as she leans down and fumbles with the jewelry case and the undergarments; I hear her shove them back in the large paper bag, at which point I finally deem it safe enough to look.

I recite the seventeen times tables until the photographer is ready for me, and by that time I'm calm, collected, and not thinking about lacy undergarments.

"Okay, groom, come stand next to your bride-to-be," she says with a smile once we've relocated to a different part of the garden. It's pretty, but flowers all pretty much look the same to me. "You guys are going to hold hands and look at each other. Both of you face forward."

I glance at Holland just as she glances at me, and I see the faintest grimace of distaste flash over her features before she smooths her expression. I shouldn't be annoyed, because I feel the same way, but I am; I roll my eyes and then hold out my hand to her.

She stares at it for a second, the midmorning sun turning her curls from blonde to fiery gold. I don't know anything about makeup, but I can tell her lashes are darker and longer, fluttering as her gaze flits from my face to my hand and then back again. I wiggle my hand impatiently, until finally she takes it.

She slides her hand into mine, her touch hesitant, her skin soft. It doesn't feel like *her* at all; she's never soft or hesitant with me.

"Good," the photographer says, practically bouncing with energy now. "Good, good. This is great. These are going to be so great. I know we're only doing two couple poses, but they're going to be amazing, all right? They're going to be so good."

"Are we only doing two poses?" Holland says to me out of

the corner of her mouth. Relief seeps from her words, the same relief I feel when I remember that I booked a mini session for this exact reason.

"Yes," I say. "Two poses and then we're done."

Her shoulders relax slightly. "Perfect." It would seem I'm not the only one reluctant to put on a loving act for a camera. "In that case..." Her grip on my hand tightens. "Let's get this over with."

I just roll my eyes, because that's what I've been saying all along.

The photographer snaps photo after photo as Holland and I look at each other, fake smiles on our faces. I'm not sure anyone would be able to tell, or at least anyone who didn't know us well—but then, one thing I can say about Amsterdam is that I *know* her.

There are no lines at the corners of her eyes, no dimples in her cheeks. That smile is fake, fake, fake.

Will she ever give me one of her real smiles? It might be nice to see one, just once. This baring of the teeth is painful to look at.

"Your eye is twitching," she mutters as the sun rises higher in the sky and the photographer continues to call directions at us.

"No it isn't," I say immediately—but I think she's probably right. I can't keep this facial expression much longer. "And if it is, it's just because your hand is gross and sweaty, Spinster Ham."

"*Spinster Ham?*" she says under her breath, her smile fermenting into something sour. "That doesn't even make sense."

"I know," I say. "But you inspired me to step up my game when you called me *Flamingo* the other day, and I liked how it sounded." My fake pleasant expression transforms into something slightly more real.

"*Amsterdam, Spinster Ham, Dumpster Ma'am, Gangster Glam*—you have too much time on your hands, Titmouse."

"Don't forget *Hamster Slam*," I say.

"All right, couple, these are looking amazing," the photographer calls, and I blink, looking at her.

I forgot she was there.

"You guys look so good. So, so good," she gushes, looking down at her camera screen. "Ugh. So good."

I don't see how those photos could possibly look good; the realization makes me wince. We got carried away, but we need to stay focused and make these convincing. "My family needs to buy this," I say to Holland, my jaw tight.

"I know," she says, her voice grudging. "They will."

Some of the tension leaks out of my shoulders.

"Let's move on to pose number two," the photographer says. "We're going to do a really adorable cheek-kiss shot. So groom, I want you to stand behind the bride—let's move over here, actually, because I want to get this sun coming through, good, perfect—stand behind the bride, groom, and then you're going to wrap your arms around her waist from behind and kiss her on the cheek."

Kiss her on the cheek?

I clear my throat. "Fine," I say with a nod. I move toward Holland, approaching her from behind; she watches me over her shoulder, her expression blank.

"Closer," the photographer calls, and I inch forward. She waves her hand for me to keep going; I grit my teeth and take another step. It's only when I feel the heat of Holland's bare back seeping through my shirt that the photographer deems us close enough.

It's *too* close. I can smell the hairspray in her loose curls and the faint sweet peppermint of whatever soap or perfume she always uses; I can feel her curves pressed up against me.

"Now wrap your arms around her waist, husband," the photographer says, "and then wife, you're going to hold your hands over his."

I comply, moving my arms mechanically around her, and just as stiffly, Holland rests her hands over mine.

"You better not take any liberties," she mutters over her shoulder, and I scoff.

"Did I or did I not tell you that I'm not interested in anything you have?" I say in a low voice, so the photographer won't hear.

"You did," Holland says, "but I look hot in this dress, Canary, and we're getting very cozy here." Her hands over mine soften, and I startle when I feel her tracing slow, lazy patterns over my skin. "So make sure nothing distracts you," she goes on. She pinches the back of my hand suddenly, and I hiss.

I free my pinched hand and angle my body slightly, leaning my head closer to speak in her ear. "Don't start games like this," I breathe—and then, finally, I give in to the impulse that's been riding me for the last hour. I lift my hand and slowly, carefully, touch one finger to the back of her neck; when she doesn't stop me, I trail that finger down, down, down her spine. "Because you won't win, *darling wife.*"

Her breath hitches at the words, and they surprise me too.

"Tilt your body just a bit, groom, and bride, give me a nice smile. Then groom, you're going to lean forward and give her a sweet kiss on the cheek," the photographer calls, blissfully unaware of our heated conversation. I let my hand fall away from the base of Holland's spine and then wrap my arm around her waist again.

"You're the mud caked beneath the hooves of a warthog," Holland murmurs through a blinding smile.

I curl my fingers around her wrist until they find her pulse. "And your heart is beating too fast," I breathe against her skin as I lean forward and touch my lips to her cheek.

Her hand twitches, and I laugh softly.

"Gorgeous!" the photographer calls as her camera erupts in a flurry of clicks and snaps. "Perfect! You guys are the *cutest*—these are going to turn out so good. A few more, just a few more and then—" She breaks off, glancing at her watch. "And then it looks like we're done for this session, but honestly, please book me again any time, because you guys are totally smokin'." She brings the camera back up to her face. "Okay, one last kiss to her cheek, groom, good, good, and…that's a wrap!"

We separate so immediately that the photographer looks startled; she glances back and forth between us for a second and then laughs. "I'm sorry," she says. "I know it's hard to stand in the same position for a long time. But I got some great photos!"

"Thank you," I tell her, trying to keep my voice pleasant. "I'll look forward to seeing what you've got." Then, once she's busy gathering her photography gear, I turn to Holland. "We're going to obtain a marriage license now, once you've changed back into your street clothes. After that you're free to go home."

I DON'T SEE or hear from Holland for the rest of the weekend; not even when I text her and tell her that half a dozen new outfits chosen by Wyatt are in the mail to her, all of them clothes my family should approve of. Normally that's something she would respond to, but all I get is silence.

She's ignoring me.

Maybe I shouldn't have touched her like that.

When I text her Sunday night to tell her we need to meet at Town Hall to get married Tuesday morning at nine, she doesn't say anything either. It's only when I tell her to answer me or I'll drag her there myself that I hear back—a single thumbs up.

The day of our wedding dawns bright and early, and the weather is mockingly perfect. There's a pleasant breeze that will heat up as the sun climbs higher, which would probably render my all-black ensemble too warm, but we should be done before the hottest part of the day arrives.

I reach the steps of Town Hall at nine on the dot, Wyatt by my side. Holland isn't here yet, as far as I can see, but that's not surprising. Given her radio silence, I can assume she's still not thrilled about our arrangement.

She can feel how she wants, I tell myself, straightening my tie out of habit more than need. *No one made her sign the contract.*

When she arrives five minutes later, she's coming from the direction of the town square; something anxious and queasy bubbles in my stomach, because there's no way she didn't draw attention on her way.

She's dressed in all black. Black, long-sleeved shirt despite the summertime; long, black skirt; I even see black tennis shoes peeking out as she walks. She looks like a wraith. Even her long, blonde ponytail seems more subdued than normal, hanging solemnly instead of swinging this way and that.

Her shuffling steps bring her closer and closer until finally she stops in front of me, and I raise one eyebrow.

"All black, I see."

"I'm in mourning," she says flatly. She jerks her chin at my clothes. "You did the same."

"Yes," I say, irritated. "Because I look excellent in black. Not because I believe my life is ending." My jaw clenches without my permission; I force myself to relax. "And what about the dark circles?" I say, pointing to the shadows beneath her eyes. "Are those for mourning too?"

She doesn't respond; she just glares.

But something slips into my mind then, a suspicion, and my lips tug into a frown. "You don't—" I break off and then go on. "Do you still have nightmares?"

She folds her arms across her chest. "None of your business," she says stiffly, turning away from me and starting up the steps to Town Hall.

That's a resounding *yes*, then.

I climb quickly after her, reaching out and grabbing the soft sleeve of her shirt. I turn her to face me. "Why didn't you tell me?" I say.

What an idiotic thing to ask.

She thinks so too. "Why would I tell you?" she says, yanking her arm out of my grasp. "What are you going to do? Ride in on your white horse and save me?" She turns away and climbs faster, hurrying ahead of me, favoring her sore knee just slightly.

"This was your choice, Amsterdam," I call. I take the steps two at a time to catch up. "I offered you work in my office."

"I needed your insurance," she says once we reach the top of the stairs.

"I would've given you employee benefits." Ironically enough, if she'd come to me and asked for money to get health care, I would have given it to her.

But she would never. She's too proud, and she would never accept something for nothing.

Her gaze darts away from mine, and that muscle in her jaw is twitching. "You should inherit Butterfield," she finally says, her words short, terse.

I stare at her. "What?"

"Butterfield," she says impatiently, and she still won't look at me. "You should inherit. You'd be a good—" She breaks off and starts again. "Your cousin is a jerk. You should inherit."

Something stirs in my chest, warm and surprisingly gentle.

But she pours icy water on that feeling the second she opens her mouth again. "Now stop talking to me, and let's just do this."

I sigh and nod, and together we make our way into Town Hall. The clerk's office is on the second floor; we climb the stairs in our funeral clothes, attracting stares from the few people we see, until we reach the little door with the clerk's sign.

"I need to get a drink," Holland says under her breath. "I'll be back."

"What—now?"

"I said I'll be *back!* Just stop talking to me." She doesn't wait for my answer; she just storms away.

So I step inside without her.

The man at the counter is short and balding with a pleasant-but-harried smile on his face; I give him a little nod and try not to picture how his expression will change when Holland comes in looking like the Ghost of Christmas Yet to Come.

"You're the nine-thirty civil ceremony?" he says.

"Correct," I say. I gesture to Wyatt, who's been following us silently this whole time. "And I brought a witness."

"Good, good," the man says, shuffling around behind the counter. "Well, take a seat. You're a bit early."

I sit down in one of the nondescript brown chairs, and Wyatt sits next to me. He passes me a water bottle, opening one for himself as well, and together the two of us drink filtered water in what might be the most boring bachelor party known to man. Then I look at the clock on the wall.

It ticks...

...and tocks...

...and ticks...

...and tocks...

...and fifteen minutes later, Holland still hasn't returned.

"All right," the bald man finally says. He smiles at me. "Where's the bride-to-be, eh?"

"No idea," I say. I take a swig from my water bottle, and then another, and then one more. "We're not currently on speaking terms."

"You're not currently—you're not—what?" He dabs nervously at his brow, hurrying around the counter. "You're —I mean to say—" He clears his throat and leans closer. "You're supposed to get married in three minutes," he says under his breath.

"Correct," I say, shotgunning the rest of my water in one gulp.

I'm about to pull out my phone and call her, but just as I'm reaching for it, the handle to the office turns.

And there she is: my bride.

The nervous little man jumps, just like I knew he would when he saw her—a grim reaper, silhouetted in the doorway, cloaked in billowing black, gathering those doomed to die.

"A short, legally binding ceremony is our preference," I

tell him, standing up and straightening my suit jacket. "I'm sure you understand."

His gaze jumps back and forth between Holland and me, and he bobs his head. "Of—of course," he says quickly. "You have the marriage certificate?"

Wyatt produces it from seemingly out of nowhere; he passes it to the man, who nods again.

"Come on," I say to Holland. She steps in and closes the door behind her; our officiant's face pales noticeably.

"Right," he says with a nervous little laugh. "Right—here, then? Is anyone else joining you?"

"It's just us," I say. "And here is perfect. Proceed, please."

I just need this part of the process to be over and done.

Holland comes to a stop at my side; she doesn't look at me. We both stare at the man as he glances at our marriage certificate and then begins to speak, his eyes jumping between us as though he expects us to stop him at any time.

"We gather here today to celebrate the joining of Phoenix Park and Holland Blakely in holy matrimony," he says.

And his words—they're just words, but somehow the already-quiet office falls completely silent; the clock ceases to tick, the paper in his hands ceases to crinkle or rustle. My whooshing pulse and the words coming out of his mouth; those are the only things I hear. A vague sense of foreboding fills me, fog creeping into my chest cavity, ghosting around my ribs and clouding around my heart. That fog thickens when the man glances up at me, questioning, but I just nod.

"Do you, Phoenix Park, take Holland Blakely to be your lawfully wedded wife?"

I clear my throat as my pulse pounds behind my eyes, against my sternum.

"Yes," I say.

The man nods and then looks at Holland.

"And do you, Holland Blakely, take Phoenix Park to be your lawfully wedded husband?"

My gaze flies to her, my shoulders tense.

Because in this moment, I truly don't know what she's going to say. Up until thirty seconds ago I would have said she would go through with this, but the *feeling* in this room—it's heavy. Significant.

I didn't think it would be like this.

"Yes," Holland says quietly, and relief, sweet and potent, floods through me. "I do."

The man stands up a little straighter; he seems just as relieved as I am. My heart beats faster still as he goes on, but it's no longer frantic or anxious; that pulse feels strong, healthy, full of life.

"By the power vested in me by the state of Florida," he says, and I could swear his words are louder, "I now pronounce you married."

Just like that, Holland Blakely becomes Holland Park.

I look at her; she looks at me. We both swallow, and I see the same weight settling on her shoulders that I feel on mine; it's something indefinable, intangible, but undeniably present. A shiver runs down my spine, goosebumps on the back of my neck; then we break eye contact, and the moment is gone.

Three hours later, she officially moves into my house.

CHAPTER 14

Holland

THE ONLY *smoking hot* part of my wedding night is Phoenix's microwave, when I'm so distracted that I put a metal cup in and start a veritable firework display in there.

I swear loudly and open the door, fanning the inside with my hand and then hunting for an oven mitt to pull the cup out, moving as quietly as I can so that Phoenix won't hear. He's been in his study for hours, and that's where I'd like him to stay.

Because it's weird, looking at him and knowing that this is our first night as a married couple. It doesn't matter that we've known each other for years or that we don't get along; it's still weird, and awkward, and uncomfortable. Phoenix Park and I are legally husband and wife.

Even though I was there when it happened, I still can't quite believe it. He told me to make myself comfortable when I moved in earlier—a transfer that consisted of me, half my closet, my shoes, and my toiletries—but how am I supposed to make myself at home when he's here?

He seems just as unsettled as I do. I've mainly been hiding in my room since I got here earlier, but the two times we have crossed paths, we just stared at each other for a few seconds, our eyes wide, like we'd briefly forgotten that we live together.

Flying under the radar seems most appealing right now. So I carry the cup to the kitchen sink, rinse it with a low stream of water, and then load it into the dishwasher with gentle, quiet hands.

We're going to skip the hot chocolate for the night and move on to the heat pack, which I know won't make the microwave angry. I stick the heavy rice pack in and turn it on for two minutes and thirty seconds, the tension easing out of my body at the low whirring sound.

I don't think I broke anything.

"Fourth of July isn't until next week, Amsterdam," a voice says from behind me, and I jump, whirling around. "So I'd appreciate it if you didn't burn my house down."

It's him, of course. How did he know? Was my electrical storm really that loud?

"Sorry," I say, because the sparking microwave is 100 percent my fault. "I wasn't paying attention."

"What's this, then?" he says, jerking his chin at where the heat pack spins round and round on the microwave's rotating plate.

"A rice heat pack," I tell him.

"It's summer," he says, stepping further into the kitchen. He's still dressed in black slacks and the black, button-down shirt he wore earlier—*to our wedding*, my brain pipes up. "Not the dead of winter."

Heat creeps up my neck and into my cheeks. "I like being warm at night," I say, sounding more defensive than I need to.

"Could have fooled me." His dark gaze roams over my pajamas, pink silk shorts and top. Then he meets my gaze again. "Just don't set any fires, please."

I nod and look firmly back at the microwave.

The one at Nana Lu's lets out three shrill, agonized beeps

when it's done cooking, similar to the sound a smoke detector makes when its batteries are running low, but the only thing I hear from Phoenix's microwave when my heat pack is done is a pleasant chiming sound; *a pleasure doing business with you* instead of *help me I'm dying*.

I hate leaving Nana Lu's, but when I move back there after Phoenix inherits, I might invest in a new microwave.

I pull my heat pack out and drape it around my shoulders, shoving aside my embarrassment. I keep my chin up, ignore the feeling of my messy bun on top of my head, and pass by him without a word.

I've only made it a few steps out of the kitchen and into the hallway when he speaks.

"Get some good sleep tonight," he says, sounding tired now. "I'm taking you to meet my grandmother at the hospital tomorrow. Some of the rest of the family will probably be there too. We'll leave at nine-thirty."

I turn to face him. "I'm going to bed anyway." Then, casting my gaze over his clothes, I say, "Do you always wear that? I figured you were probably more casual at home, or at least in the evenings. Do you sleep in a suit? Shower in a tux?"

His eyes glint in the dimly lit hallway as he steps closer to me. "Imagining me in the shower, Amsterdam?" he says, raising one eyebrow.

The *nerve*.

"Only when I feel like vomiting," I say sweetly. Then I turn around and continue on to the room I'm staying in, closing the door behind me.

It's a nice room, with plush carpet and a king-sized bed whose plain white comforter is poofy enough to swallow me whole. There's no bathroom attached, but there's one right across the hall, so that's fine. I flip the lights off and crawl into bed with the heat pack still around my neck, curling up on my side.

I'm asleep in minutes.

When I drag my still-half-asleep self into the kitchen the next morning at eight o'clock, Phoenix is already there. He's leaning against the marble countertop, dressed in a suit, sipping from a cup of something steaming—probably peppermint tea—and scrolling on his phone.

I'm still wearing my pink silk pajamas, and there's still sleep gunk in my eyes.

"When you've cleaned yourself up," he says without looking at me, "I'd like to see the clothing I had Wyatt send to you. Have you tried any of it on?"

"What, all the tweed and Ann Taylor?" I say blankly.

The corners of his lips twitch. "Yes." He sets his drink down on the counter and turns his gaze on me, tucking his phone into one of those secret suit coat pockets only businessmen know about. "My family will judge every book by its cover, and they won't change their minds after their first impressions are formed. So go shower, please, and then I'll need to see those clothes before you choose something to wear."

"I'm not a doll you can dress up however you want," I say, rubbing my eyes to try to dispel the early morning crusties.

"I'm aware of that," he says. "But I didn't check what Wyatt sent. So while it will likely all be appropriate, I need to make certain. As long as the options are acceptable, I won't interfere in your choices." He pauses. "This was part of the contract you signed, so get moving."

I don't budge. "I'm hungry," I say.

He glares at me. "I'll make you some toast, all right? Just go. Good grief."

"I don't like grape—"

"I *know*," he says, exasperated. "I have raspberry."

"But I don't—"

"Want anything with seeds that will get stuck in your teeth. I know. *Go.*"

"If you *insist...*" I say, and his grumpy eyes turn even grumpier.

"Go!" he says, pointing out of the kitchen.

I grin. It's only eight in the morning, and I've already gotten to put that look on his face. What more could a girl ask for?

I take my time in the shower, because it's way nicer than the one at Nana Lu's. Nana's shower head shoots abusive bullets of water that could probably take an eye out. Phoenix's water pressure is perfect, though, and there are two shower heads, and not once does the temperature cool down even though I'm in there for probably twenty minutes. When I step out, I slip into my fluffy white robe and then begin toweling my hair dry.

I emerge into the living room a few minutes later, both hands full of hangers. "This was too much," I say to Phoenix, who's sitting in a straight-backed chair, one ankle propped on the opposite knee, his phone in his hand again. "I'm never going to wear all these."

He buttons his phone off and exhales tiredly. "Yes, you will. You—" But he breaks off when he looks up at me, his dark brows rising. "What is *that*?"

"It's a robe," I say.

He rolls his eyes. "I know," he says. "I meant why are you wearing it?" His throat bobs as he swallows, his gaze darting away from me. "I would prefer if everyone stayed fully dressed in communal areas of the house."

"As would I," I say, "but you insisted upon seeing what

Wyatt sent before I change. So I'm not sure what you want me to do."

"I—fine." He looks back at me, and a muscle jumps in his jaw as he grits out the rest of his words. "Fine." He stands up and crosses the room in three long strides, his eyes on everything dangling from my hands. I hold out the clothes as he approaches, and he flips through them quickly like a shopper at a thrift store, the metal hangers digging into my skin as he moves. Then he backs away. "Any of that will do," he says, already turning to his chair again. "And I believe Wyatt also included jewelry. Wear pearl earrings if you have any; Mavis wears pearls only and always."

None of these things are really my style, but I did sign the contract, and I'm getting paid—the second installment appeared in my account last night—so I just nod in assent.

"I assume your grandmother knows we're coming?" I say as I try to picture what kind of woman she might be.

"Oh, yes," Phoenix says, his voice dry now. He sits back down. "She's aware. She sent me this text this morning." He holds his phone up, and I scoot forward, leaning down to get a closer look.

I almost choke when I see it. It's a photo of Phoenix—a business portrait, maybe, in which his appearance is not worth mentioning because it's too early for such things—and photoshopped next to him is a faceless bride.

The picture is as bizarre as it sounds. Just professional Phoenix and then a bride from a magazine, maybe, only there's no face on her; just a hairstyle around a blank space.

"This borders on disturbing," I say as my nerves jump. "Did she just send the image?"

"No," he says, tucking his phone away. "She also expressed how excited she was to meet the woman who would fill in this photo."

"That's weird," I say, swallowing. "She's weird."

"I did tell you," he says mildly. "Go get ready, please."

I take a deep breath, letting it out slowly. Then I return to my bedroom and blow dry my hair until it's soft, sleek, and shiny. Then I get dressed in a pink tweed skirt and a cream blouse—pantyhose are included in this outfit, and I hate every second—and return to the kitchen.

As it turns out, my new husband did make me toast, just like he said he would. He made me toast with *grape preserves* —seeds and mushy lumps included.

"We have just enough time for you to eat before we have to leave," he says, sliding the plate toward me with a smirk. "I know you're hungry." His message is loud and clear: *Make your own breakfast from now on, Amsterdam, or you'll keep getting food you hate.*

My stomach growls as I stare at the two pieces of toast, and for a second I contemplate picking both of them up and plastering them to the front of his suit coat. I resist the urge, glaring at him instead before wolfing down both pieces.

His smirk just widens before he drifts back into the living room, pulling his phone out of his suit coat. It's buzzing, I realize; he looks at the name on the screen and then answers.

"We're ready," he says without greeting or preamble. "We'll head out there now." Then he hangs up.

Wyatt, I assume.

"Wait a second," I say. It's just occurred to me that I have no idea where Phoenix's assistant actually lives. "Where's Wyatt's house?"

"Behind this one," he says wryly, straightening his suit coat. "He lives in the mother-in-law building out back. He wouldn't let me buy him his own place."

"I hope you pay him a million dollars a year," I say.

Phoenix just smiles, a genuine, warm smile that I'm not

at all prepared for. Then he jerks his chin in the direction of the front door. "Let's go," he says. "Mavis will be waiting."

I'VE NEVER BEEN to a VIP ward of a hospital before; I didn't even realize they were a thing, mostly because I'd never really thought about it. But the wing of the mainland hospital where Mavis is apparently being treated looks more like a hotel than a hospital.

"All right," Phoenix says in a low voice as we stand next to each other outside a set of double doors. "Listen carefully." His posture is almost too rigid, and there's something cold and blank shifting in his expression, like I'm watching him in the process of putting on a mask. Even the poor hospital lighting doesn't stop his bone structure from casting impeccable shadows, or his hair from gleaming darkly.

When he turns to face me, his eyes fix immediately on mine. "Don't speak to or answer questions from anyone other than me or my grandmother," he says. "Don't try to be friendly. Stand up straight, don't fidget." He pauses. "I know this seems dramatic, or like an exaggeration. But my family are wolves, Holland. They will smell fear and use it against you."

Something deep in my stomach flips, and I can't tell if it's concern over his words or surprise at hearing my name come from his lips.

And it's that, more than anything else—my name, just my name—that compels me to listen to him. I don't appreciate being told how to act, and I don't appreciate being told to hold my tongue. But the man standing in front of me is the devil I know. He's the devil I can't stand, the devil that makes

me want to scream, the devil whose mere presence sometimes feels like a knife in my gut because of the memories we
share.

And yet...I know him. I even trust him, in a way I can't
explain to myself or anyone else.

Which must be why I take a deep breath, nod, and then—
before I can stop myself—I step closer, reaching out and
touching the knot of his tie, straightening it.

His body stills.

He doesn't even breathe; I'm close enough that I can tell,
and I understand. It's a bizarre moment, intimate and
domestic in a way we never are; I tug on the knot just
slightly before smoothing the tail.

"There," I say softly as my heart pounds in my chest.

I didn't think I was actually afraid to meet his family, but
my galloping pulse and adrenaline rush say differently.

Yes. Fear, I tell myself as I take a deep breath. *That's what
I'm feeling.*

His dark gaze flits over my face as he looks down at me,
his expression still blank except for the muscle jumping in
his jaw. Then, finally, he says, "You look—nice. Mavis should
approve."

And without waiting for a response, he turns back to the
double doors and pushes them open, stepping inside.

WELCOME TO
SUNSET
HARBOR

BELACOURT RESORT

GOLF COURSE

NOAH'S HOUSE

JANE'S HOUSE

NATURE PRESERVE

DAX'S DUPLEX

SEASIDE OASIS RETIREMENT HOME

SUNSET REPAIRS

PHOENIX'S OFFICE

CITY OFFICES

SUNRISE CAFE

SCOOPS AHOY ICE CREAM

KEEVE B&B

TOWN SQUARE

BAKERY

BRIGGS'S APARTMENT

THE BOOK ISLE

CUTS AND CURLS

GULF OF MEXICO

N
W   E
S

TRISTAN & BEAU'S HOUSE

CAPRI'S HOUSE

GEMMA'S HOUSE

HOLLAND'S HOUSE

BEACH BREAK BAR & GRILL

PUBLIC BEACH

CHAPTER 15

Phoenix

MAVIS IS SITTING up in her bed, haughty and intimidating as always, with that slightly manic gleam in her eyes. The sun should be streaming in through the blinds in her giant suite, but they're closed, leaving the room in a depressing state of shadow.

I'm not fazed or surprised. This is just how Mavis is.

She's never looked like a grandmother—not soft or sweet like Nana Lu. Her brows are thin and spidery, her curls iron, her perfectly made-up face set in a faint frown. One of the earliest childhood memories I have is being scared of her. It was nothing she said or did, necessarily; she was just wildly unpredictable, and she always gave off an aura of disapproval.

She still gives off that aura, but I've learned how to deal with it now.

"Mavis," I say as I more or less burst into the suite, Holland at my heels. "I'm glad to see you're looking well."

"Don't sweet talk me," she says, raising her penciled brow at me. "You all can't wait for me to die." She gestures vaguely to her bedside, which is when I realize that my uncle Clarence and my cousin Lawrence are both here. Clarence looks as foul-tempered as ever, and Lawrence looks as cocky, his blond hair spiked perfectly.

"I'm sure that isn't true," Mavis's sycophantic assistant says—a nervous, bespectacled woman with a spine of rubber and phenomenal organizational skills.

"Of course not," an unfamiliar voice chimes in, followed by a tinkling laugh. I turn to look and discover the speaker is a dark-haired woman standing next to Lawrence—the supposed girlfriend, I assume—wearing a black dress and pink high heels. I dislike her on sight, though I have no real reason to.

"Dorothy," she says when our eyes meet. She gives me a little wave. "Call me Dot."

I don't acknowledge her—or Clarence and Lawrence, for that matter. I also don't bother denying that most of Mavis's progeny are eagerly anticipating her death. I just beckon Holland forward until the two of us stand side by side at the foot of Mavis's bed.

"You wanted to meet my wife," I say. Then I gesture to Holland, who stands up infinitesimally straighter. "This is Holland."

"Mmm," Mavis says, little more than a buzz between the thin lips on her ancient raisin face. Her advisor steps closer to Mavis's side, whispering in Mavis's ear, and Mavis nods. "Holland Blakely—" she begins, but I cut her off.

"Holland *Park*." I emphasize the word just slightly.

Mavis pretends not to hear me and goes on, flipping through the packet of papers the assistant has just handed her. "Resident of Sunset Harbor," she says. "Aged twenty-seven, employee at Cuts and Curls salon. You've been heard calling her"—she flips through her notes and then cackles—"*that woman* and *Amsterdam*." Her laugh ricochets unpleasantly, but I just grimace.

Because good grief. How did she work up such a thorough

dossier so quickly? I only told her yesterday that I was married, via Wyatt.

But I'm pulled back to the present when Lawrence's girlfriend snickers. "Amsterdam," she says.

In the corner of my vision I see Holland tense, barely noticeable if not for the fact that I notice everything about this woman. Something sours in my gut, squirming and rancid. She doesn't like being called that, and I don't like hearing that name come from anyone but me—especially someone associated with Lawrence. I turn slowly to Lawrence's girlfriend, maintaining a pleasant expression even as my fingers try to curl into a fist.

"Dorothy, was it?" I say, forcing myself to relax.

"Dot," she says with a little frown.

I nod. "Well, Dorothy." My expression doesn't change, but I can hear the ice in my voice as I go on. "You do not call her that. I will call her whatever I choose, but to you she is *Holland*. Or"—my lip curls in disgust as I look at her—"perhaps you should stick to *ma'am*."

I shoot a look at Holland, just to see how she's doing, but to my surprise, she's giving me a strange look—one I'm not sure I've ever seen from her. Her eyes have widened the tiniest bit, subtle enough my family probably doesn't notice, and her lips are parted. When my gaze meets hers, though, that look is gone, and she turns to Dot.

"*Holland* will be fine, Dot," she says, speaking for the first time. "Please forgive my husband."

I blink, my brain momentarily short-circuiting at the sound of that word.

But Holland just laughs lightly and then goes on. "You know how overprotective men can be when they're in love." She loops her arm through mine and then pats my bicep fondly. I'm hit with a twinge of pity when Dot's face falls, though; I have no doubt that Lawrence has never once tried to protect her.

"Of course," Dot says, her words strained as her eyes fall to Holland's arm linked with mine. "I understand completely."

Holland smiles at her, a brilliant, blinding, dimpled smile.

And it's probably because I just heard her call me *husband*, but...my stomach flips when I see that smile.

It *flips*.

Ridiculous.

I shake my head and look back to Mavis. "Well, we'll be off." The best-case scenario is us leaving this room in the next thirty seconds. So I tighten my arm around Holland's and then turn away from the hospital bed.

"Wait," Mavis says—one word, but the entire room stills. Holland and I both freeze. "Don't you want your wedding present?"

An uncomfortable, prickling sense of dread hits me as I turn slowly back to my grandmother. "That's not necessary," I say. "Your approval is more than enough for us."

One spidery brow lifts—daring me to protest further. "I insist," she says with a creeping, curling smile. Then, from the table beside her hospital bed, she picks up a credit card, holding it out. I step closer.

No—not a credit card. A *room key*. My heart sinks down, down, down into the pit of my stomach.

"One night in the honeymoon suite at the Vida Grande," Mavis says, and I know I'm not imagining the look of smug triumph in her smile. "For you and your beloved. You can check in today. Now, in fact. I even have your bags packed." She gestures to her assistant, who bends down and pulls two small suitcases from under the bed.

I keep my expression neutral—cold, even—but my heart sinks even further when she rolls the suitcases around the bed and over to Holland and me.

This is bad.

I stare at the card and the bags, considering carefully. If I resist, she's going to be even more suspicious than she clearly already is.

So, finally, I nod. "Thank you," I say, taking the room key from her. "We'll enjoy ourselves."

"Make sure you do," she says, her beady eyes narrowing into slits. "I have my doubts, you understand."

"I do understand," I say with a little bow. "But it's nothing more than coincidental timing."

"Mmm. *Coincidental timing.*" Her eyes somehow narrow even further. "You," she barks, gesturing at Holland, who jumps.

"Yes," Holland says.

"Come here." The command rings imperiously throughout the room, and I force myself not to let my nerves show, even though I'm pretty sure this is how my nightmare started last night.

Holland releases my arm and rounds the bed with slow steps, approaching Mavis the same way she might approach a wounded bear in the wild.

"Come," Mavis says impatiently, waving her vein-knotted hand. "Let me look at you, my darling new granddaughter." But the words are full of cynical humor, not at all welcoming or loving, and the look on her face is just shy of overtly cruel.

To her credit, Holland remains poised with her head held high, her sheen of blonde hair falling perfectly over her squared shoulders. Something about her outfit emphasizes the innate elegance I didn't realize she had; it's not a *pearls-and-old-money* elegance but rather a *watch-me-land-on-my-feet* grace that has nothing to do with her appearance and everything to do with her character.

I swallow and give myself a little mental shake. I don't need to be noticing these things.

When she reaches Mavis, she stands perfectly still, looking down at my insane old grandmother.

"Down," Mavis says to her, waving her hand again. "Down here. Don't make me stand up, Barbie. Haven't you heard I'm almost dead?"

So Holland leans down, close enough to Mavis that the woman reaches up and takes my wife's face in her hands. It startles me just as much as it clearly startles Holland, who jumps slightly. Mavis turns her face left and right, up and down, her eyes sharp, and I don't think I can breathe; the oxygen in my lungs is suddenly too heavy to expel as I watch them.

Mavis's inspection seems to last forever, though it's probably not more than a minute. When she finally releases Holland, she does so with a little push. Then she speaks.

"Take that"—she gestures at the key card in my hand—"and have a proper honeymoon." It's not a well-wish; there's a hint of a threat in there, like she's tacked on the words *I'll know if you don't* at the end.

My eyes fall on Clarence, Lawrence, and Dot; the latter two just look disgruntled, maybe because Mavis hasn't given them any gifts, but Clarence is looking at Holland with narrowed eyes.

I don't want him looking at her. Ever.

So I stride quickly to Holland's side and take her hand. I give her a little tug, and together we head toward the double doors.

"Wait!"

It isn't Mavis this time; it's Lawrence, and I'm not

surprised. I look over to see him hurrying around his father and Dot until he's planted himself right in our path.

"I have to meet my new cousin," he says, holding one hand out to Holland. His smile is pleasant, but his blue eyes are sharp. "I have to meet the woman whose name in Phoenix's phone was so intriguing that I had to call her myself to—"

"We're leaving," I say before he can blurt out anything else. I swat his hand away, and he just grins.

"Tsk, tsk," he says as we move past him with the suitcases. "So rude."

"Thank you for the suite," I call, one hand already on the door handle. "And I hope I don't see anyone lingering around the island who's not supposed to be there."

Mavis, Clarence, and Lawrence are all the kinds of people who would send someone to spy on Holland and me. My mother would too, for that matter.

I can only assume she's not here because she's protesting my marriage to someone she didn't approve first, but she'll have to meet Holland at some point. I dread the day.

We step through the double doors and out of the hospital suite, and even though I can tell Holland is bursting to speak, I hold up one finger.

"If you're going to yell, wait until we've gone further," I mutter.

"What makes you think I'm going to yell?" she says, looking affronted.

"It's hard to tell with you," I say. "You pulled out a perfect smile in there with apparent ease." A smile of the sort she never aims at me—one that made my stomach flip. Worrisome.

"Slow down," she says, ignoring my jibe. "Your legs might be a million miles long, but I'm in heels, Dodo Bird."

Great. Now I'm extinct.

"I just think your entire family needs a lesson in boundaries. And also they need to get off their high horse," she continues in a low voice as we travel the short halls of the VIP ward. "Your freaky grandma can't actually force us to go to this hotel—you know that, right? And what was that that your cousin said? Is that why he called me that one time? What's my name in your phone?"

Crap. "Holland, obviously," I say. Then I move quickly on before she can question the lie. "And when dealing with Mavis, it's best to choose your battles. She holds my future in her bony, veiny hands. So you and I"—I grimace—"can go to this hotel tonight. We don't even have to talk to each other. Fine?"

"Fine," she grumbles. "You're sleeping on the couch."

I don't answer; I can't make that commitment.

Because Mavis only gave me one key card, which means there could be another one floating around somewhere. I can't run the risk of someone barging in—I don't want to believe Mavis would do that, but in my gut I know she would —and finding us sleeping separately.

So even though she doesn't know it yet...I'm going to have to share the bed with my wife.

THE ONLY WORD for our room at the Vida Grande is *opulent.*

It's the same hotel where we took our photos in the gardens out back, but the suite we used then was not a honeymoon suite. This room has carpet so thick and soft my feet sink in, a heart-shaped jacuzzi, and a massive king-sized bed covered in rose petals—there's even a champagne bottle on ice next to the jacuzzi.

Mavis Butterfield is cruel, and she's clearly not trying to hide her suspicion.

"Are those...matching robes?" Holland says, her voice dazed as she drifts toward the completely glass shower in one corner of the room. There are no walls for privacy, and my gaze darts around to make sure the toilet isn't out in the open too; I relax slightly when I see the open bathroom door off to one side.

"Maybe," I say as I continue looking around the room. A large sliding door leads out to a private patio with a small pool; I'd be tempted by that, but Holland doesn't swim—ever. Not since she and I and Trev crashed over the edge of that bridge and into the river below. She's never said it explicitly, but I've seen her avoid the ocean and pool enough to know.

There's no couch in here, I notice, just a chaise lounge that looks like something you'd lie back in while a beautiful woman fed you grapes from a gold platter.

It's not someplace I could sleep. Even Holland wouldn't fit.

"We need to talk about the bed situation," I say firmly, turning to her. I watch as she holds a short, cream-colored robe up to her body, looking down at it; it's silk, judging by the way the light hits, and the twin of the one hanging on a hook by the jacuzzi.

I swallow, clear my throat, and then go on. "There's no couch for me to sleep on, and Mavis only gave me one room key."

"Mmm," Holland says, distracted. "I noticed that. So she could barge in here any time, theoretically." She looks up at me. "Right?"

I give a reluctant jerk of my head.

"But she's in a hospital bed."

I nod again. "She's allowed to leave for short stretches as long as a nurse accompanies her. The doctors just want her to stay for monitoring and observation; she's on hospice, more or less."

She hangs the robe back on its hook and then turns to me again. "You realize the only reason she gets away with things so invasive is that you all let her. Everyone in your family must bow to her wishes if she's doing stuff like barging into hotel rooms uninvited."

"Yes," I say slowly, "and no. It's more complicated than that." How do I explain the grip this matriarchy has on my life? "Our family is so intertwined with the company, and Mavis has always been a boss first and a grandmother second. Fighting against her doesn't just affect my family; it affects my career. And while she's unpredictable as a matriarch, she's ruthless as a CEO."

"I don't get it," Holland says, her brow furrowing, "but okay." She eyes the giant bed with its flower petals and red velvet comforter. "I'm still not sharing the bed with you."

I rub my temples. "Look, Amsterdam," I say. "I don't want to do it either. But this is one night, okay?"

She glances back at the bed, and I can see the debate going on in her mind; she doesn't want to, but she agreed to pretend.

When she turns back to me with a look of irritation on her face, I know I've won.

"Fine. But—*but!*" she says quickly as I open my mouth to speak again. "We will place a pillow barrier down the center of the bed. You will not cross it."

"Obviously," I say, rolling my eyes. "I would rather stab

myself with the thorns all those rose petals came from than sleep close to you."

"That could probably be arranged," she says with a smirk. It fades, though, as she wanders through the room. "It's the middle of the day. What are we supposed to do in here until tomorrow morning?"

I know what we're *supposed* to do. What we're going to do, though? I'm less clear on that. "Just relax, I guess. Take a nap."

"I can't nap during the day or I won't sleep well at night," she says, leaning down to examine the jacuzzi. "This tub is huge. We—"

But she breaks off as a knock sounds at the door to our suite; her eyes dart to me, gleaming with panic, and I hold up one hand. Then, straightening my suit coat, I hurry over to the door and look out the peephole.

"Oh," I say, the tension draining out of me. "It's hotel staff." I frown and look again. "With chocolate-covered strawberries."

Her anxious expression brightens. "Perfect; I'm hungry."

I open the door and nod at the man standing there.

"Compliments of the hotel," he says immediately, bowing. "To congratulate you on your special day."

"Wonderful," I say, forcing a smile at him. "Thank you."

Then, even though it's abominably rude, I take the tray from him, give one last nod, and close the door right in his face.

I have a nagging worry that Mavis could ask the hotel staff to report back to her. It's not outside the realm of possibility.

"We should get changed first," I say, crossing the room with the strawberries and setting the tray on the chaise lounge. "At least give the appearance of trying to relax if anyone else comes."

"I know," she says with a sigh. "Pantyhose are uncomfortable." She sits on the edge of the jacuzzi and stares at our suitcases. "I'm just scared to find out what's in there."

Me too.

"How about you open yours, I'll open mine, and if we don't want to wear or use anything in there, we don't have to. No questions asked," she says.

"Good idea." I'm picturing all sorts of things—tiny Speedo-sized pajamas, or maybe matching outfits, because who knows what Mavis is capable of?—and I might end up being more comfortable in my suit.

So we each open our suitcase, and I'm pleasantly surprised to find normal pajamas in mine—flannel pants and a white undershirt—along with basic toiletries.

"Oh," Holland says, her head emerging from above the lid of her case. "It's not as bad as I expected."

"Mine either."

She holds up what looks like a nightgown, silky and black with delicate straps, long enough that it will probably hit her knees. I take it in and then look away again.

If that's better than she expected, I'm not going to say anything. "Well, you can change into that if you want"— *please don't, please don't, please don't*—"or I can give you these for now." I hold up the undershirt and flannel pants from my suitcase. "I'll be plenty comfortable once I take off my coat and tie. I'll probably do some work on my phone for the afternoon; you're free to do whatever."

"Those, please," she says immediately, dropping the silky nightgown back in her suitcase and reaching for my clothes.

I pass them to her with a rush of relief, turning around while she changes.

And look—I'm not a pervert. But there's something uncomfortably intimate about listening to Holland undress. The rustle of fabric over skin, the buzz of a zipper, the *flump* of clothing hitting the floor—these are sounds I have no business hearing, not when they're coming from her.

Fourteen times two is twenty-eight. Fourteen times three is forty-two. Fourteen times four—

"Much better," she says. "I'm decent." She pauses. "I guess I'll just read a book and eat strawberries for a while. What a horrible way to spend the day."

But there's a little smile on her face when I look at her, a genuine one. I watch as she gathers her hair and pulls it into a ponytail, revealing the curve of her neck that disappears beneath the too-wide neckline of my shirt. She leans down and picks up her clothes from off the floor and drapes them neatly over the top of her suitcase; then she more or less waltzes to the chaise lounge and the plate of chocolate-covered strawberries.

"I'm going to eat every single one of these unless you specifically want me to save some," she says, settling on the lounge chair. "Even then, it will depend upon how nicely you ask."

I don't allow myself to smile at that. "Go ahead," I say. "I don't want any."

"Good." Her hand hovers over the tray as she inspects the strawberries; finally she chooses one and takes a bite, letting out a little moan.

"That's a wildly unnecessary sound you're making," I say, frowning and watching as she chews.

She moans louder, exaggerated this time, and I roll my eyes.

"Pest," I say, loosening my tie so that I can breathe. "Eat your food and read your book so I can work in peace."

"Fine," she says, pulling out her phone. "But only because I'm making my way through Sunny Palmer's backlist, and her books are more fun than annoying you. I've got my book club book to read too. I'm all set."

I hold my tongue, remove my tie and my suit coat, and then settle myself on the floor next to the jacuzzi.

No time like your honeymoon to review expenditure reports.

CHAPTER 16

Phoenix

WE PASS the afternoon in silence.

Holland is curled up on the lounge chair, her nose buried in her phone, and she smiles to herself every so often—I know this because I'm sneaking more peeks at her than I should—but she never says anything.

I do work like I said I was going to, but I'm inefficient and distracted. My eyes keep darting around the suite, at the heart-shaped jacuzzi, the rose petals on the bed, the sumptuous silk-upholstered headboard.

The level of romance expected in a room like this is almost suffocating.

When the sky starts to darken outside the sliding glass door, a knock sounds at the door to the suite.

I startle, standing up so fast my head spins. Then I groan in pain; I've been sitting in the same spot for hours.

"Relax," Holland says. "It's just room service."

I blink at her. "You ordered room service?"

"Yeah," she says, unfolding herself from the chaise lounge. "Aren't you hungry? We haven't eaten all day."

"You had strawberries," I point out.

"Fine," she says, padding to the door. "*You* haven't eaten all day. And I'm hungry anyway."

"Did you not think to ask me what I wanted?" I say, folding my arms and frowning at her.

She opens the door to the suite with a lurch and smiles at someone I can't see. "Hi," she says, sounding far more cheerful than she ever does when she talks to me. "Thank you so much." She pulls a few bills out of the pocket of the flannel pants—was there already money in there?—and passes them to the person outside. Then she closes the door and comes to me carrying two large paper bags.

"Isn't this supposed to be on a rolling cart?" I say, but she just shrugs.

"I didn't ask what you wanted," she says, passing me one of the bags, "because when I checked the menu, they had Cobb salad."

My go-to order, nine times out of ten. Especially if—

"And they let me specify that I wanted the bacon extra crispy."

Something stirs low in my stomach, something I think I recognize; it's the same feeling I had on the steps outside Town Hall, when she as good as admitted that she was marrying me in part so I could inherit Butterfield.

It's a warm feeling, slow and languid, and I'm not crazy about it—or its implications.

"Thanks," I say grudgingly, taking the bag from her. She just nods and then carries her own food over to the lounge chair. We eat in silence, and with every moment that passes, the sky darkens more and more.

That darkening sky seems to be conjuring a rock in the pit of my stomach. Because dark means bedtime, and bedtime means bed, under the covers, next to Holland.

My *wife*.

When I steal a glance at her and find her eyes on me, a

grimace on her face, I know we're thinking about the same thing.

"We just have to do it," I say, keeping my voice brisk and businesslike. The warmth she sometimes makes me feel has no place here. I gather up my trash from my meal and head into the bathroom to throw it away, speaking over my shoulder. "This will only be a big deal if we turn it into one. You sleep on one side, I'll sleep on the other, pillows down the middle."

"You snore," she says, following me.

How does she even know that? "I wear nasal strips," I say shortly. "Give me my pajamas and choose a side of the bed. I don't care either way."

"Fine," she says. She tosses her trash in after mine and then drifts to her suitcase, clearly not excited about the prospect of sharing a bed with me.

I'm not too thrilled about it either.

She pulls out her nightgown and then goes back to the bathroom, emerging one minute later looking like temptation personified. I avert my eyes and take the shirt and pants she passes me.

You are not attracted to her, I tell myself firmly. *Get it together.*

And of course I'm not—of course I'm not. A bit of bare skin is not what makes a woman appealing in my eyes. No amount of physical beauty can make a bad personality look good.

But into my mind, unbidden, pops the memory of this morning outside Mavis's hospital suite—Holland fixing my tic, her focused gaze, her satisfied nod when she finished.

And beneath that, another memory of her hand on my tie, in my office this time, pulling me closer as we battle—

And yet another memory, buried more deeply still

155

beneath years of ignoring—flashes of the one moment I never let myself think about.

A dark closet; lips chasing.

My eyes pop wide as it hits me: I think I might actually be attracted to this woman.

"No way," I mutter, shaking my head as I close myself in the bathroom. I change quickly and then step out again, my gaze seeking Holland. I find her climbing into bed, and for a second I just let myself stare.

My brows furrow as I take in her golden hair spilling over her shoulders; my mouth pulls down into a frown when I notice the slope of her neck and the vulnerable hollow of her collarbone.

I watch as she begins creating a wall of pillows down the middle of the mattress, working intently, and that warmth stirs again in my gut—it even rises up into my chest when I notice her tongue poking out between her teeth, her face screwed up in concentration as she balances pillow after pillow—

"No!"

The word rips out of me before I realize it; she jumps as she looks at me from the bed, but I can't fix my horrified expression.

Absolutely not. I can't be attracted to her. I can't be attracted to *Holland Blakely* of all people—

Holland Park, my traitorous mind whispers.

"Why are you shouting?" she says, looking annoyed. "You scared me." She resumes her pillow piling. "I'm going to bed. Do whatever you want, but this is my side"—she gestures to her side of the bed—"so don't cross over or I'll force feed you toothpaste Oreos every day for a month."

I roll my eyes and cross the room, approaching my side of the bed. "Sleeping close to you is the more disgusting option between those two," I say, but the words are forced—because they're not true.

I'm *attracted* to her. How could my brain and my body do this to me? How could I suddenly be finding her...*desirable?*

Is it really all that sudden, though? my brain whispers.

Right. Tucking that thought away forever. I shudder, shooting her another horrified look as I climb into bed. I manage to smooth my expression when she looks at me this time, though; we exchange awkward glances, sitting up in bed next to each other with nothing but pillows separating us, and then as one we lie down, turning our backs.

She clicks her lamp off a moment later, and the room falls into darkness; my last, reassuring thought is that it could be worse.

Because desiring her is one thing, but it's better than falling in love.

I AWAKE SUDDENLY, and for a second, I don't know why. It takes me a minute of reorientation to even figure out where I am or what I'm doing—or why I can hear the sound of another person in bed with me.

It all comes rushing back, though, when I hear a knock on the door. That's what woke me, I realize, and I grope around in the dark for my phone to check the time.

One-thirty-eight in the morning.

My pulse hitches and then begins to speed up. This is Mavis; it has to be.

I reach blindly to my left, shaking Holland.

"Wake up," I whisper. "Amsterdam. Amsterdam!"

Her groggy groan does not inspire confidence.

"Someone is knocking on the door," I say.

I hear a yawn. Then she mumbles, "What are you talking—"

Thud, thud, thud.

A second of silence. Then, sounding more alert, she says, "Someone is at the door."

"I know," I say quickly as I reach for the pillow barricade that has miraculously survived the night so far. I grab as many as I can with one clutching hand, tossing them aside frantically. "Come on, help me get rid of the pillows."

"I don't want to get rid of the pillows—*ouch*, Flamingo, that was my head!"

"Stop flailing around, then!" I say. "Help me get these off."

Thud, thud, thud, thud!

We throw pillows until there aren't any more; my eyes have adjusted to the dark enough that I can see them on the floor, vague light splotches.

"Now spoon," I say, hating every word. "Come on— spoon me."

"Absolutely not," she says; I can make out the shape of her, roughly, and I think she's folding her arms. "This is insane. What if we were naked in here? This is illegal, isn't it?"

"Not if Mavis's name is on the reservation," I say irritably. "Which it is. It's just scummy. Come on—over here." I pat the bed next to me. "You can be little spoon."

"I—"

"Amsterdam!"

"Fine!" she snaps. "Fine. For the record, I will only ever be little spoon," she goes on. "Never expect otherwise."

I pause, even though there's no time. "This isn't something we're going to do a lot. Or ever again, for that matter."

"I know," she says after a beat of silence.

Her voice is near now, so I reach blindly into the dark in front of me and find her—the dip of her waist, the curve of her hip. I lock my arm around her and pull her closer.

"Sorry," I mutter, because we're closer than either of us wants to be.

From across the dark room, the door beeps—the sound of a key card being accepted.

"Pretend to be asleep," I say quickly. "Now. Close your eyes. Pretend to be asleep."

She stops moving at once, her body relaxing as she falls silent.

The door to the room lurches open.

And even though every instinct in me is screaming that I need to protect her, protect myself—I do nothing. I remain motionless, my arm snaked around her waist, my breathing slow. I do nothing as I listen to the nearly silent footsteps; I do nothing when I realize that that can't possibly be Mavis, based on how quick and quiet they are.

Who on *earth* is in this bedroom, where me and my new wife are presumably sleeping?

The answer comes seconds later when I hear a dull thud, followed by a hiss of pain.

Lawrence—that's my cousin Lawrence, likely here on behalf of both himself and his father.

I hope his toe is broken.

While I recognize my cousin's pained exhale, however, Holland doesn't; she's doing her best to remain still, but I can feel her body beginning to tremble, and I put myself in her shoes.

She's listening to a strange man enter her bedroom. Of course she's terrified.

Something hot and angry rises in my chest—anger at my

family for being like this, and anger at myself for dragging her into it. I tighten my arm around her and breathe into her ear: "My cousin."

Her shaking doesn't subside, but she somehow burrows closer to me, and although I'm surprised, I don't push her away. When a beam of light falls on us, we both shift, but I keep my arm around her.

The light wanders for just a few seconds, and then it's dark again; after another moment, the door to the suite closes.

He's gone.

But we don't move.

"Your entire family is psycho," Holland finally says, her voice faint like she can't quite believe it. "You're the most normal one. How is that even possible? How did I marry into this?" She's shaking still, and when the shaking becomes more pronounced, I tighten my arm around her.

"Listen to me—Holland, *listen.*" So strange, calling her by her name like this, but...we're already spooning. Plus there's something odd about this darkness; it feels like another plane, where our normal rules don't apply. I can't see her, she can't see me, it's the middle of the night and we're in bed together; I know, instinctively, that whatever I say here tonight will stay here. Both of us will pretend this never occurred.

So I call her by her name, because I need her to pay attention. I need her to understand. "I will not let anything happen to you. Okay?"

She doesn't answer; I speak again.

"I swear," I say into the darkness. Her hair tickles my face, but I don't try to move. "Nothing will happen to you while you're married to me." Then, my voice gentler, I add, "Trust me, please."

"Impossible," she says, and I can hear the bravado she's trying to muster, but the words just come out shaky. "I don't trust you at all."

I sigh. I guess we're going to talk about the things we never talk about—more things we'll leave in this marriage bed when we get up in the morning. Because it's hitting me, all at once, the truth of what Wyatt said: that whatever Holland and I are, we're close ones. I didn't believe him, or maybe I didn't want to admit it, but...he was right.

I need her to see that. Because she's shaking in my arms, and it bothers me in a way I can't explain.

"You trust me," I say. "You do, or you wouldn't have married me. And I trust you, or I wouldn't have asked. We wouldn't be sharing this bed if we didn't trust each other, and you know it. Name one other man you would sleep next to like this."

"You wouldn't either," she says, sounding defensive.

When I hesitate, she pushes.

"Admit it," she says.

"Yes," I say finally, my voice grudging. "There's no one else. Only you."

And I'm just admitting that she's the only one I could sleep next to like this, but it *feels* like I'm saying more than that. So I take a deep breath and move on.

"I promised Trev I would take care of you. And after he died..." I swallow, clear my throat. "Anyway, I want to do something good with this company. I need to do good things. And to do that, I have to inherit. So we just need to hold out long enough for Mavis to officially name me her heir. But during that time, you'll be safe."

Holland is silent for a second. "It wasn't your fault," she says then. "The crash, I mean."

My brain, my body, my heart—they all still. "I know that,"

I say after a moment spent locating my voice. It's not entirely true.

"Then why are you trying to compensate?"

She's speaking so matter-of-factly, so dispassionately, and some part of me knows that it's because she's never grieved properly, never let herself think about Trev, never fully processed his death. She's just been running from that pain.

Aren't you tired of running, Holl?

"I'm not compensating," I say. "Or—maybe I am, I don't know." I pick through my thoughts, trying to decipher them enough to string together sentences. These are not things I ever talk about to anyone other than my therapist, and my words come out stilted and clipped. "I'm not seeking absolution, and I'm not trying to bring him back. I just...want to do good things. Isn't that allowed?"

"Of course it is," she says quietly.

"I'll happily put a dead fish in your mailbox or insult you until I'm blue in the face, but I won't actually let anything happen to you," I say. "That's my point, all right? Now go to sleep. First thing in the morning, we're out of here."

She's silent for a moment; then she speaks. "Stop saying mushy stuff. It's weird."

My lips twitch, but I don't answer.

CHAPTER 17

Holland

IT TAKES me only one week of being Holland Park to discover the most fundamental flaw in my marriage to Phoenix, and it is this: I cannot be mean to him all the time.

Because the truth is, I'm not usually a mean person. And the same is true of him; he's overbearing and overprotective and invasive, sure, but rarely *mean*.

Now we're living together. We see each other in the mornings and at night. We drink from the same carton of orange juice. And no matter how we might normally treat each other, neither of us can be petty and rude and argumentative all the time. It's too exhausting.

Which means I'm starting to see the other sides of Phoenix—the ones I've always ignored. And he's seeing the same in me; I can tell by the twitch of his eyebrows when I use basic manners like *please* and *thank you*.

I don't want to be reminded of thoughtful Phoenix or dry-humor Phoenix. I *definitely* don't want to think about vulnerable Phoenix—the one that spoke to me in the dark of our honeymoon suite, his body wrapped around mine.

Neither of us mention the things we said or did in that suite—which sounds way more risqué than it actually is—and if his psycho family has said anything more about our marriage, he hasn't told me. He doesn't tell me anything, in fact, because we barely speak at all. I work as many shifts at the salon as humanly possible over the course of the week leading up to the Fourth, just to avoid being at home with him.

I can't handle all those facets of his personality. And scary Phoenix? The one who swooped in and told Dot not to call me anything but *Holland* or *ma'am*?

That version of Phoenix was just as devastating as vulnerable Phoenix, though in a vastly different way. I will die before I ever tell him so, but there's something about a man defending your honor while also looking sexy in an uberexpensive suit.

I press my hand to my chest, frowning as I inhale and then exhale.

"What's up?" Cat says from next to me, a large plate of pancakes in front of her.

"Huh? Oh," I say, looking at my own half-eaten stack—courtesy of the Fourth of July pancake breakfast being held in the town square this morning. "Just feel a little—funny." But something twisting and anxious is starting to squirm in the pit of my stomach.

I'm imagining things, right? My heart didn't *flutter*. Not for Phoenix.

Not again.

Food poisoning, maybe, or pneumonia, or the stomach flu. It's probably one of those.

And this is why I've been avoiding the house: because my heart is doing things I don't like, randomly, and for no reason at all.

"If you get me sick and I end up throwing up all these pancakes, I'll never forgive you," Cat says.

"Oh, don't talk about throwing up," Ivy says with a groan, looking at her own pancakes. "Not while I'm trying to eat."

"No one will be throwing up," I say as I collect another bite and then shove the whole thing in my mouth, syrup dripping off my fork. "I don't think I'm sick. Just a little... off."

"Off how?" Cat says.

"I don't even know," I say with a sigh.

She gives me a questioning look, but I don't have an explanation for her. I just shrug, and then we chat for a while as more people join us at the table.

The Fourth of July is an all-day affair in Sunset Harbor, and most of the town comes out to celebrate. There's a breakfast to start out, and then a parade, then games on the beach, and finally music, dancing, and fireworks.

I'm not really interested in games, but I do love free breakfast, and I'll probably go listen to Mo and the Kokomos later. They're headlining the show tonight for the billionth year in a row, and they're always good.

"Where should we watch the rest of the parade this year?" I say once we've finished our pancakes.

"There's a nice place in the shade that we went to growing up," Cat says, looking at Ivy. "Let's try that."

"I'm good with shade," I say, because the sun overhead is already uncomfortably warm, and it's not even nine yet. We make our way through the town square and then north up the island until we reach a sandy little hill, shaded by palm trees and facing one of the streets the parade will travel.

We settle in and watch from there, listening to the music and watching the floats. I've seen some of these floats every year since moving here, but I'm still not tired of them; it's just hard to be anxious or upset when a giant silver star is rolling by, accompanied by a spangled, festooned marching band.

Even if you're stressed about your errantly fluttering heart, like I am.

Once the parade is over, the three of us part ways; Ivy and Cat head to the beach, and I head home.

And by *home,* I mean Phoenix's house.

I haven't seen him yet today; he was gone when I got up this morning, and because we're not actually in a romantic relationship, he didn't leave a note telling me where he was. I considered texting to ask, but that felt clingy.

I shiver as I step through the front door, the AC kissing my sweat-sheened skin; my white-eyelet sundress was perfect for the heat outside, but not so much in here. I'm just slipping off my sandals when Phoenix rounds the corner into the entryway, a large cooler in one hand, his eyes going wide when he sees me.

"Do we have any of those popsicles I bought?" I say, fanning the back of my neck. But when I take a closer look at him, my jaw drops. "Are you wearing a *t-shirt?* Will you be okay without your emotional support button-down?"

Phoenix just stares at me, and I'm about to ask what his problem is when two more people follow him around the corner: Beau Palmer and Dax Miller.

Phoenix's wide eyes are nothing compared to Beau's when he sees me; Dax just looks vaguely confused.

"Ah." The word slips weakly from my lips. But what else can I say? I've just let myself into the house with my own key, and I asked if *we* had any popsicles left.

"Hi," Beau says, a smile spreading slowly over his face as he looks back and forth between me and Phoenix.

"Hi," I say. "I—didn't know you were here."

"Clearly," Phoenix says with a strained expression. He

sets the cooler down and runs one hand over his face. "Yesterday you said you were going to the parade."

"I did go to the parade," I say dumbly. "The parade is over. Cat and Ivy went to the beach"—Dax straightens up when I mention Ivy, I can't help but notice—"and I decided to come back home."

"Are you two *living* together?" Beau says. He looks happier about this than Phoenix and I have ever been.

I don't want to lie, so I pass the buck and stay silent.

"We're married, actually," Phoenix finally says, his voice resigned. "And we'd prefer to tell as few people as possible, because we're only doing it to take care of some family stuff, and then we'll separate. So keep your mouth shut, please."

"We're only doing it to take care of some family stuff." Hear that, heart? I tell myself. *Stop fluttering.*

"I have so many questions," Beau says, and Phoenix rolls his eyes.

"I thought you were in a hurry?" he says.

"I am."

Phoenix nods shortly. "Then let's go. Dax, we'll drop you off on the way."

Dax nods too, and the three of them move past me, each carrying a cooler. Beau shoots me a smile over his shoulder as they leave, but he's the only one; the door shuts, and I'm alone again.

I SPEND the rest of the afternoon reading a book and icing my knee—which, according to the doctor I saw two days ago, just needs moderate activity and physical therapy. I hear Phoenix come home late morning, but I stay in my room.

Only when six o'clock rolls around do I venture out, like a hermit going into public for the first time.

"Are you coming to the beach?" Phoenix says when I reach the kitchen. He's still got on his light blue t-shirt, and it looks stupidly good on him.

"Yeah," I say, drifting over to the counter by the fridge. "I like Mo and the Kokomos."

"Is that what you're wearing?"

"Why?" I say as I reach for an apple. I look down at my sundress and grin. "Do you want to borrow it?"

He just rolls his eyes. "I didn't know if you needed time to change. If you don't, let's go." Then, after a pause, he adds, "You know, I've been paying attention for the last week, and you only smile at me when you're making fun of me or when you're pretending to be a devoted wife."

"So?" I say with a snort. He said something about this after we met with Mavis. "Why are you bringing up my smile again? You don't smile at me at *all*."

"Yes I do," he says, looking offended.

I just shake my head and start toward the door. He mutters something under his breath about *not true* and *ridiculous* as he follows, but I ignore it.

Mo and the Kokomos are already in full swing when Phoenix and I arrive at the beach. Several groups of people are getting bonfires ready up and down the stretch of sand, though they won't actually light any fires until later. We separate as soon as we arrive, Phoenix heading to hang out with Beau while I search for Cat and Ivy.

It's hard to hear much over the music, but we dance and snack as the evening wears on; Ivy leaves about an hour in. When she and Cat have both gone to do their own things, I look around for someone to talk to—Capri Collins and Tristan Palmer are here, I notice with a smile, but they're looking *very* cozy, so I decide to give them their privacy. I see Briggs Dalton a second later, so I head in his direction. Briggs isn't my type, but even I can admit he's cute. He's got a nerdy-hot thing going on, and he looks perfectly suited to his job at the book shop.

"Hey, Briggs," I say, smiling as I approach him.

"Hi," he says with a little nod.

"How's it going?"

He shrugs, looking around. "Well enough," he says. "How have you been?"

What a question. "I've been okay," I say, because the truth is complicated and uncomfortable. "Just—"

But I break off when I see Phoenix. He's talking to Jane, the two of them a decent stretch of beach away. He cuts an imposing figure even in a t-shirt and shorts, and Jane looks as cute as always.

"Sorry," I say, pushing aside the weird little twist of my stomach at the sight of his expression.

He says he smiles at me, but I don't think we've ever had a conversation that looks like that—chatting politely, pleasant expressions, and—yes—smiles. Real, genuine smiles.

"Yeah, I've been good," I manage to get out. "How's the shop doing?"

Briggs smiles a little; it seems like asking him about the shop is a good way to get him talking. "It's doing all right. A lot of steady, repeat customers—like you," he says with a nod.

I watch over his shoulder as Jane laughs at something Phoenix says, and my stomach sours.

What's wrong with me? I *like* Jane. Jane is totally great. We're friends.

It's because Phoenix and I are legally married now; that

must be it. His ring is on my dresser. That would make anyone feel a little possessive. I don't *actually* care if Phoenix is giving his smile to another woman; it's just a wife thing.

I nod to myself. That makes sense.

"You work at the salon, right?" Briggs says, pulling me back to our conversation.

"Huh? Oh, yes," I say with a nod before stealing another glance at Jane and Phoenix.

I'm barely paying attention to what Briggs says; I catch him mentioning something about the book shop, but all I can really focus on is Phoenix's face as he talks to a woman who isn't me.

This is insane. Completely insane. I *cannot* be possessive over a man I don't love or even like.

But no matter how many times I tell myself that, the acid in my stomach continues to eat holes through my insides until finally, I can't take it anymore.

"I'm so sorry," I tell Briggs. "I've got to go."

"Sure," he says with a nod, his glasses glinting in the light of the bonfires spotting the beach around us.

I turn toward Phoenix and Jane, my heart pounding in a way that doesn't make sense. My hands are clenched into unnecessary fists, and my feet are all set to carry me to the two of them—to do what, I'm not certain.

I'm surprised to see, then, that they've stopped talking; Jane has disappeared into the crowd, and Phoenix?

Phoenix is moving toward me.

He's moving in my direction, and even in the orange light of the fires I can see his eyes darting back and forth between me and Briggs before finally, dark and burning, they settle on me.

Something swoops low in my stomach, something antici-patory, something *wanting*. It's a feeling that's both foreign and faintly familiar—a book that was shelved long ago, dusty and hidden, now being rediscovered.

There are people mingling everywhere, dancing all around us, but they fade into the periphery as he stalks closer. He's a magnet, pulling my eyes, pulling the breath from my lungs.

This should not be happening. He should not be storming toward me with that look in his eyes, and my pulse should not be tripping.

Keep things business-focused, I tell myself.

"I think we should add something to the contract," I say as soon as he comes to a stop in front of me.

"I agree," he says, his voice low and silky. He's too near; but the music is loud, and the people around us are dancing, and somehow I find myself taking a step closer, until we're separated by mere inches.

"Even though this marriage is in name only—" I begin, but I break off, trying to find the words I'm so embarrassed to say. Because I can't tell him not to *smile* at other women if he's not going to smile at me. That's ridiculous and stupid and I shouldn't care.

When I look at him for help, though, Phoenix only raises his eyebrows—like he's daring me to go on.

"Yes?" he says, clasping his hands behind his back.

I exhale roughly, frustrated. "You know what I mean."

"Hmm," he hums. He tilts his head as he looks down at me. "Do I?"

"I just think that while we're married, we should refrain from—from—"

He moves impossibly closer, his dark eyes holding me captive. "Say it," he breathes. It's not a request; it's a command.

But I can't make myself speak. I can't bring myself to spit

those words out, because they'll mean something—it will be as good as admitting that I'm jealous.

"As my *wife*, Amsterdam," he says in a low voice, "you're the only person in the world who has the right to ask this of me, so just say it."

I narrow my eyes, annoyed. He already knows what I'm trying to say, and he's making me speak the words anyway.

But you know what? He's right. I am his wife. I can't tell him not to smile, but I'm allowed to ask for more reasonable things. So I take a deep breath and straighten up, the sand soft beneath my feet as I shift. Then, trying to ignore the heat I feel in my cheeks, I speak. "I think we should refrain from extramarital relationships for the duration of the contract."

"I agree," he says immediately. "I'll have Wyatt add it first thing in the morning."

My shoulders relax as relief trickles gently in, a cool breeze after uncomfortable warmth.

But Phoenix notices—and something wicked flares to life in his eyes. "Never thought I'd see you get jealous," he says, cocking one brow at me as his lip curls like the smoke rising to the heavens around us.

I stare at him, lost for words, until finally I manage to splutter something out. "I'm not jealous. I just think you're giving a lot of attention to other women when you're not actually available—"

"And you've been smiling at Briggs Dalton an awful lot for someone who comes home to me every night," he cuts me off smoothly.

"*Comes home to you*—" I begin, my eyes widening. It sounds so intimate when he phrases it like that. "Are you—wait." I break off as his words register.

He knows who I've been talking to. He knows I've been smiling.

He's been watching me, just as much as I've been watching him.

"*You* were jealous," I realize, my eyes wide.

"You wish, Amsterdam," he says with a snort. But he breaks our eye contact, and the words are too casual to be convincing.

"You were," I say again, my certainty growing. "You've been watching me. You're jealous." Something like triumph rises in my chest, and my lips pull into a smile of my own.

"Absolutely not."

"Really?" I say, leaning closer to him, close enough that I can smell leather and mahogany over the scent of the bonfires. "So if I asked Briggs to dance, you'd have no problem with it?"

"Of course not," he says, scoffing.

"Mmm-hm. And if I hugged him, you'd be fine?"

He rolls his eyes. "Friends hug all the time."

I nod slowly. Then—I don't know why I do it. I really don't. It's stupid and impulsive.

But the next thing I know, I'm rising up on my tiptoes, steadying myself with my hands on his shoulders. His grip finds my waist, probably instinctively—because the look on his face tells me he's not paying attention to his hands right now.

His eyes flare wide, his lips part, and those are the last things I see before I lean in and kiss him.

The lightest touch of my lips to his, and I don't stay for longer than a second, but it's enough to set off a pleasant fizziness in my stomach.

"What about if I kissed him like that?" I say when I lean back. I don't let go of him, and I don't stand down from my tiptoes.

Phoenix's hands on my waist tighten, and he glares at me,

his eyes full of fire as he speaks. "You could kiss fifty men like that, Amsterdam, and I still wouldn't be jealous."

I kiss him again—firmly this time, and longer, my lips against his, hunting for the answers I want, because he doesn't respond *at all...*

Until he does.

A low sound leaves him as his lips come to life, moving suddenly, slanting impatiently over mine as his fingers dig into my sides. I don't even notice the pain, because this kiss is telling me something—something I can't quite grasp no matter how desperately my lips chase his.

He's there for three seconds, and then he's gone—his mouth rips away from mine, and when I lean away, he's already shaking his head.

"No," he says, his chest rising and falling rapidly, his eyes locked on my lips. "Still wouldn't be jealous."

"Liar," I say, just as short of breath as he is.

The word is barely out of my mouth before he's back. He comes as close as he possibly can without actually kissing me, and even though he doesn't speak again, I can feel the debate raging inside of him; his lips hover so close to mine that I can feel their heat, feel every breath, feel every rise and fall of his chest. His hands slide from my waist to my back, but he doesn't close that last bit of space.

When I speak again, it's so soft that I question whether he can even hear. "And if I wore a silk nightgown and spooned with him in a honeymoon suite on a bed covered in rose petals?" I say.

"That would fall firmly under the *extramarital relationship* category, so try it and see what happens," he whispers against my lips, the words clipped.

"Admit that you're jealous," I whisper back. Somehow my

arms have wound around his neck, and his arms have snaked all the way around my waist. When did that happen?

Phoenix's black eyes glitter with challenge as he looks down at me. "You first," he says.

I swallow, and I can't stop my gaze from darting over his features. Fire light does great things for his bone structure.

"I was jealous," I finally say, so quietly I can barely hear myself. Then I go on. "It's because you've been saying all that stuff about smiling at each other. You got in my head," I finish, accusation in my voice.

"I got in my own head, too." His words are reluctant, but when he goes on, his voice gets stronger. "Smile at whoever you want. But you will kiss no one else, in any way, while we're married—"

"No one *else?* As in...only you?"

His cheeks flush.

"No one at all," he corrects himself. "I'll abide by the same rule." He swallows. "No romantic relationships for either of us."

"Do you actually think I would cheat?" I say with a scoff, letting my arms drop to my sides again.

"No," he admits, and he takes a few steps back. The cool air is a welcome relief. "But it's still good to have a contract in place." He hesitates; then, looking at me, he says one more thing. "This is your last warning, Amsterdam," he says, his eyes dark. "Don't start a game you can't win. Don't kiss me whenever you feel like it."

The words slam into me, unexpected, a blow to the solar plexus that makes it difficult to breathe.

"Or what?" I say.

"Or I'll kiss you back," he says, looking suddenly tired. "And we'll like it, Holland. You know we will. We'll start kissing, and we'll never—" He clears his throat, his gaze darting away. "We'll never want to stop. Things will get messy and complicated. So don't do it, not unless you know what you're getting yourself into." He gives me a little parting nod before turning silently and disappearing down the beach.

A single tear slips down my cheek, and I have no idea why; I swipe it angrily away.

But another one just falls in its place.

CHAPTER 18

Nine Years Ago

Holland

EVERY YEAR for New Year's, my parents travel to New York City. And while they're gone, my brother holds a party—every single year. He did it in high school, and he's continued to do it in college when he comes home for winter break.

Every year he holds his New Year's party, and every year I hide in my room with Maggie. We have a girl's night where we watch movies and eat snacks and I paint her nails—blue, usually, because that's the only color she really likes. Trev checks in on us throughout the night, and he brings us more snacks so we don't have to venture out into the social hubbub. He's a people person, a Golden Retriever; I am not.

But this year is different.

I mean, not *horribly* different—I still hide with Maggie. But usually I go to sleep after she falls asleep, the two of us snuggled up on the bed in my childhood bedroom. Tonight I don't do that.

Because I know for a fact that Phoenix Park is here tonight, and I also know Trev invited some girl in a few of Phoenix's classes, a girl Phoenix has had his eye on.

I've gotten to know Phoenix a bit better—since it turns out he's Trev's roommate. He's not a partier or a flirt; he's an observer, and if someone catches his eye, he watches them intently. He's serious a lot of the time, but he has a dry sense of humor that comes out every now and then. He's smart. He's loyal.

He was rude about the tampon thing when we first met, but he's warmed up a bit. Mostly he's just impatient, with a low tolerance for anything he deems dumb or stupid or wrong.

I shouldn't like him, but I do—just a little crush. And if I have to watch him get together with that girl from his classes, I'm going to cry—but at least I'll be able to see it for myself, and then maybe I can put these silly feelings to rest.

Because a large part of my brain knows it's never going to happen. He's Trev's best friend, three years older than me, and way out of my league in every way. His family owns some sort of company, so they're filthy rich, and he's tall and handsome and he wears a lot of suits.

The girl from his classes—Jewel, Trev said—is about his age; I saw her briefly when she first got here, before Maggie and I went to the bedroom. She's pretty, and she and Phoenix clearly have similar interests if they're in classes together.

She'll be perfect for him.

I just…need to know for sure.

So I wait until Maggie falls asleep—my sweet, precious Maggie, whose cheeks are still the slightest bit round because she's only twelve—and then I slip out of the room, making sure she doesn't wake at the sound of the door opening and closing.

The hallway is cooler than the bedroom, and it's a welcome relief. I fan my face with my hands, lifting my hair off my neck and fanning that too. I shouldn't have worn this cardigan. I'm doubly irritated because Jewel is wearing one almost exactly like it.

It looks better on her.

I tiptoe down the hallway, listening for voices; as I expected, the party has congregated downstairs, in the basement. There's someone clanking around in the kitchen, but other than that, it's silent up here. So I round the corner and head down the stairs on gentle feet, making sure to skip the squeaky step, even though I know no one will hear me with how loud they're all being.

The temperature drops several degrees by the time I reach the bottom of the stairs, and the lights are off; the only illumination is the glow of my parents' TV, large and shining blue as Trev conducts a conversation about what movie to watch—or maybe they're debating which game to play? I don't know. I'm too busy hovering there, scanning the clusters of people, looking for Phoenix and Jewel. I try to look casual, like I belong with this group that hasn't even noticed my presence; I lean against the wall, my arms folded, as my gaze roves around the room.

I don't see Phoenix anywhere, and I don't know Jewel well enough to tell. Why did Trev have to turn the lights out?

I sigh. Everyone continues talking about what movie they're going to watch, and that's when I decide to take my pity party elsewhere. My cardigan is itchy and there's a weight in my stomach and I keep looking for Phoenix and Jewel, but now that I'm here, I'm not sure I actually want to find them. So I push off the wall and stand up straighter, running my fingers through my hair again. I tug at the hem of my cardigan, trying to stop it from riding up.

"All right, ladies," Trev says loudly from next to the TV. "Come look at our movie selection and pick something."

The gaggle of girls go crowd around the entertainment

center, but I don't bother; I know Trev's not talking to me. I just look at the TV as the screen changes and opening credits start rolling, watching vaguely as I try to place what movie they've chosen.

But I jump when I feel a hand on my shoulder, and I jump further when I hear Phoenix's voice whisper in my ear from behind me.

"Meet me in the coat closet next to the stairs upstairs," he says, and I shiver at the feeling of his breath on my neck.

Forget speeding up; my heart just stops altogether as he slips past me and heads toward the wet bar with two cans of soda in his hands, not looking back at me.

Meet him in the coat closet?

My mind reels, but my body automatically obeys, and I begin climbing the stairs. Why does he want to meet me in the coat closet? Does he want to talk to me?

Or—what if—

No. No way.

I reach the top of the stairs and slip quietly into the coat closet, closing the door behind me. I leave the light off, because I can't even begin to fathom what my face looks like right now. Flushed, definitely. But also bewildered and confused and stupidly hopeful.

No; the light will stay off.

I wait for only thirty seconds before the door opens. A sliver of light shines into the closet, and then it's blocked as Phoenix slips quietly in. I can faintly smell his cologne, and it's heavenly.

When he's closed the door and the closet is black again, he whispers, "You here?"

I swallow. "Yes," I whisper back.

I hear him hum, a deep, vibrating sound. "Good."

I fold my arms across my chest. "What do you want?" I whisper, sounding much more confident than I feel.

"Mmm. Isn't that obvious?" he says with dry amusement. "I've been thinking about kissing you."

My brain screeches to a halt. "I—what?" I forget to whisper, and I can hear my incredulity.

"You sound...strange," Phoenix says immediately, and I can tell by his voice that he's frowning. There's silence for a second—while my mind implodes—and then he goes on, sounding less certain. "Did I misread this?" He clears his throat. "My apologies."

Brain. Not. Working.

"Right," he says, sounding unsure of himself. It's a voice I've rarely heard. "I'll leave."

And that does it. My mind springs back into action, because Phoenix wants to kiss me, and he's about to walk out of this closet.

My hand darts out, reaching blindly for him. When I make contact with his chest, I grab a fistful of his shirt and tug him closer. I hear his breath catch.

Am I doing this? I am. I'm doing this. I've been intrigued by this man for months.

"How long have you felt like this?" I whisper, because I need to know. I don't want him to think I'm pathetic, to think I've been pining for him, but what if he's been just as interested in me as I've been in him?

"How long have I wanted to kiss you?" he says, and from his businesslike tone, I can tell his confidence is back. I feel his hands suddenly, like the darkness itself reaching for me, and his fingers trail lightly from my arms to my shoulders to my face. One of his thumbs traces my lips, his touch softer and gentler than I ever would have imagined. My legs are approximately as steady as jelly.

"Yeah," I say, trying to breathe. But riots of butterflies are fluttering inside, and electricity is coursing through me from his touch.

"Long enough," he says, his voice low. "Since shortly after we met and you—"

"Stop talking," I whisper, cutting him off. "Stop talking and kiss me." My words are breathy and impatient, but I've heard what I wanted to know, and I'm done waiting.

He doesn't care. He exhales roughly, and the next thing I know, his lips collide with mine.

And I've died and gone to heaven. I've kissed guys before, but none of them have ever kissed me like this. Phoenix's lips are firm, unyielding, and perfectly in sync with mine. His hands move from my face, and I feel his arms wrap around me, pulling me flush with him. I slide my hands up his chest and around his neck, holding onto him desperately, running my fingers through his hair. It's so much softer than I ever thought it would be.

The kiss goes from intense to downright scorching, and as his lips move beneath mine, I can't stop the tiny little sigh that slips from the back of my throat. His hands clench in response, digging into my sides as he deepens the kiss further.

All I can think about is the feel of his arms supporting me, the taste of him, the leather-and-mahogany smell of his cologne, the hard planes of his muscular body pressed against me. The sensational overload is almost too much for my brain to handle, and my mind goes blissfully fuzzy.

I gasp as his lips break away from mine, as I feel the oxygen rush into my lungs. There's silence for a second, broken only by our ragged breaths intermingling. I can feel his chest heaving, and I know mine is doing the same. I rest my forehead against his, waiting until I can breathe steadily to speak.

But he beats me to it. "That," he says, sounding shaken, "was..."

"I know," I say. With a tinge of regret, I go down off my tiptoes, because my legs are starting to get shaky. He tugs me close, and when I rest my head against his chest, I can hear his heart racing.

I smile. *I* made his heart race. And he's being so *gentle*.

"Jewel—"

I push away from him, and he breaks off.

A sick understanding is suddenly dropping like lead in the pit of my stomach, a dull roaring in my ears.

Jewel.

Jewel.

"Jewel?" I manage to say.

Silence. Terrible, condemning silence.

I feel blindly above my head until I find the string hanging from the ceiling. I pull it, and the closet light snaps on.

And his face, his beautiful face, morphs from wary confusion to complete and utter horror. "Holland?"

We stare at each other for a few seconds until I can't stand to see his expression anymore. I look at the floor, only looking back up at him when he swears under his breath.

"This—it wasn't supposed to be you," he says, his voice tight, his jaw clenching. "It was supposed to—"

"To be Jewel," I say, ice spreading rapidly through my veins. "Yeah. I get it."

"I thought—her shirt looks like yours. And her hair—" He gestures to my hair, which I guess is similar in color and length to Jewel's, now that I think about it.

To my horror, I feel tears stinging my eyes. And despite

the cold numbness spreading through me, my whole body is on fire—from humiliation, from embarrassment, from that stupid kiss. I begin tugging at the buttons of my cardigan, and Phoenix's brows fly to his hairline.

"What are you doing?" he says. "Don't take your shirt off—"

"I have something on underneath," I snap. I tug the cardigan off, and the temperature becomes moderately more bearable.

"That hardly qualifies as a shirt," he says, gesturing at my tank top. His eyes linger on it for a second, and then they dart away. He swears again.

"Language," I say, not bothering to keep my tone polite. This might be the worst day of my life. I put my hands on my hips. "And for someone so clearly opposed to kissing me, you seem to like how I look."

A muscle jumps in his jaw as he clenches it. "I don't have any particular feelings about how you look." His eyes fly back to mine, dropping to my lips and then away again. "And even if I did, I'd still know that kissing you is a stupidly bad idea."

Well, if that isn't just the loveliest slap to the face.

He shifts his weight. "I made out with Trev's sister," he mutters, staring at the floor and running his hand through his messy hair.

This is a nightmare.

"Nothing happened," I say, staring fixedly at the wall. I hate how tremulous my voice is, that my weakness is so obvious. "You've made it perfectly clear that it was an accident. Just forget about it."

He's silent for a second. "Holland," he says, his voice strained but surprisingly kind. When I look up at him, I see the worst thing I've seen from him yet, far worse than his horror: pity. "It's not personal. But—you're only eighteen. And I'm—"

But I can't stay. I can't listen to any more. So I push past him, out of the closet, and rush to my room. I lock the door behind me and cry myself to sleep while Maggie slumbers peacefully on.

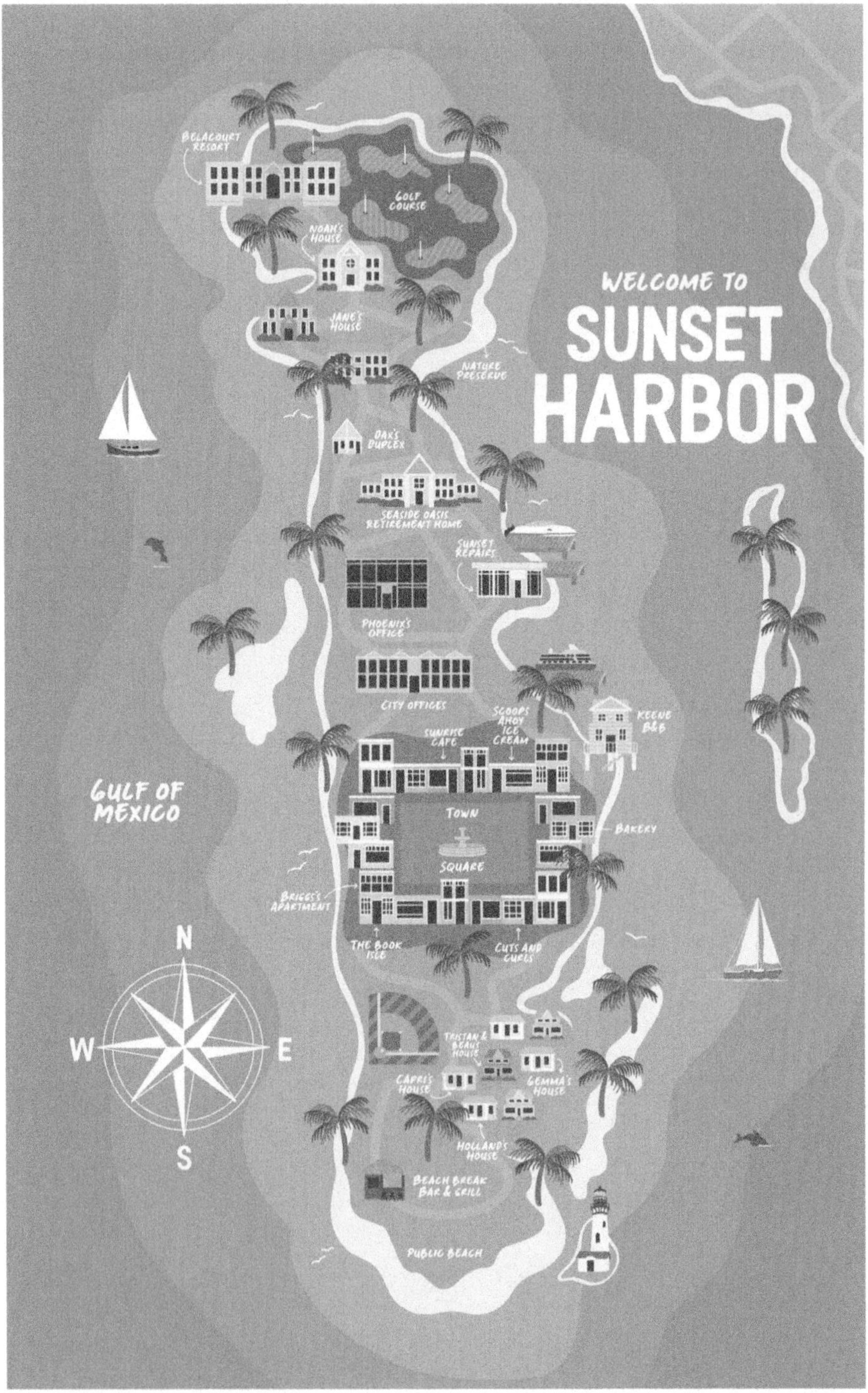

CHAPTER 19

Phoenix

ONCE UPON A TIME, many, many years ago, I kissed Holland Blakely.

It's not something I let myself think about, because it was an accident. If it wasn't an accident, it would have been a bad idea anyway. She's younger; she's Trev's sister. I'm self-aware enough to admit that I've never viewed her like a little sister, but I've never had feelings for her, either. I've never wanted to date her.

Right? I'm sure I haven't.

She has an explosive personality, and when I'm with her, she brings out my explosive side, too. So how did I go from "kissing her was an accident" to "we're married and we've kissed several more times"?

I thought she was Jewel that night—a girl in one of my classes who I've long since forgotten—but somehow when I realized it was Holland, the kiss made more sense.

Holland kissed me like she'd been waiting her whole life to do it; that's not a feeling that's easily replicated. She doesn't do anything by halves—kissing included.

No more kissing, I tell myself firmly. *She won't kiss you, you won't kiss her, and everything will stay neat and safe.*

"Judging by the way you're sighing, you're thinking about your wife," Wyatt says, pulling me out of my thoughts.

I look up at him, surprised. "I am. How did you know? Do I sigh differently when I'm thinking about her?"

"You have a specific furrow in your brow," Wyatt says, pointing to his own forehead. "Right here."

It's late on the evening of the Fourth of July, and I told Wyatt he didn't need to come to the main house tonight, but he did anyway. Just to help me organize things for tomorrow, he said, but I think he gets lonely—and he knows I get lonely, too.

Work is good. Work is safe. Work distracts me from the tingling feeling in my lips and the phantom body I can still feel in my arms.

Why did she kiss me? And why did I kiss her back?

She's asleep now, I think; the light under her door turned off hours ago, and the only sound coming from her room is the whirring of a fan. We came home together, but we didn't say a word to each other; we didn't even make eye contact.

Her eyes looked red, and it caused something horrible and heavy to shift in my stomach.

"Well, you're right," I say as that heavy feeling returns. "I'm thinking about her."

"Mmm," Wyatt says, keeping his eyes on the folder in his lap. The lamp in my home office casts a warm glow over the room, and my assistant's glasses glint when he shifts in his chair. "Anything in particular?"

"We kissed," I say dully. "I guess technically she kissed me. I tried not to kiss her back, but…"

I didn't try that hard.

Wyatt hums again, but he doesn't say anything. I watch him from behind my desk, waiting, but he remains silent; finally I speak again.

"You don't have anything to say about that?" I find it hard to believe.

"I have several things to say, but I'm not certain you're ready to hear them."

I blink at him. "What?"

"I have several things to say," he repeats, "but I'm not certain you're ready to—"

"I heard what you said," I cut him off. "I was just surprised. Tell me."

He shoots a skeptical look at me, his brow more lined than usual, and I let out a tired breath.

"I mean it," I say. "Tell me." Nothing he can say will make this situation any more confusing than it already is.

The indifferent shrug he offers is not comforting; *If you say so*, it says. "It is my belief," he begins, "that you and Miss Blakely—"

"Mrs. Park," I correct him without thinking.

A little smile twitches at his lips. "Of course. It is my belief that you and *your wife* have been in a committed relationship for many years."

My jaw actually drops.

But Wyatt just nods and continues to smile; there's even a bit of amusement in his expression, like he knows he's upsetting me with how ridiculous he's being. "Your love language is arguing. You take care of each other—"

"Because I told Trev I would," I say incredulously.

Another nod from Wyatt. "You did," he says. "And you've been very faithful to that promise. But I suspect that even if you'd made no such vow, you would still be taking care of her, and she you."

"She doesn't take care of me," I say with a snort.

"Look more closely," Wyatt says, completely nonplussed. "I think you'll find she does, and in ways you're so used to you don't even notice them."

Into my mind pops the image of her handing me my bag

of food in the honeymoon suite, my Cobb salad with extra crispy bacon; the image is replaced with her voice, weeks ago, telling me to buy some vegetables so I don't get scurvy.

"Ridiculous," I mutter, reaching for my throat to loosen my tie—only to realize I'm wearing a t-shirt.

"She's the only woman you would have considered marrying, even if you won't admit it"—I did admit it; to *her*—"and if she married another man, I'm very sure you would lose your mind."

"That's a bit of a stretch," I say, but my voice is too defensive, and the memory of her smiling at Briggs earlier is too fresh. She teased me, taunted me, and I lied to her.

If she hugged someone else, danced with someone else, kissed someone else, I would be jealous.

Because she's my wife, I tell myself. *No one wants their wife to do those things with someone else. It's wrong. That's all.*

"I don't want to date her," I say to Wyatt, leaning back in my chair. The leather squeaks, a sound that normally annoys me, but I'm not paying attention.

"I believe that," he says. "I don't think you want to date her."

"Then what could you possibly be going on about?" I say, sighing.

"I don't think you want to date her. Going out in public, taking her to dinner, going to the movies—I don't think you like dating at all, no matter who the woman is. But I believe your heart has been ready and waiting to fall in love with her for a very long time. And if she gave the slightest indication that she wanted a life with you, you would be gone, just like that." He shakes his head. "Dating wouldn't be enough for you. You would want everything, always. You don't do things by halves."

The exact same thing I thought about Holland, not half an hour ago.

"I think this is good for the night," I say, standing abruptly. I should have listened when he said I wasn't ready for what he wanted to tell me.

Because he's saying absurd things.

"Anything else can be left for tomorrow morning," I go on. "We should get some sleep. It's been a long day."

I see Wyatt look at me from the corner of my eye, but I don't meet his gaze. I keep my attention fixed blindly on my desk, because I don't want to see his expression—be it pity or disappointment or concern.

To my relief, he doesn't insist on staying or continue to speak; he just stands up as well. "I'll see you at seven, then," he says in a completely normal voice.

"Sounds good," I say.

Even after he leaves, though, I keep staring at my desk; once I've changed and gotten into bed, I stare at the ceiling.

I fall asleep to the faint sound of fireworks from the mainland.

WHEN I WAKE UP, it's still dark outside, and something is wrong.

I flip my phone over to check the time; two-thirteen in the morning. Much like the night in the honeymoon suite, at first I can't tell what's woken me. I sit bolt upright in bed, my heart pounding, but nothing seems amiss in my room. Black comforter, white carpet, wood furniture, everything in its place.

Then I hear it, though: a sound coming from Holland's room, low and ragged.

Those are cries. She's crying.

No—she's *sobbing*.

I'm out of bed before I realize what's happening, and I've never left my room that fast in my life. I don't knock on her door before I enter, though I should; but there's a frantic urgency driving me, one that tells me this isn't normal crying.

I don't turn on the light in her room. I fly to her bedside, where my gaze can only make out the shape of her figure in bed; the light mess of her hair on her pillow, the curled form of her body because she's kicked all her covers off.

"Holland," I say, reaching for her. I find her shoulder in the dark and give it a little shake, but there's no response; just her continued sobs, low and ragged.

Something dangerously close to compassion rises in me as my suspicions are confirmed: she's not awake. This is a nightmare, and it's so much worse than I expected they would be.

"Holland," I say again, shaking her harder. When she fails to respond, I don't think or plan or consider—I just act, instinct driving me.

I lean down, slide my arms beneath her shaking body, and lift her into my arms.

Her skin is somehow clammy and hot at the same time, but I hold her closer anyway; I carry her out of her room, opening the door wider with my foot, and into my own room. I sit on the edge of my bed and shift her slightly so that her head is resting higher on my chest, near my shoulder, and then I rock back and forth as though she's a very large baby.

I have no idea what I'm doing, but it feels right, so I keep going.

"Holland," I say, louder this time, my voice tense. I free one hand and click on my lamp, the dim light spilling into the room. Then I reach for the glass of water I keep by my bed, dipping my fingers in. I bring them to her face, smoothing water over her forehead and her cheeks. "Holland, wake up. You're having a nightmare."

She flinches at the feeling of the water on her skin, so I get some more. As I get her face wet, her cries begin to fade, and her pained expression begins to twitch—relief crashes over me when she begins actively shying away from the water.

"Holland," I say again, patting her cheek. "Wake up. Wake up—there you go."

Her lashes flutter for a second, and then her eyes open; only slightly, and she's clearly not fully aware, but she's awake.

My racing heart calms a bit as I take a deep breath.

"Oh. This is better," she says after a moment of looking around. Her voice is sleepy and slow, and the sheen of tears still clings to her lashes.

"What?" I say.

She snuggles into my chest, pressing her cheek against my skin as she makes herself more comfortable. "This is a better dream," she says, and her eyes drift closed again. "I like you better in my dreams than I do in real life."

I blink down at her, taken aback. "Do you?"

"Mmm. You're less annoying." One hand reaches up to rest on my bare chest. "And more shirtless, I guess."

I sigh, stroking her hair, my hand moving of its own accord. "This isn't a dream, so stop talking," I say. "You're going to regret saying these things." I'm going to have to pretend I don't remember any of this—it's all I can give her. Maybe I could say I was drunk?

No. She knows I don't drink.

I'll just tell her I was half-asleep myself.

"Of course it's a dream," she says in that sleepy voice, her eyes still closed. "We would never do this in real life. You hate me too much."

An odd mixture of surprise and pain pierces me somewhere around my solar plexus. "I don't hate you," I say. "You hate me."

"No. I hate that when I look at you, I remember watching the paramedics wheel Trev's body away." She inhales deeply and then lets out a shuddering yawn. "I feel so guilty. It hurts —*you* hurt."

Down in the depths of my heart, something shatters. The memories rise before I can stop them—she and I huddled together, silver shock blankets wrapped around our soaking bodies, Trev lying between us.

A knot rises in my throat; I swallow it, along with those images. Is that what she sees when she looks at me? Is that what I make her feel—pain and guilt?

She snuggles closer, and when she sighs again, I can feel her puff of breath against my chest. "You hurt," she mumbles. "But you make me—feel. You make me feel so—so alive."

And another image floods into my mind, one I haven't thought about for a long time.

Holland, sitting on the side of her ER bed, staring blankly off into the distance—a large bandage on her forehead, limp arms and legs, eyes devoid of light and life.

I remember watching her from my own bed and realizing that I would do anything to take that look out of her eyes— even poke and prod and nag and annoy until she found fire to burn me with. For Trev, I would do that.

But as I look down at her, asleep on my lap now, it dawns

on me that Wyatt was right once again: somewhere along the line, taking care of her stopped being about Trev.

"I make you feel alive, huh?" I say, the words reluctant. "That's good." I pause, and then I voice the ridiculous question that's nudging me over and over. "Do you think I could ever make you happy?"

But I'm pretty sure I know the answer to that one.

I stand up, holding her carefully, and take her back to her own room.

"We're quite the pair," I say as I settle her into her bed, pulling the covers up around her. "Just a couple of sentimental fools, feeling guilty for something we couldn't change." I smooth her hair out of her face. "Sleep well, Holl."

I don't hear her for the rest of the night, but I never fall back asleep.

CHAPTER 20

Phoenix

I WAKE up the next morning with a sick sense of dread in the pit of my stomach at the thought of looking at Holland, talking to her, figuring out exactly how much she remembers from the night before. She'll realize she wasn't dreaming, and no matter what I tell her about how much I remember myself, she'll worry.

Then things will grow even more uncomfortable than they were last night coming home from the beach.

I take the coward's way out by sequestering myself in my study before she even wakes up. I could just go into the office, but that idea is as stressful as the idea of seeing her; I ask Wyatt to meet me here instead of in the driveway since I've decided not to leave.

My brain doesn't like the idea of seeing her *or* being away from her while things are so tense, it would appear.

Why did she kiss me?

Why did I kiss her back?

But when she looks at me, she remembers her beloved brother's death. When she looks at me, she feels pain and guilt.

Is being married to me pure hell for her?

I rub my temples and try to push the question out of my mind, even though I know it will keep coming back. The computer screen swims in front of my eyes, likely because I'm so tired, but I blink and try to focus. I have to look at the same set of numbers three times before they register, but I continue on anyway.

I've been working this inefficiently for thirty minutes when my mother calls and drops a bombshell of epic proportions on me.

I know something is up because instead of simpering or buttering me up, she cuts to the chase immediately.

"The doctors let your grandmother go home," she says in a high-pitched, high-strung voice.

The words don't make sense at first; not really. They wouldn't let her go home; she's more or less on hospice, and she would never condescend to pass away peacefully at her own house. She wants her life stretched out to the last limits, by any means necessary.

But surely—she isn't *better*. There's no way.

"What do you mean, they let her go home?" I shove one hand through my hair, clutching my phone with the other hand. My fingers are starting to feel slippery with sweat, despite the fact that this conversation began only thirty seconds ago. "Doesn't she need to stay for observation or something like that?"

On the other end of the line, my mother titters nervously. "I guess they've already observed everything they need to. Dr. Harvey says her recovery is nothing short of miraculous. Mavis says she actually feels stronger and better than she has in months."

Mavis Butterfield needs more strength like I need a hole in the head. What kind of higher power is running around handing out miraculous recoveries to people like her?

This is bad. This is bad, bad, bad. I have a contract with

my *wife* that is contingent upon the idea that Mavis will pass away soon.

"Well, what about a psych eval?" I ask, feeling more irritated by the second. "Did they do a psych eval? No one would dream of turning her loose after getting a good look inside her head."

"Phoenix," my mother says more nervously still. "Speak respectfully."

"I will not," I say through gritted teeth.

I know—I'm horrible. I'm awful. But I don't actually wish death upon my grandmother. All I wish is consistency—I need to know what's going on, because I'm married to Holland Blakely, and the plan is to *stay* married until Mavis passes and I can inherit.

My heart sinks as my brain rushes through the implications of this development. It sinks all the way down to the pit of my stomach, and then it keeps going.

I can't ask Holland to stay married to me indefinitely. Whether or not I would be interested in exploring that option is irrelevant; she didn't sign up for forever, and she doesn't seem to be in the headspace where a relationship with me is even *good* for her. If I make her miserable—my heart somehow sinks further—I can't force her to stay.

"Phoenix," my mother says. "Phoenix, are you listening to me, baby boy?"

"Don't call me that," I say, suddenly ten times more exhausted than I was before. "I have to go. Thank you for telling me."

I hang up. Then I glance at Wyatt, who's just let himself quietly into the room.

"Your facial expression is concerning," he says, a little frown pulling at his thin lips.

"Mavis Butterfield appears to have made a miraculous recovery," I say. I give in to the urge to slump forward, letting my forehead rest on my desk. Then I go on, my voice muffled, "The doctors have sent her home with a relatively good bill of health."

Wyatt is silent for a moment. "Shall I assume you're currently working on a plan for your marriage situation?" he finally says.

"Yes," I say wearily. "I can't ask her to stay married to me forever. She doesn't want that."

"Assumptions are how major miscommunications begin," he says after another pause. "I would be sure before you make any significant decisions."

He's right, I can grudgingly agree.

This timing is terrible. Could Mavis not have waited a bit?

"I would recommend going for a run at the moment," Wyatt says, and it's only then that I realize my leg is jumping, my entire body tense, as my thoughts spiral.

"A run," I say, my voice strained. I lift my head and nod absently; there's a treadmill in the lower level of the house. "Yeah. Good."

"Clear your head." He looks more closely at me, and a little crease appears in his brow. "Consider taking a nap as well. Reset and approach this with a clear mind."

I stand up and leave the room without another word.

I MAKE my peace with my next course of action somewhere around mile three.

Holland can stay if she wants to, but I have to give her an

out. It would be wrong to keep her with me now that the situation has changed so drastically.

My feet pound rhythmically on the treadmill, my thoughts louder even than the grinding sound of the machine, and it feels good to be pushing my body like this—to be exhausting myself so thoroughly that my mind slowly lets go of its worries and holds instead to only those things I need to survive.

Breathe in; breathe out. Keep moving forward.

When I was a kid, my favorite movie was *Beauty and the Beast*—something Wyatt and Wyatt alone knows. I loved all the talking household items; I loved the industrious chaos of Maurice's inventions. I loved the magic and the music.

I never thought I would find myself relating to the Beast.

But Belle is in my castle, and I have to let her leave if she wants to. I can't keep her here forever; not when she only agreed to a few months.

After mile five, I finally allow myself to be done; it's been a long time since I ran this far, and my legs are shaky when I step off the treadmill, my vision swimming as my eyes readjust to a surface that isn't perpetually zooming away.

I lift my shirt and wipe my sweaty forehead, forcing myself to breathe deeply instead of panting. Then I grab my phone and send a message to Holland before I lose my nerve. I press send with a sinking feeling in my stomach, one that weighs me down as I head up the stairs, my muscles protesting every step of the way.

When I reach the top and see Wyatt, I'm expecting a small smile or a hint of approval—not the wide-eyed look of concern he gives me.

"What?" I say, frowning at him, and he hurries closer.

"Your mother and the CEO are here," he says, his voice

tense. "They're parking the cart they rented, and then they'll be at the door."

I stare at him for longer than I should, considering the urgency. "What?"

He nods, his normally neat hair a little ruffled. "Make yourself presentable; I'll stall as long as I can."

"Please do," I say, rushing past him.

This is just like them—both my mother and my grandmother. My mother is afraid of Mavis, and when they're together, she becomes a child—not ingratiating but pouty and entitled. She's difficult to deal with at the best of times, but when she's around her own mother, her inferiority complex shines glaring and bright.

This is the last thing I need today.

But, because no one asked my opinion, I take the fastest shower of my life—two minutes flat—and then dry off and get dressed. I almost line the buttons up wrong in my haste, realizing at the last minute.

Mavis is not a woman who can be easily stalled; if I can get out there before she has a chance to make it all the way in, Wyatt won't have to do as much. He's never said so, but being around her makes him uncomfortable.

But even though I rush, even though I set personal speed records for everything I do to get ready, it's no use—by the time I reach my study, the leather seats are occupied by none other than Marshana Butterfield-Park and one very disapproving Mavis Butterfield.

"Thank you, Wyatt," I say, watching as he passes a cup of tea to each of them.

He ducks his head, his expression as bland and passive as I've ever seen it, calm and unruffled. When our eyes meet, he raises his brows just slightly—asking if I want him to stay or go. I nod subtly to my desk, and he bobs his head again too.

I don't *need* him to stay. But I want him here anyway.

"Please forgive my tardiness," I say to my mother and Mavis, keeping my voice distant but polite. "If I had known you were coming, I would have been prepared."

Mavis smirks her thin lips; she understands the censure for what it is, and she's amused. She's dressed impeccably, of course, in a tweed suit and blazer with a string of pearls. Her steel curls are set perfectly, and her painted-on brows have a little more arch to them than usual.

My mother, on the other hand, is flashier; she's wealthy because of the family, but she doesn't actively participate in the business, and I think it's something she's always been insecure about. She wears shinier jewelry than Mavis, brighter colors, thicker makeup. Her hair is much lighter than mine—I get my coloring from my father—and it's curled neatly around her face, brushing her shoulders.

I don't like seeing either of them in my home—my sanctuary. All I can do is try to get them to leave.

I straighten my suit coat and then round the desk; Wyatt follows me silently, standing behind my chair and off to one side.

"Do you want to sit?" I say, but he shakes his head, so I take a seat. Then I look at Mavis. "To what do I owe the pleasure?"

"Can't I check in on my grandson?" she says. "And his new wife?"

"Of course you can," I say, offering up a prayer of thanks that Holland is still asleep. "But there's not much to report." I hesitate and then risk the question: "Unlike yourself, I hear?"

Mavis adjusts her pearls with bony fingers. "How do you feel, knowing I'll be living for longer than expected?"

I want to tell her I'm frustrated and exhausted from all

the games she plays. I want to tell her that it's cruel and petty to hold the company over our heads and make us dance like puppets.

I open my mouth to speak—I don't know what I'm going to say—but in the end, I don't get the chance anyway. Because at that exact moment, moving like a whirlwind of thunder and lightning, one very tense pajama-clad Holland comes bursting through my office door. She doesn't knock; she just barges into the room, her eyes spitting fire, her cell phone thrust out in front of her with my earlier text displayed on the screen.

"What is *this* supposed to mean?"

CHAPTER 21

Holland

WHEN I BECAME a victim of the human-sized dog bed internet scam last month, I experienced a brief moment of deepest shame and humiliation.

Realizing I'd been scammed was embarrassing enough, but it was the actual act of reporting it to Beau Palmer at the police station that made me feel like crawling under a rock. Every detail I gave him was excruciating; I wanted the floor to swallow me whole. I wanted to dive into the top of a volcano and never come out, as long as it meant I wouldn't have to show my face again.

I didn't expect to feel a similar level of embarrassment so soon afterward. But as I read the text message Phoenix sent me earlier—and then reread it, and reread it again just to make sure I'm not imagining things—an unpleasant heat creeps up my neck, and a little flame of humiliation starts to burn in my chest, growing larger and larger until it's become an all-consuming bonfire.

I learned earlier this morning that Mavis's condition is no longer believed to be terminal, the message says. *She may in fact live much longer than initially expected. Since these are not the expectations that were in place when you agreed to marry me, I am willing to dissolve our arrangement. If that's the course you choose, I will still provide*

Maggie's tuition as well as any health care fees you need. Please consider the options and let me know of your decision by EOD today.

I sit on the edge of my comfortable, fake-wife bed for probably five full minutes, just staring at my phone, reading the message over and over and over. Then I get up and rush to the bathroom, because I really have to pee—but when I return to my room, I pick the phone back up and read the message once more.

Is he…breaking up with me?

That's what it sounds like. Mavis isn't dying after all, which means we could be married indefinitely, and he doesn't want that.

The roaring fire of humiliation somehow grows higher until I can feel the flames licking at the back of my throat, hot and miserable.

Is this because I kissed him? Did he hate it that much?

Would it kill him to talk to me about this in person? Who does this kind of thing over text? And why do I feel *hurt?* I have no right to feel anything but relief—not after how we treat each other; not with our history.

But there's no relief to be found, not even when I scrape the deepest corners of my mind until my nails tear and my fingers bleed.

My thoughts whirl, chaos of the highest degree, half-formed ideas and questions and cobwebs of confusion that trap all the little kernels of logic trying to take root. I shake my head and stand up, giving my cheeks a few firm pats.

I can't just sit here stewing. It will only make things worse.

So I grab my phone, take a deep breath, and then force myself out of my room. I fortify my defenses as I hurry down the hall, every step I take louder and stompier. I peek around as I pass the living room and kitchen area, but he's not there, and I don't expect him to be.

If he's at home right now, I'll find him in his study.

When I turn the corner of the hall and see light coming from under his study door, I know I'm right.

You are not a child, I remind myself, *so don't shout or throw a fit.*

I have big feelings. I always have. Usually that means my anger and hurt and frustration are bigger than normal, too.

I don't knock on the door, because I'm too impatient, but I do resist the urge to throw it open. I just let myself in (with admittedly more energy than is helpful) and hold the phone up, reigning in the urge to yell.

"What is this supposed to mean?" I say instead, crossing the office in several strides until I'm right in front of his desk. My voice is hard, but it is normal in volume, which I think is to be commended.

Except I swear, Phoenix could not look more horrified to see me if he tried. His eyes widen, his brows fly up—but the expression lasts for no more than half a second, replaced almost immediately by a blank, neutral mask.

Something happens then, little tendrils of memory niggling at the back of my mind, and for a second, they elude me—I chase them, my brows furrowing as I study his face, until—

Last night.

The memories flood in—the nightmare. Phoenix. The dream that wasn't a dream; the things I said. And a question from him, murmured absently as I was drifting off to sleep against his bare chest: *Do you think I could ever make you happy?*

The words ring in my ears as I stare at him, his unflinching gaze, his lips pressed into a tight line.

Sleep well, Holl. He said that, too.

"You—" I begin, my mouth moving without permission. "You called me *Holl*. You asked if you could ever make me—"

But I break off as his expression changes, and I watch, fascinated; his eyes dart away, his throat bobs as he swallows, and his cheeks begin to flush red.

Understanding hits me then, not gradually but all at once. Because whatever else can be said, I know Phoenix Park. I know him well. I know the parts of him I try to ignore and the parts of him I choose to focus on.

He didn't send that message this morning because I kissed him. He sent that message because I told him last night that looking at him hurts. And now that Mavis is supposedly feeling better, he doesn't want me to have to be his wife with no end in sight.

I don't have proof; I don't have confirmation.

But I know I'm right.

Just like I know that he never meant for me to hear what he said.

My embarrassment, my humiliation—they fade as something else unfurls in my chest, something hesitant but curious.

"Mrs. Park," Wyatt says, and I startle. I hadn't even realized he was there. But he steps up from behind Phoenix now and speaks again. "Please welcome our guests," he says, gesturing to something behind me. "They dropped by to visit."

I whirl around and find, to my dismay, that there are two women here already: Mavis Butterfield and a woman who can only be Phoenix's mother. She doesn't have his dark hair or dark eyes, but considering the distaste on her face as she looks at me and the faint resemblance to Mavis, I don't see who else she could be. Wyatt's subtext is clear, too; they came uninvited and without warning.

Perfect. Just…perfect. I am *fresh* out of bed, my hair a mess, my body clad in pink pajamas—not a pearl in sight, and not my wedding ring, either. It's still on top of my dresser, where it usually lives.

"Hi," I say faintly, giving a stupid little wave. I let my arm drop quickly and then turn to face Phoenix again.

And I don't know what I'm feeling; there's too much going on. I'm embarrassed to look like this in front of these women, and I have the strange desire to stand in front of Phoenix so he'll be shielded from their sight. Even more confusing is what *he's* feeling; I'm going to have to unpack all that.

What I do know is that this is my chance—my chance to get away. Away from him, away from his family, away from the feelings that keep cropping up.

This is your chance, I tell myself. *This is it. Run.*

So…why am I hesitating?

I can't stop myself from inspecting him, taking him in, especially his face; he's trying not to let anything show, but there's a desperate question in his eyes, one he doesn't want me to see.

A question—and a truth.

He wants me to stay. He wants me to stay, but he'll never ask. Because he knows how hard this arrangement is for me.

A strange feeling filters into my chest—a grim sort of relief. And even though my brain is telling me to run, run, run, my heart makes a unilateral decision: No matter what he and I are working through, I *will not* abandon him to these people.

I'll stay with him, and we'll figure out the rest later. That's how it's going to have to be.

But if I'm going to do this, I need to commit—really commit. Not fight and whine and complain and participate half-heartedly. And what I said last night was true: sometimes looking at him hurts.

How can I move past that?

I don't know, but it's not something I'm going to figure out right this second. So I straighten up and tell myself that confidence is 90 percent of how people perceive you. Then I look over my shoulder at the Butterfield women.

"I'm so sorry I was unprepared," I say, gesturing to my hair and my clothes as I make my way around the desk to where Phoenix sits. "If I'd been informed of your visit, I would have taken the time to make myself more presentable."

A suspicious-sounding snort comes from Wyatt—I think it's a laugh, though I don't know what's so funny—and Phoenix clears his throat loudly, his eyes on me as his lips twitch. When I reach him and hold my hand out, however, the wariness enters his eyes again.

I wiggle my hand at him, and he takes it, standing slowly when I give a tug.

His face is back to its neutral mask as he looks down at me, but I can tell his jaw is clenched. I don't let myself hesitate; I close the space between us and wrap my arms around his neck in what might be the first *real* embrace we've ever shared.

And as his arms encircle my waist, his body curving around mine, something deep inside of me sighs in relief.

This is how it's supposed to be, that little part of me urges. *This is what Phoenix Park is supposed to feel like.*

I tighten my arms, going up on my tiptoes as I breathe him in, pressing my face into his neck, and he pulls me closer, his arms banding further around me. He's warm, and solid, and his grip is strong.

Despite all his strength, he still needs someone on his side.

I will be that person.

"I'm not leaving you," I say in his ear, barely a whisper.

"What?" he murmurs.

I tighten my arms, because I can hear his disbelief, his hope. "I'm not leaving you," I repeat, more firmly now.

For a second, he doesn't react to my words; but then his hold on me changes, going from tight to desperate—grasping and bone-cracking. And even though it's painful, it's also strange and warm and...nice.

It's *nice*, being held like this. What does that mean? Do I *like* him?

Someone clears their throat; not Wyatt but one of the women. I release him more reluctantly than I expected, letting my hands trail down his arms as I step back.

And at the stunned look on his face, the heartbreaking hope in his eyes, a smile tugs at my lips; it pulls and pulls until finally I stop fighting it. I smile at him, *really* smile—and he smiles back.

My stomach flips, and the warmth inside glows a little bit brighter.

I'M NOT one to judge, but Phoenix's mom is a piece of work.

It's immediately clear that she doesn't like me, based on the twitch of her lips into a subtle sneer and the side eye she keeps employing. Even after I go change out of my pajamas into a perfectly respectable set of cropped black pants and a boat-neck top, her gaze follows me like she's a lion and I'm a gazelle.

So. That's pleasant.

Phoenix just takes it in stride; he's obviously a master at dealing with these women, because not once does he lose his temper, not even when his mom keeps calling me *Holland Blakely* instead of *Holland Park*. He corrects her coolly and moves on.

I just try to remember what he told me before we visited Mavis in her absurdly big hospital suite: *Don't try to be friendly. Stand up straight, don't fidget.*

I can be an ice queen. So that's exactly what I do; when he sits back in his desk chair after our embrace, I stand by his side and smile with serene detachment while he and the Butterfield women play verbal volleyball.

Never thought I would be playing the part of a silent wife, seen and not heard, but that's how I feel safest in this situation—I don't particularly want to deal with the Butterfield women. He told me they were wolves; I trust him to know best how to handle them.

When his mother turns a toothy smile on me and asks how I met her son, though, I don't bother holding my tongue. I can answer this one safely, and maybe even in a way that will support our story.

"Phoenix was best friends with my brother in college," I tell her. "We've known each other for years."

His mother's heavily lined eyes pop wide. "Have you two been dating for that long?"

"Oh, no," I say with an airy laugh. "We haven't been dating the whole time we've known each other. We were on and off for a long time." The lie has my voice going high-pitched; I clear my throat and go on. "But we had our very first kiss…" I trail off, thinking, and in the corner of my eye I see Phoenix look over at me so fast he'll have a crick in his neck. "I guess it would have been eight or nine years ago," I say.

I finally give in and look at him; his eyes are wide, and I can clearly hear the thought he's projecting: *I can't believe you went there.*

Oh, yeah, I think with a little smirk. *I went there.*

The kiss we have literally not talked about in years—not once since the crash. We haven't acknowledged it. It seems very on-brand for us that we're bringing it up now, in front of his mother and grandmother.

"And," I announce, because I'm not done yet, "he called me by another girl's name afterward."

His mother gasps, looking scandalized, and her hand flies to her chest. "That's *quite* enough," she says to me. "He would never do something so—"

"I assure you, I did," Phoenix breaks in. He's rubbing his temples, and he shoots me a look.

Silence falls for one awkward second; Mavis looks back and forth between Phoenix and me with sharp, all-seeing eyes, but Phoenix's mother doesn't bother. She rallies immediately.

"Well," she says with a sniff. "Perhaps you just weren't very memorable, dear."

"My wife," Phoenix says, "has always been memorable."

My wife. The words ring in my ears, play in my mind, again and again and again. He's said them before, so why do I have goosebumps?

His mother is not so afflicted; she just gives a little twitch of her shoulders, and then she busies herself with the shiny bangle bracelet she's wearing.

"Tell me," Mavis says, using her cane to thump against the floor, and my eyes jump to her. "How do the two of you get along? Do you argue?" She directs her question at Phoenix, but she raises her eyebrows at me, too.

"Of course we do," Phoenix answers easily. "All couples argue sometimes."

"Bertrand and I never did," Mavis says.

I guess Bertrand was Phoenix's grandpa?

"I can only assume that's because he was scared of you," Phoenix says with a little dip of his head.

Mavis's thin lips curl into a smile, not entirely pleasant. "That he was," she says. "He knew his place." But as her gaze comes to land on me, her smile vanishes, and her eyes narrow. "Do you know yours?" she says to me.

Do I know my *place?* Is she serious?

She is; I can see it plainly. She's serious.

"I know my place," I say, keeping my voice light and professional even as anger snaps inside.

My place is wherever I dang well want it to be. I belong wherever I choose to belong.

"Ooh-ho-ho," Mavis says as her grin returns—one of delight and amusement. "Does that get your goat, girlie? Does that make you want to rage at the injustice?" She gasps theatrically. "How dare I, an old woman, remind you that things are done a certain way at Butterfield?" Her grin disappears like a switch being flipped, and her voice is cold as she goes on. "How dare I tell you there are behavioral expectations I expect you to uphold? Is that it? Is that what's going through your mind—lovely, liberated Holland Blakely?"

"Holland *Park*," Phoenix says through gritted teeth, and when I pull my horrified gaze away from Mavis and look over at my husband, I'm not surprised to see his hands clenched into fists in his lap.

Because he was right. He was absolutely right. His grandmother is insane. She is insane and bizarre and *terrifying*.

She looks back and forth between us for a second, while Phoenix's mom continues to stare sulkily at her hands in her lap. Mavis's eyes are shrewd and mocking, and I don't know what they're searching for. When she finally throws her head back and cackles loudly, I feel my lifespan shortening by at least three years.

"Marshana will be taking me home now," Mavis says.

Phoenix's mother blinks at Mavis. "Now?" she says.

"That's what I said, isn't it? Your head isn't just for decoration, Marshana. Use your ears."

It's both funny and sad, the way Phoenix's mom hurries to do Mavis's bidding—deference and proverbial bowing and scraping are involved, and it's hard to watch. Wyatt and I wait as Phoenix leads them out of the study; I hold my breath until I hear the front door open and close. Only then do I relax.

"Finally," I say, exhaling loudly as I flop down in one of the leather chairs. "That was torture. My heart is still beating too fast." I look over at Phoenix just as he enters the study again. "Do they do that a lot? Just show up, uninvited?"

He hums, rounding the desk and sitting back in his seat. "Not much, but it has happened before, and it will probably happen again," he says, running one hand through his hair. "Mavis has no respect for boundaries or niceties, and my mother will just follow along."

"It's too early for that kind of nonsense," I say. I let myself slump further in the chair. Then I add, "I shouldn't have doubted you. She's nuts."

"She is," he says with an affirmative nod. "Highly unpredictable, often cruel, razor-sharp business instincts."

"I feel like I need to call Nana Lu and talk to her to cleanse my mental palate."

Phoenix doesn't respond, and for a moment, silence

stretches between us, heavy and uncomfortable. When he finally sighs, I'm almost relieved.

"I guess we should talk about last night," he says, and even though his face remains neutral, I can hear the reluctance in his voice.

I straighten up, my pulse skipping.

Don't be stupid, I tell myself. *It's fine. You can talk about this.* So I open my mouth and force out the words. "I guess so," I say.

Phoenix's expression shifts as he looks at me, his eyes narrowing thoughtfully. "Are you sure you want to do this?" he says after a few seconds of staring at me. "I assume that's what your little display meant earlier—that you want to remain married?"

My little display—I guess that's how it would look to him. I don't know how much of it was for show and how much of it was real.

But that's not what he's asking.

"Yes," I say, trying to keep the nerves out of my voice. "We should stay married. For now, at least."

He sighs again, still looking unconvinced. "You said last night that looking at me hurts. You said that every time you look at me—"

"I know what I said," I cut him off. I swallow and raise one eyebrow at him. "*You* asked if you could ever make me happy. Are we going to talk about that too?"

He leans abruptly forward in his chair, his eyes flashing. "If you think you can handle it, sure."

And even though my pulse is pounding in my ears, a deafening *whoosh, whoosh, whoosh,* I scoff at him. "Of course I can handle—"

But he interrupts me, standing up so suddenly that I startle in my chair.

"Be very, very sure before you finish that sentence, Amsterdam," he breathes, his gaze still full of electricity. He rounds his desk in three long strides, and several more bring him to where I'm seated. "Let go of your pride for once and tell the truth," he says as he looks down at me.

He's impossibly tall from this angle, and even though he's standing and I'm sitting, I can still smell leather and mahogany.

The intoxicating scent grows even stronger when he crouches down in front of my chair.

I'm just opening my mouth to speak—I have no idea what I'm going to say—when I hear the faint sound of a throat clearing.

Phoenix and I whip our heads toward the sound at the same time, only to see a very stressed-looking Wyatt—pressed up against the wall as though he's attempting to make himself smaller—and clearly in the process of trying to inch past us unnoticed.

"Please let me leave the room before you continue," he says, looking supremely uncomfortable.

I blink at him, surprised; I forgot he was here. He's so *quiet.*

"Of course," I say, my voice faint. "Sorry, of course. But you know—you don't have to sneak around," I add with a little frown. "Speak up if you're uncomfortable. We're not going to get mad at you."

"It felt like the kind of conversation that should be allowed to play out," he says, ducking his head apologetically. "But thank you. I'll take my leave."

And I've never seen him walk as quickly as he does leaving this study. He scurries past both of us, his folder tucked under one arm, and slips out the door in a flash.

I stare at the office door as it closes behind him, and then I look at Phoenix, just as he's looking back at me.

I don't know who cracks first, but it happens—first we're smiling, and then we're laughing, the electric spell between us lifted and replaced by something light and free. Phoenix's laugh is deep and pleasant and *rare*, so rare; you're more likely to get a snort and a grin. I let myself bask in the sound, just for a moment, taking in the genuine smile spread over his face and the bright shine in his eyes.

Somewhere inside, that warmth stirs—warmth and a little jolt of something I can't identify. So I'm glad for Wyatt's interruption, because honestly, I don't know if I can handle a conversation about what Phoenix said last night.

I change the subject before he can return to his previous question, letting my laughter die. "I'll stay married to you," I say, still smiling. "But..." Then I shake my head. "I don't know. I think I should maybe get a therapist or something."

Phoenix's smile vanishes, and he blinks at me. "Are you serious?" he says.

"Why?" I say. "Do you think it's a bad idea?" I don't know what else to do about the issues I'm having.

"No," he says quickly, his eyes widening. "No, I think you should do it. Absolutely. Our insurance covers mental health care."

"It might be good for you too," I say. I lean forward, closer to him. "To see someone."

"I do," he admits, surprising me completely. "Once a month now, but I went every week for years."

Huh. I'm...impressed.

"I'm not going to lie," I say. "My opinion of you just went up. Just a little tiny bit."

"Yeah?" he says, his lips twitching. "A man in therapy really does it for you, huh?"

I grin. "I guess so."

My grin vanishes two seconds later, though, when I realize what's happening. I shrink back in my chair, slapping my hand over my mouth.

Flirting. We're *flirting*.

I stare at Phoenix, my eyes wide, my hand still over my mouth, but he doesn't even question it. He just flashes a brief smile—amused, like he knows what I'm thinking—and then stands up.

"Don't you have work today?" he says.

I check the time, squawk, and then dash out of the study.

ONE WEEK LATER, I attend my first therapy session. The woman—Dr. Samson—is maybe in her sixties, with a soothing voice and bright green eyes. I feel weird walking in and dumping all my trauma on her, but that's why I'm here, so after I fill out the questionnaire she gives me, I get down to the meat and potatoes.

"I'm here because my brother died," I tell her when she asks what prompted me to seek help. "In a car crash. We went over the side of a bridge." I swallow past the knot in my throat and then lay bare my deepest shame to this complete stranger: "I was the one driving."

WELCOME TO
SUNSET
HARBOR

GULF OF
MEXICO

BELACOURT RESORT
GOLF COURSE
NOAH'S HOUSE
JANE'S HOUSE
NATURE PRESERVE
OAK'S DUPLEX
SEASIDE OASIS RETIREMENT HOME
SUNSET REPAIRS
PHOENIX'S OFFICE
CITY OFFICES
SUNRISE CAFE
SCOOPS AHOY ICE CREAM
KEENE B&B
TOWN SQUARE
BAKERY
BRIGGS'S APARTMENT
THE BOOK ISLE
CUTS AND CURLS
TRISTAN & BEAU'S HOUSE
CAPRI'S HOUSE
GEMMA'S HOUSE
HOLLAND'S HOUSE
BEACH BREAK BAR & GRILL
PUBLIC BEACH

N
W E
S

CHAPTER 22

Nine Years Ago

Holland

"THIS IS STUPID," I say, tugging the neckline of my dress up so it will cover more skin.

The dress I'm wearing doesn't actually belong to me. It's my roommate's, because I can't afford to buy a fancy new outfit if I'm only going to wear it once. So she let me borrow one of hers—a little black dress that hits just above my knee, fitted, with a sweetheart neckline and thin straps. It's simple, which I prefer, and it's definitely better than the other option she presented me with, which was mossy green with lace.

"It's not stupid," Trev says, his voice blaring into my room as we chat on speaker. "And what do you have to complain about, anyway? I bought your ticket. You're basically just getting free food, Holl."

"My dress is too tight," I grumble.

"Suck it up," he says, as cheerful as ever. "We're almost to your place. Come wait outside."

"It's raining—"

"But we're like two streets away. Come outside. I don't want to wait thirty minutes for you to walk down three flights of stairs in heels."

"Fine." I hang up on him, grab my little black purse, and leave my room, waving goodbye to my roommate.

It doesn't take me thirty minutes to get down all three flights of stairs, but that's only because I take my shoes off to walk. Trev isn't far off on his guess; I love cute dresses, but I've never been good at heels. The staircase is outdoors, so I'm already contending with the wind and the rain; no need to stack the odds against myself.

Trev and Phoenix are just pulling up when I get to the ground floor. I walk carefully through the light rain, dreading every step that takes me closer to Trev's black car.

Phoenix and I haven't seen or spoken to each other since the disastrous closet kiss two weeks ago. I wouldn't say I'm avoiding him, exactly, but I've been happy not to see him. Since he's Trev's roommate and best friend, however, that can't last forever.

Trev pops out of the driver's side, looking dapper in his suit. His light hair blows in the wind as he jogs over to me. "I need to use your bathroom really fast," he says, and then he goes right past me. I hear him taking the stairs two at a time, an obnoxious *clang-clang-clang* sound that I'm sure my neighbors will appreciate, and I roll my eyes as I climb in the back seat of the car.

Phoenix doesn't turn to look at me; he doesn't even speak. All I can see of him is that he's wearing a suit, like Trev, except his is probably tailored and more expensive.

When I finally can't stand the silence anymore, I clear my throat. "You didn't say anything to Trev, did you?"

Phoenix's eyes jump to mine in the rearview mirror. "No," he says, sounding horrified. "And you can't either. Don't even think about it, Holl, or I'll—"

"Threaten me? Are you serious?" I say, scoffing. "Or are

you going to blackmail me? Because if you do that, I'll have no choice but to tell Trev about the tampon incident."

Phoenix snorts. "He wouldn't care about that."

"Yes he would," I say. "You were a total jerk, and I'm his beloved little sister."

Silence from the front seat, accompanied by his dark-eyed glare in the rearview mirror.

"We'll both keep our mouths shut about anything that's happened between us in the past," I finally say. "Tampons and closets included. No threats or blackmail will be necessary. Deal?"

Phoenix just grunts, which I take to mean *yes*.

Trev fills the car with his chatter as we drive to the event. He's always talkative, but more so tonight; he's part of the university's outreach organization, so he's been helping plan this benefit gala for months, and he's more excited than I've ever seen him. All proceeds will go toward local disaster relief, which I guess is a good cause.

I just wish he hadn't dragged me along with him. But he paid for my ticket and begged me to come, so here I am. I can only assume he forced Phoenix to come too, because Phoenix doesn't strike me as the kind of person who enjoys dinners and galas and fancy events.

A shame, because that man in a nice suit is a sight to behold.

When we arrive at the hotel where this thing is taking place, an actual valet takes our car and gives us a ticket. I've never used a valet in real life; it's counterintuitive to me, letting a stranger drive away in your car, but Trev doesn't seem to mind. He just hops out, and we follow suit, taking the ticket and then going in.

There's a large sign that points us in the right direction, but Trev obviously knows where he's going; he and Phoenix stride across the lobby like they were born to stride across lobbies, and I scurry along after them in my uncomfortable heels, following until we reach the entrance to Ballroom A.

It's huge. So big, and there are so many people, and all of them are wearing fancy dresses and suits. There's vaguely familiar classical music playing, and there are even a decent number of couples dancing.

"Food," I say as my eyes find the table on the other side of the ballroom, full of silver platters with what look to be appetizers. There will be an actual meal served later, but for now...

"Have at it," Trev says with a smile. "We'll go get settled at the table."

"Are there assigned seats?" I say, looking around.

"Yeah. We're over there somewhere, I think," Trev says. He points to one corner of the ballroom, and I nod.

"I'll meet you there."

I hurry to the table of appetizers—hors d'oeuvres, if we want to be fancy—and fill one of those nice plastic plates that look like scalloped glass. I grab mini cheese balls, a mini puff pastry with spinach, and I even brave some sort of mushroom cap. Then I head back to the table where Trev and Phoenix have seated themselves; Trev is speaking animatedly to an older couple at the table, while Phoenix nods politely.

My plan of action is to pretend I'm invisible and somehow will it into being, so I can sit and eat my food in peace. I hold my plate in one hand and try to discreetly pull up the neckline of my dress with the other as I make my way to our table. My feet are definitely suffering in these shoes, but I remain as steady as possible.

I more or less collapse into the chair next to Phoenix, letting out an embarrassing little *oomph* as I land. Phoenix looks over and raises one dark brow at me; I'm sure to him I seem like a cavewoman wearing heels for the first time, but whatever. These death traps are four inches high. Mr. *I-Sleep-In-My-Suit* can suck it.

"Stop staring," I snap at him when I notice in my periphery that his eyes are still on me. "I'm sure you have better things to look at."

"Don't speak with your mouth full," he says.

By the time I turn my head to glare at him, he's already looking away.

I make my way through my plate of food—the mushroom caps aren't my favorite, so I leave them—and then stare wistfully when everything is gone. When the people Trev is talking to meander away, I turn to ask him if I can get seconds, but he speaks before I have the chance.

"All right," he says, standing up. "I need to go mingle. You two—go dance or something."

When Phoenix and I just stare at him, he waves his hand.

"Dance!" he says again. "Go dance."

And I don't know why neither of us protest; it's clear we don't want to dance, much less with each other. But that's part of Trev's magic; he's hard to say no to, because he's so enthusiastic and excited about everything.

"Go," he says when Phoenix and I both stand as slowly as humanly possible. "Come on; go dance. We need people to dance or it will just be an awkward empty dance floor."

He shoos us away from the table, and we grudgingly go, weaving around tables until we reach the dance floor.

"We don't have to dance," I tell Phoenix as he positions himself in front of me. "Trev isn't actually going to force us."

"It's fine," he says.

"It doesn't seem fine," I say, my voice skeptical. Because his expression is blank, his body stiff as he rests one hand on my waist and holds the other out for me; I take it, putting my other hand on his shoulder. "You seem like you would rather be tortured than dance with me right now."

"I don't like to dance," he says. "But I can stomach one song."

I roll my eyes. "I'm flattered," I say. "Really. You know, maybe *Jewel* is here tonight—"

"Don't start, Holl," he says, and he rolls his eyes too. "It was a mistake. I'm sorry. But there's nothing else I can do."

I don't respond, because he's right.

"Sorry," I say—though I have to force the word out.

"It's fine." He doesn't look at me as we sway back and forth to the music; in fact, his eyes are everywhere but on me. "You'll find someone, you know? Don't worry about it."

"Hang on." I stop before remembering we're on a dance floor, and we have to keep moving or we'll look weird. So I resume dancing, letting Phoenix guide me as I speak. "You seem to be under the impression that I'm—I'm *pining* for you or something. Is that what you think is happening?"

"What? No," he says, his gaze finally resting on me. "I didn't say that."

"Because I'm not," I say with a little frown. "I was vaguely interested in you, Phoenix. I wasn't in love. You're not the only fish in the sea." I'm not even lying. I had—maybe still have—a crush on Phoenix, but that's it. I wasn't naming our future children. I wasn't planning our wedding.

Phoenix shifts uncomfortably, his hand flexing on my waist as the slow drone of music continues to play around us. "I'm not sure how I feel about you making out with someone you're only *vaguely interested* in, but okay—"

"I can kiss who I want."

"I know you can," he says with a sigh. "And I guess I don't care. Just—be careful."

"You be careful!" I laugh incredulously. "You were the one kissing the wrong girl."

He snorts. "Believe me, I've learned my lesson."

His lesson. Perfect.

"Let's stop talking," I say. "I've now been referred to as a *mistake* and a *lesson,* and while I get what you're saying, my pride is severely wounded."

His exhale seems to take several inches off his height. "Holland—"

"I'm serious," I say, swallowing the knot in my throat. *"Please* let's stop talking about it."

I don't look away as his gaze darts over my face, because my shredded dignity won't let me; I just hold his eyes until finally he nods.

"Fine," he says.

We finish the dance in awkward silence, and when the music ends, we let go of each other as though we've been electrocuted. Though we don't discuss where we're going, somehow we both gravitate toward Trev, who's waving to someone and smiling as they head for the ballroom doors.

"I need to keep mingling," Trev says when we reach him. "I still need to go thank a few of the donors who weren't here yet earlier. Come with me," he adds to Phoenix, looking anxiously around the room. "Stand next to me and look dignified and wealthy."

"Dignified and wealthy," Phoenix says in a dry voice, a hint of a smile flitting over his lips. "Got it."

"We'll be back, Holl," Trev says. "Eat some more hors d'oeuvres."

"I ate everything but the mushroom ones," I say. "Am I allowed to get more of the little cheese balls?"

He nods and waves toward the long table in the back of the ballroom. "Go. Get more cheese balls."

More cheese balls. Excellent.

I lose track of how long I sit at the table by myself, but it feels like forever. I'm too embarrassed to get a third helping of cheese balls, so I don't; a while later dinner is served anyway, and everyone returns to their seats. I eat my salad quietly and speak only when someone talks directly to me; the hours pass painfully slowly until finally, *finally*, people begin to leave.

Not us, apparently, but other people. Trev, Phoenix, and I stay until we're some of the last, and my toes are numb in my shoes, and there are blisters on my heels.

The blisters feel bigger than they actually are—like they're covering my entire heel—and by the time we've helped take down a large portion of the decorations, they're throbbing painfully. I'm also feeling very stupid, because this must be the real reason Trev begged us to come along: he wanted help with take-down duty.

When we finally head outside and get our car from the valet, Trev passes me the keys.

"We've both had champagne," he says when I look blankly at him. "So you're driving. Why are you glaring at me?"

"Have you ever tried driving in a dress and heels?" I say to him, narrowing my eyes. Then I sigh. "Get in, I guess. Come on—everybody in."

"You don't need to herd us," Phoenix says with a frown. "We're not completely inebriated."

"Just say *drunk* like the rest of us," I mutter under my breath. "Get in; I'm tired. I want to go to bed."

The shoes finally come off when I've settled myself in the driver's seat, Phoenix in the passenger seat and Trev in the back.

"Take care of my sister up there," Trev says sleepily from his seat, patting Phoenix on the shoulder.

"I promise," Phoenix says, his voice dry.

I give Trev ten minutes before he's asleep.

We begin the drive home, the car dark and silent. The roads aren't great; it's not raining anymore, but there's standing water that makes me nervous.

A tickle of foreboding crawls up my spine.

I slow our pace, and Phoenix either doesn't notice or doesn't care; I think he's awake, but he's staring out the window.

I slow some more. He glances at me briefly, but he doesn't speak.

We're only a few miles from home when it happens.

Rain begins to fall.

And rain is fine, rain is normal, but there's something about this night that feels different; an icy hand squeezing my lungs. Visibility is worse now, and although I'm driving slowly, it doesn't seem to make much difference. We're halfway over the river when the wheels catch a patch of water, and awfully, horribly, terrifyingly—I lose control of the car.

"Phoenix," I say immediately; I don't know why his is the name that comes to my lips.

I grip the steering wheel tighter, dig imprints of the seams into my palms, but everything is happening in slow motion and I don't know what to do. We're hydroplaning as though we're weightless—the middle of the road, the edge of the bridge, and horror like I've never known in my life—

Screaming, yelling, shouting, a cacophony of wordless terror—

And finally darkness as the car crashes through the guard rail and plunges into the river below.

WELCOME TO
SUNSET HARBOR

GULF OF MEXICO

BELACOURT RESORT

GOLF COURSE

AIDAN'S HOUSE

JANE'S HOUSE

NATURE PRESERVE

DAX'S DUPLEX

SEASIDE OASIS RETIREMENT HOME

SUNSET REPAIRS

PHOENIX'S OFFICE

CITY OFFICES

SCOOPS AHOY ICE CREAM

KEENE B&B

SUNRISE CAFE

TOWN

SQUARE

BAKERY

BRIGGS' APARTMENT

THE BOOK ISLE

CUTS AND CURLS

TRISTAN & BEAU'S HOUSE

CAPRI'S HOUSE

GEMMA'S HOUSE

HOLLAND'S HOUSE

BEACH BREAK BAR & GRILL

PUBLIC BEACH

N W E S

CHAPTER 23

Phoenix

HOLLAND IS quiet when she comes home from her first therapy session.

We decided that it would be weird if she saw the same therapist I see, so she's going to someone different in the same clinic. It's a little place on the mainland, discreet, and I've liked them a lot.

But it's hard to tell if Holland likes them.

When I pick her up from the ferry, she looks horrible; haunted, almost, and her whole body is listless, dragging.

Was therapy a bad idea?

It's not that I expect change after one session—or even have the right to expect change at all—but she looks exponentially worse than she did when she boarded the ferry two hours ago. And I'm smart enough to know that you don't ask someone what they talk about with their therapist, but when I ask her vaguely how it went, she doesn't even give a verbal response. She just shrugs and gives a noncommittal humming sound before turning to stare out the golf cart.

I keep my thoughts to myself, and the rest of my questions, and my concerns. She might be my wife, and we might have reached a tentative peace, but we're not close enough that I can broach these things with her yet. So I settle for keeping my eyes on the road and sneaking occasional glances at her.

She goes to bed less than thirty minutes after we get home.

And I shouldn't be so worried; I shouldn't feel this anxious. She's a grown woman; she doesn't need me meddling into her mental health, and I don't have the right to meddle. But I find myself drifting down the hallway every so often, listening intently when I pass her door, just to make sure...

What? What am I trying to make sure of?

On my third such trip, I finally sigh and tell myself to get a grip. I'm all but pacing, and it's unlike me.

I go to the living room instead and pick up a magazine I've been meaning to read, last week's Forbes. I flip it open randomly, latching onto the first article I see, trying to force myself to be interested—but my eyes do little more than skim the words. It's almost a relief when my phone rings.

I answer without looking at the caller ID, which I regret immediately, because it's Clarence.

"Yes," I say.

"Come to dinner next week," he says. "At your grand-mother's."

His voice, gruff and impatient, tells me that he doesn't want to be calling me any more than I want to be hearing from him; these are the kinds of tasks Mavis offloads to other people.

"I'm busy," I say. It's true; I'm always busy.

"On Monday," he says, ignoring me completely. "Be there. Bring your wife."

Then he hangs up, leaving me staring at the phone, clenched tightly in my hand.

Deep breath.

I toss the magazine to the side; then I stand up and head to my study, my steps determined.

Mavis's miraculous recovery means I need to make some adjustments—major adjustments. And though I never foresaw her return to health...I do have some ideas.

They're intimidating ideas; scary, even. But, oddly, they feel good, too—in a way I can't describe. When I think about my options for the future, I mostly feel dread; only one path fills me with any sort of excitement.

I always envisioned my future at the company. I wanted to open a humanitarian branch. I wanted to do good things.

But I don't know how much longer I can remain under Mavis's thumb. I don't know how much longer I can stand the mind games. And I definitely don't know if I can justify keeping Holland around an environment so toxic.

I think...it might be time.

So I call Wyatt as soon as I'm seated comfortably in my desk chair. The phone rings twice before he answers.

"I've been forcefully invited to have dinner with Mavis on Monday."

"Noted," he says. "I'll add it to your calendar."

"Thank you. Also," I add—I take another deep breath—"I think it's time to plan for some changes."

Wyatt hesitates for just a second. Then he says, "I wondered."

"Do you remember the contingency plans we discussed briefly when Mavis first sent out the copy of her will?"

"I do," he says, and I can imagine him nodding, his glasses flashing, his hair combed neatly into its side part.

"Let's get the ball rolling on that." Even just saying the words fills me with something like adrenaline, the same kind of nervousness you feel before performing on stage or giving a presentation.

Wyatt pauses once again. But when he speaks, he only asks one question: "Are you certain?"

I think about my phone call with Clarence; I think about Lawrence. I think about Holland and my mother. I think about Mavis Butterfield.

I straighten up in my seat before I even realize I'm doing it. "Yes," I say, my voice stronger. "I think so."

DINNER THREE DAYS later is not quite a disaster, but it's not good, either.

All of my aunts and uncles are present, gathered around Mavis's long dining table. It's made of shiny, dark wood, and Mavis sits at the head, a queen surveying her kingdom from her throne. My mother and Clarence and Aunt Rita and Aunt Barbara all look like Mavis, and they all wear similar expressions—haughty, entitled, thoroughly unpleasant. It's like sitting at a table with a bunch of Mavises; Lawrence and Dorothy-call-me-Dot are here too, and Lawrence wears the same expression as the rest.

There's still no ring on Dorothy's finger, I can't help but notice, and I'm not surprised; Lawrence's pathological need to remain uncommitted must be locked in battle with his desire to inherit the company. He won't be able to hold his father off for much longer, though; my guess is they'll be engaged by the end of the summer.

I think I might feel some pity for Dorothy, even though I don't like her.

I stick close to Holland from the second we enter the house—a giant, sprawling home that edges into mansion territory. There's a sweeping staircase that I doubt Mavis can travel anymore, lots of dark wood, and ornate light fixtures in every room; it's objectively nice, even if it's tainted by its inhabitants. I can tell Holland wants to gape at everything—her eyes go wide as soon as we step into the foyer—but she doesn't; she maintains a cool, almost bored expression, her posture perfect, not a hair out of place.

She was made to wear this dress—navy blue, knee length, with a high neckline and sleeves that come down to her elbows. It shows very little skin, but it's fitted to every curve, and the dark color somehow makes her hair seem brighter, more golden.

I'm getting distracted, though only partly by her appearance; she still isn't quite herself. She's better than she was right after her therapy session, but some of her fire seems to be gone. So I stay by her side, because my family is unpredictable, and she doesn't need their nonsense right now.

There seems to be little point to the gathering; I keep waiting, but Mavis doesn't make any announcements, and no one gives any official family updates. There's no business talk. We just sit around the table and eat for forty-five minutes in near silence, and Mavis appears to be the only one who enjoys it. I'm half waiting for her to cackle, but she doesn't.

A power play; that's what this is. *Look at how alive I am. Look at what I can demand from you.*

I swallow my beef bourguignon with grim satisfaction. *Not for long, you old witch.*

"Hey," Holland says out of the corner of her mouth, leaning closer. "We should poach your grandma's cook. This is amazing."

"I don't want to employ anyone who's worked for Mavis this long," I breathe back.

She turns her head to look at me, surprised. "What about Wyatt?"

"Wyatt worked for my father until he died," I say quietly. "He took care of me after that. He's never been with Mavis."

She smiles slowly. "I knew I liked him."

"What are you lovebirds chatting about over there?" Clarence cuts in, his voice blaring and intrusive, his smile ribbon around ice. Every head at the table turns in our direction.

"I was asking Phoenix what size of pads he recommends," Holland says just as loudly—and without missing a beat. Further up the table, Lawrence chokes and coughs into his beef bourguignon. Mavis snorts with something that might be amusement.

"He says jumbo size is good for days of heavier flow," Holland goes on. "The overnight ones with the wings."

Clarence hums coldly, his lips twisting in distaste—*wrong line of business, Clarence*—and Holland returns to her food and her quiet.

Every now and then she casts a questioning glance around the table, though, and I try to picture how strange it must seem, a large family eating in tense silence, no under-lying warmth to be felt.

She sighs audibly when Mavis excuses herself without a word ten minutes later, waving her assistant over to help her stand. Everyone disperses after that, and we're the first ones to leave. My mother tries to get my attention on the way out, but I ignore her—rudely, maybe, but I have limits. I grab Holland's hand without thinking, pulling her along to get out faster; she hisses at me and yanks on my grasp until I slow down again.

"Look at me, I'm the big alpha male, dragging my helpless

female along," she mutters under her breath as we stride through the foyer, and I roll my eyes.

"Then *hurry up,*" I say over my shoulder.

She makes a face at me, and I halt with tired feet.

"You signed the contract," I say in a low voice. "Cooperate, please."

"Signing the contract does not equal letting you drag me around," she snaps; her voice echoes around the marble foyer, and I make a hissing sound at her.

"Quiet," I say. Then, because she's right, I add reluctantly, "I'll stop dragging you. Sorry."

She bristles but nods, and we resume our path.

Both of us are exhausted by the time we get home; she kicks off her heels immediately and then beelines for the couch, flopping face-first and not moving for several seconds.

"I just don't understand how you're the easiest person to be around in your entire family," she finally says, rolling over. "In any given situation, you should be the most insufferable."

"Bold words for a woman who kissed me in a closet all those years ago," I say, leaning back against the kitchen counter and loosening my tie. "And then agreed to marry me."

She sits up. "For *pay,*" she says. "I agreed to marry you for *pay.*"

I cock my brow at her. "Yeah?" I say. My tie undone, I begin unbuttoning my shirt. "What about the closet? Was that for pay too?"

"I—it wasn't—" She swallows, her eyes falling to my shirt. "Are you taking that off out here?"

"Why?" I say, smirking at her expression. Something shifts in my chest at the way her eyes are trained on me, something that pushes the next words out of my mouth. "Want to find another closet?"

She scoffs, pulling her gaze away from my half-bare chest. "You wish."

"Maybe sometimes," I murmur.

Her head whips back toward me, her cheeks rosy pink. "What?"

"I said *You're dumb sometimes.*" I push off the counter and head toward the hallway where our bedrooms are located. "I'm going to bed. Try not to snore tonight."

She gapes at me, her eyes narrowing. "You're the one who snores. I've never snored a day in my *life—*"

"But you wouldn't know, would you?" I pull my shirt off just before I round the corner. "Sleep well," I call, grinning.

She doesn't snore. But it's fun to get that look out of her.

I fall asleep almost immediately, and I dream of closets with my wife—of kissing her and never stopping.

I WAKE up suddenly and with a pounding heart; part of that is from the dreams that have been haunting me all night, but the other part is that I can hear Holland. It's another nightmare, judging by the sound, torn and desolate.

As soon as I open her door, the light from the hallway illuminates her, and I see that tonight is different. She's not asleep anymore, or even half-asleep; she's fully awake, sitting up, curled in on herself. Her head is hidden, buried in her knees, and her arms are wrapped around her legs. Even in the weak light I can tell that she's holding herself too tightly, a woman clutching a life raft.

The sound of her cries is one of the worst things I've ever heard. They're sobs pulled not from her throat but from her soul.

I sit on the edge of the bed, my hands hovering awkwardly in silent debate until I finally rest one on her shoulder.

"Holland," I say. I can hear my uncertainty; sometimes people need to fall apart in private, with no one watching. I don't know what she wants right now. "Holland?"

When she speaks, I don't understand. The words are muffled, spoken into her knees and blurred by her tears.

"I can't hear you," I say.

Her shoulders continue to shake as she lifts her head, and I barely stop myself from rearing back.

Devastation. Bottomless, unseeing eyes.

"Trev is dead," she says—broken, gasping, desperate.

It's a blow to the chest, physically painful, and my heart falters and then plummets. I swallow and answer her anyway. "Yes," I say, my voice quiet. "Trev is dead."

She fights for more air, a tight, horrible sound. "I couldn't stop the car."

"I know," I say with a slow nod.

"I tried—I tried—"

"I know." I tighten my grip on her shaking shoulder. "I know you tried."

She's close to hyperventilating now. "I couldn't—I couldn't—" She breaks off, and I scoot closer to her.

"You couldn't," I say. "You couldn't have done anything. If I had been driving, I wouldn't have been able to do anything either. We couldn't have changed anything, Holl. We couldn't change the road. We couldn't change the car. We couldn't change the river." I swallow as a tangled knot rises in my throat. "Rivers are always going to flow. Sometimes they're icy. We just swim anyway."

She finally releases her death grip on her knees, swiping at her eyes. "I'm tired of swimming," she says. Her entire body is still shuddering with her cries, but she sounds frustrated now too. "I'm *tired.*"

I lean forward and wrap my arms around her, pulling her close. "I know," I say heavily.

She doesn't resist; she melts into me, sobbing, hot tears on my bare chest—sorrow past words, jagged and sharp, grief like a knife.

And I wonder: Is this the first time she's cried about Trev? Surely not. My guess is that this is what she talked about in her therapy session, but was it the first time she'd ever talked about the crash in any detail?

Something deep in my soul whispers that these tears have been a long time coming—that I'm witnessing the destruction of a dam she built around her broken heart years ago.

It's probably twenty minutes before her tears subside and her body stops shaking in my arms; I figure she's fallen asleep, until she shifts and a question filters toward me.

"Do I really snore?" she says in a tired little voice, slow and drowsy.

I smile gently as something warm stirs in my chest. "No," I say, stroking her hair.

"I knew it."

I just pull her closer. When she finally falls asleep, I ease her back onto her pillow; then I crawl under the covers and curl up next to her, dozing off to the sound of her soft, even breathing.

CHAPTER 24

Holland

I WAKE UP TOO EARLY.

The world is still bathed in golden-orange light, the sky stained pink—I can see it out my window. As early as it is, though, I'm glad to be awake, because as memories of the nightmare I had last night filter in, I realize it was the worst I've had in ages—vivid in a way I had forgotten. They all used to be like that, but they grew fuzzier around the edges as the years wore on.

I blink a few more times, my eyes still bleary. Then I stretch and look vaguely over at the other side of the bed— where I find a sleeping Phoenix, his arm behind his head, his face peaceful. I smile at the sight; there's something beautiful about the way he looks in sleep, so carefree.

I reach for him, tracing one finger down his jaw and then over his cheekbone. His bone structure is nothing short of a masterpiece. His dark lashes flutter open as I trail my finger over his lips, and I smile.

"Hi," I murmur.

"Mmm," he says, inhaling deeply and then yawning. "Hi." It's a deep, gravelly voice, one that sends pleasant shivers down my spine.

"Who told you you could sleep shirtless in my bed?" I say

softly, fighting my own yawn. I poke his bare bicep, and he responds with a sleepy smile.

"I took my own liberties," he says. "How are you feeling?"

"Better," I say, snuggling into my pillow. "I'm sorry about last night."

"Don't apologize." He stretches one hand toward me, as though to cradle my face or tuck my hair behind my ear, but then he freezes suddenly; his eyes widen as their sleepy haze disappears, and his smile vanishes as he stares at me.

And it hits me, clearly right as it hits him: We don't do things like this. *Ever.* We don't wake up next to each other; we don't have murmured, sun-soaked conversations in bed.

I scramble away so quickly that I fall off the mattress and land painfully on the hard floor, banging my head on the corner of the nightstand.

"Ow," I moan as the sharp pain ricochets through my skull. "Ow—" Tears spring to my eyes, and I roll sideways on the floor, feeling around beneath my hair. When I brush the spot and my fingers come away bloody, my vision swims. "*Ouch.*"

"What are you—good *grief,* Holland," Phoenix says when his eyes land on me. He frowns right up until he sees the blood on my hand; then he swears and hurries out of bed and to my side. "You have to *be careful—*"

"Why are you in my bed?" I say as my pulse pounds behind my eyes. "Ouch—"

"Stop whining," he says, sounding irritated. He kneels by my side and tilts my head carefully, pressing gentle fingers to the bump. "Does it hurt?"

"Yeah, obviously it hurts," I snap. "Did you not hear me saying *ouch?*"

And I'm telling the truth; my head hurts. But that's not

the reason my heart is still racing and my thoughts are so frantic.

We were acting like a real couple—a genuine, loving couple.

"I mean when I touch it," he says, rolling his eyes. "Come on—up. Stand up."

"Ow," I say as he tugs on my arm. "I don't want—"

"We have to clean it, Holland," he says as he pulls me up. For all his grumbling, his hand on my arm is gentle as he leads me into the bathroom across the hall. He gestures to the shower. "Get in. Come on," he adds impatiently. "Go." His face is pale, his jaw clenched, and his gaze seems fixed on the side of my head.

I watch, dumbfounded, as he opens the shower door and turns the faucet on, holding his hand under the water until he's satisfied with the temperature. Then he pulls the little lever that sends the water to the showerhead.

"In," he says as he gestures once again to the running shower, his eyes still lingering on the bump on my head. "Let's go." He places gentle hands on my shoulders and pushes me toward the shower.

And honestly, I'm too shocked to do anything but comply. I'm still in my silk pajamas; he's still in basketball shorts. But he leads the both of us into the shower anyway with me stepping in first, followed closely by him.

What on earth is going on right now?

"Turn around," he mutters, taking me by the shoulders again and spinning me around. I'm facing him now, and he is *so shirtless*, and he doesn't seem to notice or care at all; all of his attention is focused on me as he steps close and reaches around me, tilting my head under the stream of the shower.

I wince as the water finds the bump, and his eyes dart to mine.

"It's not terrible," I say quickly when I see the muscles tense in his shoulders. "It stings a bit, but I'm not in excruciating pain."

He relaxes slightly and nods before returning to my hair; he rinses it gently under the water, his hands slow and soft, and my heart is going a million miles an hour. No, a billion. A trillion, even.

"Your face is turning too red," he says, the words stiff. "Breathe properly, please."

"Sorry, but we are *in the shower,* Phoenix," I say in a tight voice.

His hands freeze, and I realize belatedly that I've called him by his name.

Gonna pretend that didn't happen. "We're in the shower in our clothes," I go on, "which is uncomfortable." Uncomfortable because he's so close to me, and his hands are so gentle, and—perhaps the most disturbing—he seems legitimately worried.

He's taking care of me.

Think about something else, I tell myself. And my nightmare from last night jumps into my mind; I guess talking to the therapist about what happened pulled it all to the surface. The feel of the steering wheel, the slide of the tires, the endlessly bizarre sensation of falling with no road beneath us —I pull in a shuddering breath and blink rapidly, trying to dispel the thoughts and images that years later still haven't left me.

"Water in my eyes," I say when Phoenix raises one brow at me.

Breathe in; breathe out. The memories and the fear and the sorrow are overpowering, but something else is rising in my chest, too—something just as powerful: a savage sense of pride and satisfaction.

Because I'm *doing* something. I'm reliving this trauma more vividly because I'm in the process of rooting it out. I didn't realize how powerful that knowledge would feel.

My heart is heavy. My eyes are swollen. I have a headache. But I'm doing a good thing.

I let my eyes trail over Phoenix as he stands in front of me, tilting my head this way and that, working the blood out of my hair. This is twice, now, that he's found me having a nightmare in the middle of the night—twice that he's seen me at my absolute lowest, my most broken. It's not something I want anyone to witness, but especially not him. I almost wish he would laugh at me, because I could respond to that with anger. It would be easy to handle his teasing or his mocking.

But he holds me instead. He holds me close and lets me cry and strokes my hair and makes me feel so inexplicably *safe*. How am I supposed to react to that? What am I supposed to do with that behavior? How is it supposed to make me feel? Because what I find inside myself right now is something dangerously like hope—although hope for *what* is harder to put my finger on.

All I know is that he can't keep holding me while I cry. He can't wash my wounds so tenderly. I can't handle behavior like that. It makes me feel…things. So many things.

I sigh as the inevitable question creeps into my mind: Do I *like* him? Do I actually like Phoenix Park, my husband—this man who takes care of me in the most begrudging of ways?

Of course not, my brain says.

You agreed to stay married to him, a smaller part of me whispers. *And your pulse is racing right now. What do you think that means?*

"I think you've got it," I say as my feelings twist into knots low in my stomach.

"Head wounds bleed a lot," he says, turning my body to the side so he can look. "But this doesn't actually seem too bad." Then he turns me to face him again. "Do you feel okay?"

I nod.

"Don't lie," he warns, his hand clenching on my shoulder.

"I'm not," I say softly. "It's a little tender, but other than that, I feel fine."

His gaze darts over my face for a second, searching for the truth, until finally he nods. Then he leans past me and turns off the water, plunging us into silence broken only by the sound of dripping water and our mingled breaths.

I'm completely soaked; under the stream of the warm shower it was fine, but now I shudder. Phoenix's eyes flit over me before he squeezes them shut, exhaling roughly.

"Get out," he says as his hand clenches tightly on the handle of the shower door. He slides it open, his eyes still closed, and I step carefully out. I wrap a towel around myself and then turn back to him.

"Thank you," I say before backing out of the bathroom.

He doesn't respond.

WORK CRAWLS by at a glacial pace; I enjoy the salon, but today I can't wait for my shift to be done. I make absentminded conversation with my clients, paying just enough attention to do a good job. I leave at two o'clock on the dot, and I barely pause on the way out to say goodbye.

I spend the afternoon with Nana Lu, which is much more enjoyable than work, even if it doesn't keep my mind as occupied as I'd like. We video call Maggie, who we catch on her way to class; Nana listens with genuine interest as Maggie tells her about the last test she took, smiling and bobbing her head and asking questions in her feeble voice.

I want Nana to live forever, sweet and full of unwavering love. It's selfish, I know. And I want Maggie to be happy forever—I want her to be happy, and I want her to know she's loved, and I want the sun to shine on her always. I want every good thing for her, and then some.

"Nana," I say after we're done talking to Maggie. "I think there might be a guy I like."

Nana Lu gasps and turns her head slowly toward me. "Is there?"

"Maybe," I say. I lean closer and tuck the blankets around her further; she spends a lot of her time sitting up in bed, and she likes to stay warm. "I can't really tell right now."

"Is he handsome?"

I'm tempted to say no, just to revolt against my feelings, but the lie probably won't come out as anything more than a high-pitched squeak. I think of Phoenix's flawless bone structure and the way his eyes flash when we argue. "I guess so," I say.

Nana shifts, trying to sit up straighter; I stand up quickly and help her adjust the pillows behind her back. She's so frail, so feeble, but she still makes time to be with me and chat about stupid things.

"Is he a nice boy?" she asks once we've eased her body back against the pillows.

"He...can be nice," I say, my voice grudging. I don't want to lie to Nana, even if I'd like to lie to myself. "But sometimes he's a jerk."

The lines in Nana's aged face grow even more pronounced as she frowns. "But you're such a nice girl. Don't like him if he's a jerk, sweetie."

247

But you're such a nice girl.

Heat creeps up my neck—the heat of shame and guilt. I'm not nice to Phoenix; not really. I'm petty and rude. And I'm not sure I know how to interact with him any other way.

Nana and I move on to other topics, but her words stay with me even after I leave for the day. The wind is formidable outside, and the sun from this morning is nowhere to be found; a storm is coming. So I pick up my pace as I walk, lost in thought, the chilled air driving my steps faster and faster.

And I don't realize where I'm going until I'm there.

"Good grief, Holland," I mutter as I look up at the two-story building with rock beds and palm trees. "Really?"

But you're such a nice girl.

I exhale roughly. I'm about to turn around and go straight home when the first rain drop hits me, a fat *splat* right on top of my head. The brisk wind blows harder, pulling my short dress this way and that, trying to lift it to inappropriate heights. So I accept my fate—if I had been paying attention to where I was going, I wouldn't be in this situation—and then hurry up the sidewalk, past the rock beds, and to the entrance of Phoenix's office building. The stupid wind likes this direction; it pushes me from behind, an invisible hand shoving me toward the husband I'm not all that nice to.

The husband who got soaked head to toe this morning to make sure I was okay after hitting my head.

I'm coming to your office for a bit, I text him as a heads up, and then I go in.

Inside the office I find the quiet hustle and bustle of closing time; people are pulling on jackets and organizing desks and packing up briefcases.

I wonder if they know how hard their boss works, long after they've left for the day.

Several of them smile or wave as I pass the rows of cubicles, and I smile in return, trying at the same time to feel my hair and make sure it's not too crazy from the wind and rain. I head for the back and then climb the stairs, hurrying left down the hallway until I reach Phoenix's office.

A few of his blinds are open, so I lean closer to the window, trying to see if he's in a meeting, but there's only him. I open the door and stick my head in, the blinds rattling.

We're going to pretend this morning never happened.

"Yes," Phoenix is in the middle of saying. He gives me no more than a glance before he waves me in, returning his attention to whoever he's on the phone with. "I think that would work."

I slip in and close the door quietly behind me. Then I turn my eyes to the ceiling, looking for a vent; once I find it over by the bookshelves, I position myself directly beneath it and pull my dress away from my body, trying to speed the drying process. I do this for a few minutes and then run my hands through my hair, airing that out too.

When I glance over at Phoenix, I'm startled to find his gaze already on me; he raises one brow and mouths *What are you doing?*

"It's starting to rain," I whisper, pointing out the window behind him.

He swivels around and then turns back to me, nodding. "And what about the lease?" he says into the phone.

The lease? Is he moving?

Whatever. I continue my airing-out process until I'm feeling marginally dryer; Phoenix is still on the phone, so I decide to check out his bookcases. I peruse down the row—there are a lot of classics, some business books, and a few that even look like old college textbooks. I ignore my fluttering pulse as I pass the shelf he pressed me up against when we kissed, because I'm not sure now is a good time to indulge in those memories. So I move resolutely on, until I reach the desk.

I scoot past it and continue searching for anything that I might like to read, but there's nothing. I turn my attention to the large window instead; the wind is blowing harder now, and the rain is coming down in sheets. A twinge of nervousness plucks at my insides, but I force it down and turn away.

I'm sure the weather won't get too bad.

I poke around the books a bit more until I'm bored out of my mind; then I pick up Phoenix's cell phone from the edge of his desk. He's not even looking at me—his phone conversation has moved on to square footage and maximum capacities—so I press the home button to sneak a peek at his lock screen.

You can tell a lot about a person based on their phone wallpaper.

"Figures," I say with a snort when I see it. It's just plain dark blue, no patterns, no designs, which ironically does say a lot about his personality. He's not the kind of person who would take the time to set a specialized photo; he has too many other things to do, most of them more important than what his phone looks like.

The lock screen is plain dark blue...and yet I don't look away; I even squint, bringing the phone closer.

Because my text is displayed there too—and accompanying it, the name he's given me in his list of contacts.

I'm coming to your office for a bit. That's what I said. But my message isn't attributed to *Holland*, which is what he said was my name in his phone. Apparently I'm not even listed as *Amsterdam* or one of its many derivatives. No—at the top of the text is nothing more than the word *Her*.

I frown and grab my phone from the pocket of my dress; then I punch his number in and press *call.*

Sure enough, when his phone begins to buzz, the caller ID reads simply *Her.*

"What are you doing?"

I startle so violently I almost drop both phones. "Nothing," I say, my head jerking up to face Phoenix, whose forever-long call is apparently over. My heart is pumping faster than it should be, and something strange and fluttery is flitting around in my stomach.

"How's your head?"

"It's fine." I hold out his phone to him, swallowing hard. Then I say, "Am I just *Her* in your contacts?"

He freezes in place, half out of his desk chair, his hand outstretched to take his phone. But that stillness only lasts for a brief second; he snatches his cell out of my grasp and sits back down, tucking it into his suit coat. "Yes," he says, his voice casual. "Because I couldn't be bothered to type in your whole name. So what?" He eyes me, raising one brow. "Why? What am I listed under in your phone? Cockatoo? Chicken?"

"Your name isn't in my phone," I say—*stop admitting things!* my brain screams, but my mouth keeps going— "because I have your number memorized."

That cocky raised eyebrow of his is joined by the other as his expression turns to one of surprise.

And I think there must be something wrong with my eyes, because they can't seem to move away from his; we're staring at each other too long, too intently, and the space between us grows viscous as my pulse pounds in my ears.

Breathe; I need to breathe. Why can't I breathe?

But I know exactly why I can't breathe. Because of all the

female contacts he has, of all the women he knows—I'm the one he didn't need to name.

I'm the one he would think about when he saw the word *Her*.

From outside, a violent crash of thunder shatters the sky; both of us jump, and the moment is gone.

A second later, the lights cut out.

They don't disappear only in this room, but out on the floor as well; the whole building has lost power. And, as I whirl around and look out the window once more, I see that it's not just us; through the slanting rain I can make out that the nearby buildings are dark as well.

From his desk behind me, Phoenix sighs. "Great."

"Look at that." I tap the window, and the squeak of leather sounds before Phoenix joins me.

"This might be a bad one," he says, his voice grim. "I guess it's good it's happening now; everyone else has already gone home, and Wyatt is over on the mainland today."

I eye the rain still coming down in sheets. "Should we wait it out, I guess?"

"Yes," he says, settling back in his desk chair. "It won't last for long."

He's wrong.

One hour later, the rain is still torrential, and the palm trees are losing leaves to the wind. The power isn't back, and we've lost internet and cell service too.

"It's not like I'm a weatherman," he says irritably when I give him a look that clearly says *You were way off*. Then he leans his head back in his seat and closes his eyes.

Night is falling, so we've dug up some flashlights; one of them is propped up in a leather chair, casting its light on the ceiling. There's food down in the refrigerator in the break room too, Phoenix says, food that will need to be eaten soon anyway now that the power is out.

Food and light aside, however, I am not reassured. It's looking like we might have to stay the night here.

"Does this not at all concern you?" I say when I see how relaxed he looks in his chair, his eyes still closed, his arms folded comfortably over his chest.

He shrugs. "My employees are long since gone home. You're safe here with me. What else is there to worry about?"

You're safe here with me. Can he hear himself?

And into my mind pops the tense look on his face as he examined my head this morning, the gentle ministrations of his hands.

I watch him for a while from my chair across from the flashlight; when he's been still and silent for maybe fifteen minutes, I allow myself to stand up and move closer.

I just want to look at him; that's all. I want to see him more clearly.

So I stand up and walk around his desk, hopping up to sit on the edge slightly to one side.

He lets out his breath when I seat myself. "Can I help you?" he says, keeping his eyes closed.

"Mmm," I say, because I don't have a good answer. I narrow my eyes as my thoughts swirl. "I don't know."

"Want to explain?"

"Not really," I admit. How am I supposed to explain that I can't tell if I have feelings for him? "It's embarrassing. And" —I sigh, swinging my legs—"confusing." I shake my head and tear my eyes away from him. "I'll leave you alone. Sorry."

"Just tell me," he says, finally opening his eyes. When I hesitate, he goes on, "Come on. I won't laugh."

His gaze is pitch black in the darkened room, a vacuum

that threatens to suck me in. And as often seems to happen, the darkness seems to free my tongue.

"You said that we would like kissing," I say hoarsely. "And that we would never want to stop."

He nods slowly, his expression serious.

"Do you really believe that?" I say.

His throat bobs as he swallows, but he gives me just one word: "Yes." He doesn't look so relaxed now; his arms are still crossed, his head still resting on the back of the chair, but his whole body is radiating a tense, tight energy.

"Do you think we have feelings for each other?" I don't know where these questions are coming from, but I don't stop them. I'm not sure I can, any more than I can make myself breathe as I wait for his answer.

"I think...it's possible," he says.

I clear my throat. "Maybe we're just attracted to each other."

Another nod. "Undoubtedly," he says, and I snort—a blissful snap of humor that I clutch with desperate hands.

"So modest."

He shrugs as some of the tension drains out of his shoulders. "I know I'm handsome. And you..."

My breath catches as he studies me, his dark gaze sweeping from my head to my toes and then back again.

"You are very beautiful," he finally says, the words reluctant.

The edge of the desk digs into the back of my thighs when I speak; I try to keep my voice normal and unaffected, but it doesn't work. "I thought you said there was nothing appealing about me," I say.

The corners of his lips twitch, and his eyes flutter closed again. "I lied."

Butterflies. So many stupid butterflies taking flight in my stomach, all of them drunk and out past curfew.

When Phoenix sighs, his body relaxes further. "Why now for all the soul-searching, Amsterdam?" he says, shifting comfortably in his chair.

And I should change the topic. I should say something—anything—to steer this conversation into safer waters. But only one thought is going through my head right now, and I find the words escaping without my permission.

"Say my name," I whisper.

The room is even darker now; the sun hasn't set completely, but with the raging storm, most of the light outside has died. Still, when Phoenix's eyes open again, I see every second of it. I see the subtle shift in his expression as his gaze flares; I see his dark brow lift.

"And why should I do that?" he says, his voice low and silky.

"You know why," I say, swallowing thickly.

Slowly—so slowly—he pushes his chair back and then stands up. All it takes is one step to the side, and we're face-to-face. There's a familiar challenge in his eyes as he looks down at me, one that spikes electricity and adrenaline into my blood.

"You think hearing your name is going to make every-thing suddenly clear?" he says, leaning down and placing one hand on the desk on either side of me so that I'm caged in. "You think it will answer all the questions you keep asking yourself? It won't—*Holl.*" He caresses the name, lets it roll sensually off his tongue, and I shiver.

"I think—" I can't believe I'm saying it, but I go on, my eyes wide. "I think I might have a crush on you."

He shakes his head, his gaze never leaving me. "No," he says slowly. "You and I are well past that stage."

"I don't know what you mean." It's a half-hearted denial at best.

"I mean that you might find a lot of things with me," he says, his voice still low, "but a little *crush* won't be one of them."

I can barely find the oxygen in this room, but every inhale brings me the scent of leather and mahogany; his features aren't crystal clear in the dark, but I can feel his arms on either side of my body, strong and warm.

And he's magnetic. He pulls me in always but especially now; I lean forward, closer, moving my hands to trail my fingers up his arms.

He shudders at my touch.

"I told you no more unless you were ready for everything that came with it," he breathes, and I can feel his words against my lips. "I know myself, and I know you. If you kiss me right now, everything will change, and we won't be able to go back." He pauses before going on. "We'll sleep in the same bed. I'll call you *sweetheart* instead of *Amsterdam*. We'll argue when you use my nice razor to shave your legs. And I will love you, Holland, because every single emotion you make me feel is intense. There will be no crushes or infatuations." He spits those words out like he's never heard anything so ridiculous. "If you kiss me now..." he says, trailing off as his gaze darts over my face. Then he shakes his head. "If you kiss me now, you're *mine*."

Mine.

"What if I don't want you to call me *sweetheart*?" I whisper as my arms twine around his neck.

"The name is negotiable," he murmurs, his hands finding my waist.

"And the razor thing—"

"If you try to use my razor to shave your legs, we *will* argue."

I exhale, looking at him, my fingers playing absently with his hair. "You really think you would fall in love with me?"

"I think *we* would fall in love with *each other*."

"From one kiss? Are you insane?" I hesitate. "We've kissed before. In this very office, in fact."

He snorts, a little puff of breath against my jaw as his lips hover. "Tell me you didn't think about that for days."

He's right. And I know the truth; I feel it in my bones. I have loved this man in every way *but* romantic. I have made him a part of my life; I've made him a part of *me*. I've given him all of my most overwhelming emotions—my anger, my frustration, my fear.

Negative emotions, but I still gave them *to him*. He's the one I trusted not to walk away.

It would be easy, so easy, to fall in love with him. And although I don't know what that love would look like, I do know that this precipice we've been dancing on is sharp and jagged and painful.

Falling for him is scary...but trying not to fall for him has been torture.

So I spread my wings and prepare to jump.

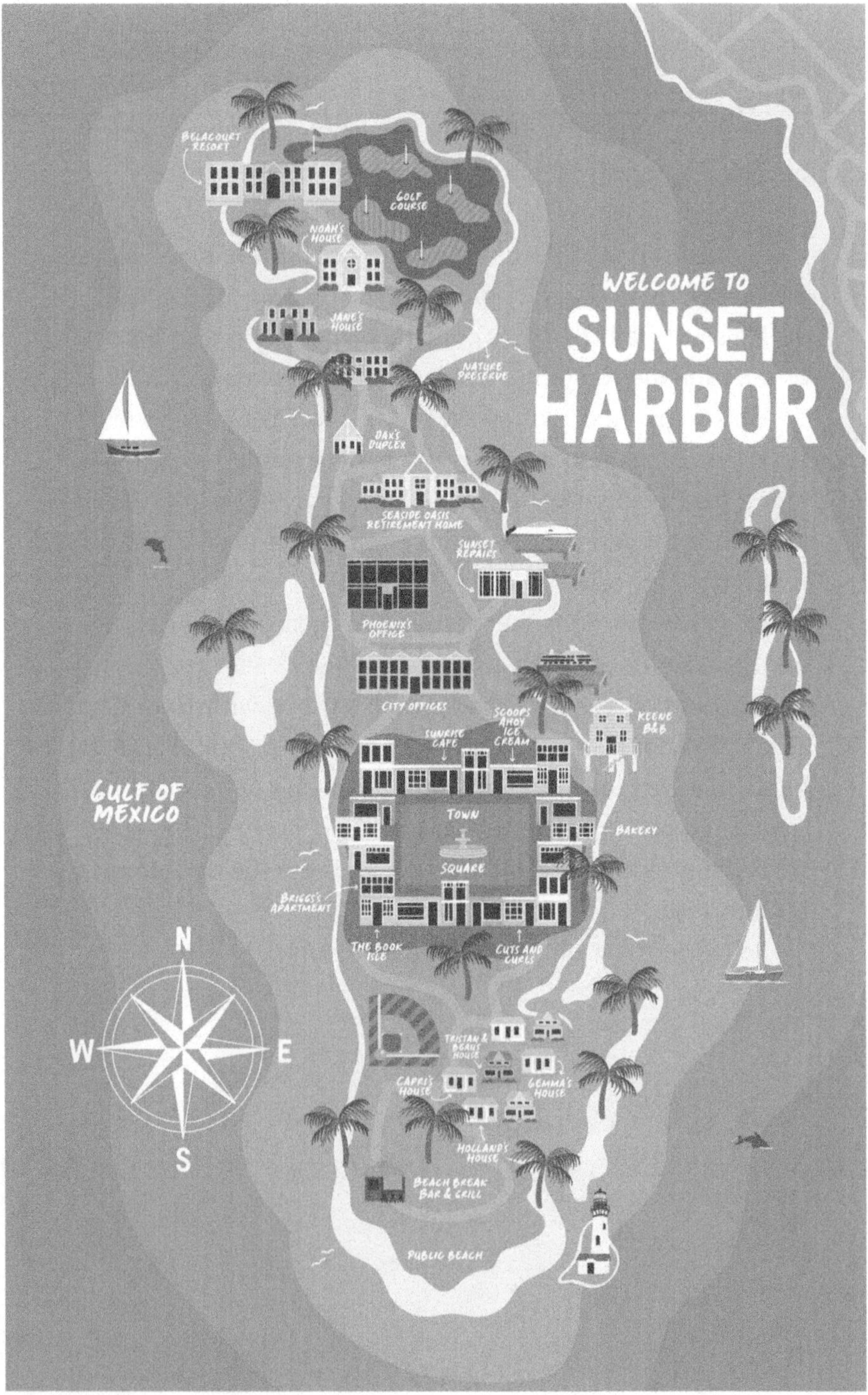

CHAPTER 25

Holland

THE STORM ROARS OUTSIDE; rain pounds a deafening rhythm against the window. But somehow, in spite of all that, the world feels silent. Phoenix's hands are tight on my waist, his lips centimeters from my own, and the only thing I can really hear is the sound of our breathing.

"So the razor thing," I say again, and Phoenix rolls his eyes.

"What about it?" he says impatiently. "You can't use my razor to shave your legs. Buy your own."

"It's just that I sort of already did," I admit, tightening my arms around his neck. "Use your razor, I mean. The one you keep by the sink in your bathroom."

His head rears back; even in the shadows I can see him blink at me.

I nod, trying not to laugh at his indignance. "Just once, because mine broke. So...is that a dealbreaker?"

"Good *grief*, Holland," he mutters under his breath, looking pained. "You can't use my stuff like that."

"It's just a razor—"

"It's not *just a razor*," he says hotly. "It's a *boundary*—" But he breaks off and glares at me. "And didn't I tell you we would only have this argument if you kissed me?"

"You also said that if I kissed you, I would be yours."

There's something light and airy bubbling up in my chest, something giddy.

"Yes," he says, his eyes still narrowed on me. "You'll be mine. So what? You still can't use my razor."

"So we'll have a joint bank account, right?" I say with a shrug. "Which means what's mine is yours and what's yours is mine."

He puffs out a little laugh of disbelief. "You have two seconds to drop it, you complete *menace*," he says against my lips then, "or I'm going to—"

"What?" I say with a smirk. "Throw me over your shoulder? Pin me to a bookshelf? Put a dead fish in my mailbox?"

"Kiss you," he says, grinning; I can feel every word he speaks. "Kiss you first and forever and I *swear*, Holland, if you use my razor again—"

"*Sweetheart*," I say, pressing the word to his lips. "I like *sweetheart*."

"*Sweetheart*," he says, his hands on my waist pulling me to the edge of the desk. "Fine."

Silence, stillness, for the space of two long seconds— infinity suspended in an hourglass, my pulse thrumming at the glaze of sheer longing in his eyes.

I don't know who moves first. One instant our eyes are locked, our breath mingling, and the next we're kissing— desperate, determined, the breaking of a dam. We fall into the motions with ease, the back-and-forth tug, the tilt of our heads, the slide of our lips.

"Such a pain," he breathes as he breaks away and skims his lips up my jaw.

"At least I'm not in a secret relationship with my *razor*— ow!" I say, laughing as he nips at my ear.

"Don't be rude," he murmurs between the kisses he trails back down my jaw. When his lips meet mine again, they're hungrier, more demanding; his hands slide up my sides, and I scoot closer until I'm about to fall off the desk.

And it hits me just as his tongue traces the seam of my lips: he's right.

I think I'm going to fall in love with my husband.

THE STORM LASTS through the night.

We search all the supply closets in the building when it's time to go to bed, but we can't find any blankets or pillows—not surprising, but still disappointing. So we end up lying on the hard floor in Phoenix's office, our heads propped on the cushions we've removed from his leather chairs.

"So now that you're madly in love with me," I say—Phoenix snorts from next to me—"I have some questions."

"No questions," he says, his eyes closed. "Go to sleep." He's lying on his back, one hand resting neatly on his stomach; his other hand is by his side, fingers tangled loosely with mine.

"You don't really think I can sleep on this floor, do you?" I say with a frown. "It's like granite."

He hums. "Such a snob."

"I'm not a snob!" I say. It's mostly true. "I just can't rest on surfaces this hard. So let me ask my questions." When he doesn't answer, I roll my eyes. "Don't pretend. I will pay you actual money if you fall asleep, because I don't think it will happen. You sleep on a million-dollar mattress."

"*We* sleep on a million-dollar mattress."

My heart stutters in my chest.

"Fine. Yes," I say. "Now *we* sleep on a million-dollar mattress. My point is that we're not going to be able to sleep here, so we may as well chat to pass the time. So tell me. Did you—"

"If you're going to ask me questions, I'll get to ask you some too, and you'll have to answer honestly," he says, his voice lazy, his eyes still closed. "Can you handle that—*sweetheart?*" His lips quirk at the word—which is going to take some getting used to.

I hesitate for only a second. "Yes. Deal." Then, wanting to clarify, I add, "And you'll be honest too?"

"Mmm...yes," he says with a little tilt of his head. "I'll be honest." His eyes flutter open as he turns his head to look at me.

"I don't even know where to start," I say. "I have so many questions."

He snorts. "You can't have *that* many. I'm not particularly mysterious."

What a liar. "Okay, I have my first one. When we kissed in that closet—"

"By accident—"

"Did you like it?"

He's silent for a second; his eyes narrow as they flit over my face. "How old were you then? Over eighteen?"

"Yes," I say, rolling my eyes. "I was legal."

"Then yes," he says. "I liked it, much to my chagrin. I thought about it more than I should have."

When I raise my brows at him, he shrugs. "You were Trev's little sister, just a kid. I wasn't supposed to think about kissing you."

"Ah, yes," I say as a particularly loud boom of thunder sounds outside; I startle and then go on. "You were ensnared by my charm."

He snorts. "Hardly. But you did make an impression. It was...not at all what I expected."

"Were you expecting it to be bad?"

"No," he says slowly. "I was just expecting someone else. So I wasn't expecting it to feel personal. But it did." He pauses and then says, "You kissed me like you liked me."

"I did," I say with a sigh. "A little bit, anyway. Poor baby Holland."

"You turned out all right."

Considering that our fingers are tangled together and our hair is mussed and one of the buttons on his shirt is still unbuttoned...he's not wrong.

"So I'm yours, huh?"

He hums, his eyes flashing. "I made that clear." His voice is reluctant as he continues. "I'm not a romantic man, Holland. I don't buy flowers or write poetry. And I've never been shown what a healthy marriage looks like. But you're mine. I'll keep you safe; I'll treat you well."

A laugh slips out of me. "Yeah, right—" But I break off when his hand clamps over my mouth.

"I've always treated you well," he says as I try to lick his palm. "You're the one who treats me terribly. Stop—that—gross, Holl—"

"What did you think was going to happen?" I say when he yanks his hand away, wiping it on my shirt. "No—don't wipe that on me!"

"Reap what you sow, sweetheart," he murmurs with a grin, reaching for me. "Now answer my questions."

"One question," I say quickly as he pulls me closer, until his arm rests over my waist and our faces are separated by mere inches. "If I only got one question, you only get one."

"You can have more," he says. "But it's my turn first. Do you want kids?"

I blink at him in surprise, but he just waits for my answer.

"Yes," I say. "Not right now, but someday. Do you?"

"Sure," he says, his arm tightening around me, his fingers tracing lazy patterns on my back.

"Now my turn," I say. I clear my throat. "What did you think of my wedding dress?"

"Are these the only questions you're going to ask?" he says. "You just want to know what I've thought of you in the past?"

"It's not all I'm going to ask, but I want to start there. I want to see how long you've been pining after me—"

He lets out a short bark of a laugh that cuts pleasantly through the dark office. "You're going to be disappointed. There's been very little pining involved."

"Just humor me," I say, nudging him with my elbow. "Answer the question."

"The wedding dress was perfect," he says with a sigh, but there's still a sparkle of amusement in his eyes. "I first admitted I was attracted to you that night in the honeymoon suite. And your pink silk pajamas are the bane of my sanity. Is that good enough?"

"Close," I say, and I can't stop my own smile spreading over my face. "Are you in love with me?"

"Hmm," he says, looking thoughtful now. He doesn't point out that this is my second question in a row, and I don't bring it up. There's a little furrow in his brow as he looks at me, his gaze darting over my features. "It's difficult to say," he says finally. "I'm not sure our relationship has ever been conventional." He pauses, and something shifts in his expression—a flash of hesitation, or maybe insecurity, that disappears as soon as I spot it. "Are you in love with me?"

"I don't know," I admit. "Can you be in love with someone who drives you crazy?"

"I think most couples would say yes," he says dryly. "You trust me, enough to marry me. Enough to—" He breaks off, and heat floods into my cheeks as his gaze skims down my body. He grins but doesn't finish his sentence.

"I trust you," I say quickly. "I *guess*—"

"Oh, please."

"And I guess I like being around you sometimes—"

"*Sometimes?*"

"And I can admit that you have some appealing character traits," I finish.

"Such as?"

"You're competent," I say, because I did promise I would answer truthfully. "Which is weirdly attractive. You're straightforward. You know right from wrong. You're smart. And I just—" I let out a gust of breath, finally allowing myself to be vulnerable. I let go of the flippant compliments, and when I speak again, my voice is softer. "I think I like you."

"Mmm," he says, nuzzling my nose with his. His expression is more gentle now. "Do you?"

"Yes," I say. "You give me butterflies, you excite me—but you also make me feel secure. I like you."

"I'm a likable man," he whispers, and the hand around my waist moves to my face, brushing a few strands of hair off my forehead. A cocky smile twitches over his lips, and I roll my eyes—even as contented relief spreads over me.

I wasn't sure how it would be, taking this step. Because Phoenix is right; nothing about our relationship is conventional. Suddenly choosing to be together, choosing to own up to the feelings stirring between us—I wasn't sure how that would change us or our interactions.

But the only thing that feels different is my confidence that he doesn't actually dislike me, even when we're arguing.

He couldn't touch me as tenderly as he does if he really disliked me. Being physical with him feels very natural, and this isn't the first time he's showing me a softer side.

"Let's try to get some sleep," he says, pulling me closer. "Tomorrow will come soon enough, and you're a monster when you're tired."

"Excuse you," I say, but my eyes are already drifting closed. "I am delightful always."

He snorts. "I have quite the array of evidence to the contrary." Then he drops a tiny kiss on my nose. "Go to sleep."

I tuck my head under his chin, and he adjusts immediately, shifting so the position is more comfortable for both of us.

"We need to redo the contract," I murmur into his chest. "Or just get rid of it."

"Get rid of it," he says with a nod. "We will." Then he sighs, his hand playing absently with my hair. "I never let myself think about stuff like this—holding you, touching you. But..."

"It's nice," I finish for him. I snuggle further into him, and his arm tightens around me.

"It is," he admits.

"Hey," I say as a question pops into my mind. "What am I supposed to call you?"

"I don't know," he says after a second. I can feel his jaw moving against the top of my head as he goes on. "Just not *Flamingo*."

I smile, pulling back slightly and tilting my head up. "*Honeybuns?*" I say.

"Pass," he says in a dry voice.

"*Sweetie Pie?*" I press a kiss to the base of his neck.

"Also pass."

"What about *Baby?*" Another kiss, longer this time, right over his Adam's apple. His breath hitches.

"Holland," he says, warning in his voice.

"Hmm?" I move up to his jaw, skimming my nose over his skin until I find a good place for my lips. *"Babe?"* Kiss. *"Lover?"*

"We're supposed to be sleeping," he says as his hands clench convulsively, digging into my skin.

"Mm-hmm." I press a kiss to the spot just below his ear— and that's when he snaps.

He curses softly and hauls me up, his lips finding mine in a searing kiss. "Call me whatever you want," he growls.

I just smile and kiss him back.

BECAUSE THE STORM has knocked out cell service, Phoenix doesn't receive Mavis Butterfield's raging message until the next day. I can tell something is wrong immediately; his face hardens as he listens to what sounds like an angry tirade, and when he puts his phone down, he looks as grim as I've ever seen him.

"It would seem that Mavis has somehow gotten hold of our contract," he says.

My heart sinks as a jolt of panic hits. "She did?"

Phoenix gives a clipped nod as his lips turn down even further. "And now she's demanding an immediate audience with me..." He trails off, his eyes flying to mine. "And my fake wife."

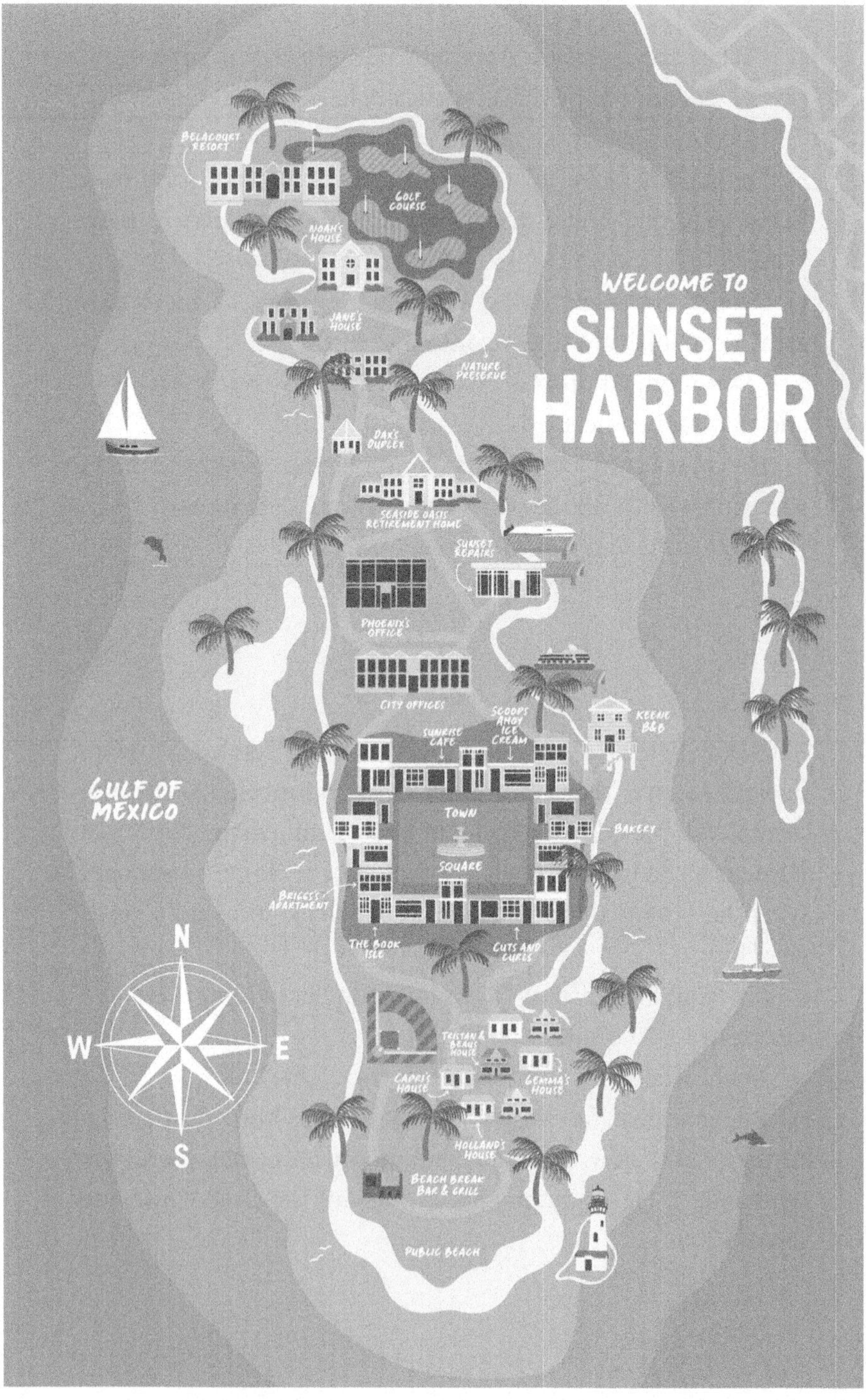

CHAPTER 26

Phoenix

"WHY AREN'T you stressing about this?" Holland asks me three days later, her fingers drumming nervously on her thigh.

"Because depending on what Mavis has to say, things aren't going to go her way," I tell her, putting my hand over hers so the finger-drumming will stop. "Just calm down for now."

She slaps my hand away. "Are you familiar with the Venn diagram of women who were told to calm down and women who subsequently *did* calm down? It's something you should take a look at," she says. "Let me be antsy. It relieves stress."

"Could have fooled me," I say under my breath, but I don't attempt to calm her again. I just let her stew in her agitation, her foot bouncing nervously in the passenger seat of the golf cart, her hair blowing in the wind as we drive.

The whole island has been in chaos mode after the storm, but even though things aren't completely back to normal yet —cell service is still spotty—the ferry is finally up and running.

Which means we're headed over to the mainland to visit my dear grandmother.

Soon. Soon I won't have to jump when Mavis tells me to;

soon I won't have to bow and scrape and live on the edge of my seat waiting for the other shoe to drop.

Wyatt and I have moved our timetable up, now that Mavis has questions about the validity of the marriage.

How did she get that contract?

Not just a copy, either; she has the original hard copy that was supposed to be in my file cabinet at home. The one in my work office was still in place—I checked after I got her message—but when we got home, the one at the house was gone.

Something simmering and hot rises in my chest, anger like lava, but I keep a check on it. We finish the drive in silence, and it's only once we've boarded the ferry that Holland speaks again.

"Okay, so walk me through this," she says, turning in her chair to look at me. Her nose and cheeks are pink from the wind and the persistent drizzle, a sheen of humidity on her skin. "What's the worst that could happen here?"

"There's nothing that could happen that I haven't made provisions for," I say truthfully. "But Mavis will likely object to our marriage and refuse to recognize it. I guess she could also disown me."

Holland gapes at me, her eyes wide. "Would she actually?"

"What, disown me?" I say, pulling my phone out of my suit pocket. "Not likely. I'm the best candidate to inherit and she knows it. More than that, though, she likes having all of us under her thumb." I shoot off a message to Wyatt, hoping it goes through, and then I tuck my phone away again.

When I look back at Holland—my *wife*, who's so much more than I ever expected or hoped—her eyes are on me, a little grimace on her lips.

"What?" I say blankly.

She clears her throat and scoots closer to me. "So listen," she says in a low voice that I can barely hear over the sound of the ferry's horn. "You're not going to like—*off* your grandmother or anything, right?"

"Of course not," I say calmly. When she continues to look skeptically at me, I roll my eyes. "Would I do that?"

"Absolutely," she says without missing a beat. "Under the right circumstances, you absolutely would."

"Anybody could kill under the right circumstances," I say. "You could too. But that's not the point—I'm not going to *off* my grandmother."

"You're just really, really chill about this. So I'm concerned."

"Maybe instead of being concerned, you could *also* try to be really, really chill," I point out. "Not one week ago you were waxing poetic about how much you trust me—"

"Shut up."

I point at her. "And I remember something about my moral compass as well—"

But I break off as she raises one hand toward my face as though to clamp it over my mouth.

"Try it and see what happens," I say, a jolt of heat flashing through my veins as I remember doing the same thing the night of the storm.

She freezes in place as her eyes fly up to mine; then a slow, amused smile unfurls over her lips. "You can dish it, but you can't take it?" she says softly, her eyes sparkling with laughter. Her hand shifts and comes to rest on my cheek, her thumb stroking my skin, and it's bliss—it's bliss feeling her touch without trying to convince myself I don't enjoy every second or long for more.

Because I do. I do enjoy every second, and I long for more. She sets my blood on fire, in so many ways and with

GRACIE RUTH MITCHELL

so many emotions. So when she tugs my face down and presses a soft kiss to my lips, I don't fight, even though we're in public.

"Doesn't it feel weird, though?" she says, leaning back. "We never used to kiss, and now suddenly we're doing it all the time—"

"'We never used to kiss'?" I say with a snort. I cover her hand with mine and then pull it away from my face, interlacing our fingers and resting them on my leg instead. "I would say we kissed an abnormal amount for two people who didn't get along. In fact—" I break off, thinking.

How much we kissed each other should have been a clue.

I shake my head and sigh. "Anyway—you should be prepared. I don't know what Mavis is going to say or do or threaten, but I might be making a lot of changes very soon. *Very* soon."

"Do those changes involve sucker-punching your cousin in the gut?"

My lips twitch. "That could be arranged if you really insist."

"I'm going to rest my head on your shoulder," she says, scooting closer. "I want to see what it feels like."

"I—" It's all I can get out before she's there, her hand still in mine, her head dropping gently on my shoulder.

"Oh—I like it," she says, making herself more comfortable. "And I won't insist on punching your cousin," she goes on. "But he deserves it. They all do."

I look down at her, at the blonde hair now spilling over my arm. "Are you not going to ask what my plans are?" I say with a little frown.

She shrugs but stays right where she is. "As long as you actually have a plan, I'm not worried." She pauses and then glances up at me. "You do have a plan, right?"

272

"I—of course." I always have a plan. More than one, in fact.

Her head rests on my shoulder again. "Then it's fine."

Huh. She actually *does* trust me. I...like that.

I like that a surprising amount.

So with only slight hesitation, I rest my head on top of hers.

And I like that, too.

WYATT MEETS us at the ferry stop with a change of outfit for both of us, since we've been out helping with clean-up all day and we only barely made the ferry.

"Wyatt," Holland says as soon as he passes us our clothing and ushers us into his car. "Do you have a Mary Poppins bag full of all this stuff?"

"It would seem so, wouldn't it?" he says dryly. "But really I'm just very good at being prepared."

"You're amazing. If you ever get annoyed at Phoenix, just come to me," Holland says as she scoots into the back seat and buckles her seatbelt. "I'll help you plot some good pranks. I've got one I've been dying to try that involves personalized stationery and a long mailing list."

I narrow my eyes at her in the rearview mirror, but she just smiles sweetly.

Wyatt simply chuckles, the traitor. Then he says, "I assume you both made it through the storm with no problems."

My gaze flies to the rearview mirror again, just in time to see a smile spread over Holland's face—small but genuine and warm.

"We did," she says. "How was it over here?"

"Nothing we couldn't handle," he says with a dip of his chin. Then he looks over at me and speaks in a lower, more serious voice. "I've changed our timeline like you asked. We're still waiting on a few things, though."

"That's fine," I say. "My guess is I'll end up announcing today, but I don't think it can be helped. Oh," I add as I remember. "Let's go through the home security footage later. Mavis got hold of our contract somehow. I think it was probably Clarence and Lawrence, but I'd like to be sure before I take action."

Wyatt nods, a tight grimace pulling at his lips.

"And speaking of the contract," I say, because there's no point in putting this conversation off—even though Wyatt will get that knowing look in his eye when I admit that he was right and I was wrong. "I think we can terminate it. It won't be necessary any longer."

Wyatt's graying eyebrows fly to his hairline, and he shoots a look at me before turning his eyes to the rearview mirror. "So you're..." he says, trailing off like he doesn't dare ask.

"My husband is in love with me," Holland says in a bland voice. "And I find him tolerable enough to tempt me—"

"Shut up," I say, reaching blindly behind my seat and swatting her legs—except I have to force myself not to smile.

My assistant does no such thing. When I look over at him, he's beaming—the biggest smile I think I've ever seen on him. Something unexpectedly warm and affectionate stirs in my chest, and I speak again.

"Thanks to you, in part," I add to Wyatt, my voice grudging. I'm not good at expressing my emotions, but it should be said. "I appreciate your advice."

And I swear his eyes actually get a little glassy.

By the time we reach the Butterfield building, though, he's regained his composure, as stoic as ever. He drops us off at the entrance to the headquarters—twenty-three stories high—and we pass through the rotating doors. The lobby is nearly empty, thankfully; Holland and I take the elevator up to the employee lounge, where I direct her to the women's changing room.

"This is so nice," she says as she looks around, her eyes wide. "There's exercise equipment over there." She moves to stand closer to me, though, when she sees the people staring —two guys over at the coffee station, three women eating at a small table. Most of the employees know who I am, even vaguely, and a decent amount probably also know that I don't work in this building anymore.

My guess, though, is that they're more interested in the way Holland's fingers are intertwined with mine. She seems to be a hand-holder, and I can't say I hate it.

"Don't get too used to it," I tell her, pulling my hand away. "Now go change. Meet me back here. You have five minutes."

"I have however long I need," she says, rolling her eyes at me. "And you're not going to spontaneously combust if you go too long without bossing someone around. Take a deep breath and fight the urge." Then, before I can respond to her snark, she's gone, disappearing through the door to the locker room.

I shake my head and go into the men's room, debating before I finally decide to take a lightning-fast shower. I feel significantly better after I do, and I make it out of the changing room about ten minutes before Holland appears, also freshly showered.

Office clothing isn't her natural style, but there's something incredibly appealing about the way she wears it; the buttoned-down shirt, the slim-fitting skirt, the heels she probably hates.

Amazing that I can notice these things now instead of pointedly ignoring them.

"Pencil skirts are the worst," she says with a frown on her face as I approach her. "And so are pantyhose. I need to tell Wyatt that."

"I'm sure he'd love to know," I say. "Let's go."

"And the heels—I can walk in them, I guess, but they're just uncomfortable. It feels like my foot is contorting into unnatural shapes."

"Well, you look great," I say dryly.

"Do I?" she says, looking startled.

"Yep." I don't feel the need to deny it—not now. "Something about the buttoned-up look."

"Huh," she says. "Like the sexy librarian thing, kind of?"

Good grief. "I can't talk about this with you right now," I mutter. "Come on."

Her heels *click-click-click* on the floor as we return to the elevators, the *ding!* echoing quietly through the hall. I pull out my employee badge when we get in and scan it before pressing the button for the twenty-third floor.

It still works, which is something, at least. We'll see how long that lasts.

"You should know," I tell her as the elevator begins its ascension, "that I might become very rude up here."

She lets out a loud, theatrical gasp. "You? Rude? *Never.*"

"Believe it or not," I say, a smirk tugging at my lips, "I've never treated you scathingly."

"I know," she says, sounding exasperated now. "You don't need to warn me. I'm prepared, PheePhee."

My head whips toward her so violently that my neck muscles protest. "Excuse me?"

"You said I could call you whatever I want, didn't you?"

I turn my body to face her and advance slowly, stepping closer and closer as she backs up until finally she bumps into the elevator wall.

"I did say that," I tell her in a low voice, "but I spoke under the assumption that you wouldn't abuse my permission." I've put up with a variety of bird names, but I draw the line at *PheePhee*.

"Fine," she says as her eyes sparkle up at me. She wraps her arms around my waist and tilts her head up and to the side; because of her heels, this puts her lips right at my ear. "How do you feel about being called *Husband?*" she whispers.

"Much better," I say as my hands come to rest on her shoulders. Then I let them trail up her neck until they cradle her face. I allow myself to indulge in one display of workplace PDA, pressing my lips softly to hers.

"Should we make out in this elevator?" she says when I lean back again.

Yes. Immediately.

"Probably not," I say with a sigh. "Cameras"—I jerk my chin at the small blinking light in one corner— "and professionalism in general."

"I bet they'd love to watch," she says, turning her gaze to the camera.

"I have no doubt," I say, my lips twitching again. "But it's still a bad idea."

"Fine," she says, but she's smiling too.

When the elevator eases to a stop and the doors open, however, her smile fades as quickly as mine does.

"We're here," I say as I reach for her hand. Then I grimace and offer one last piece of advice before we get out: "Be ready. Things might get uncomfortable."

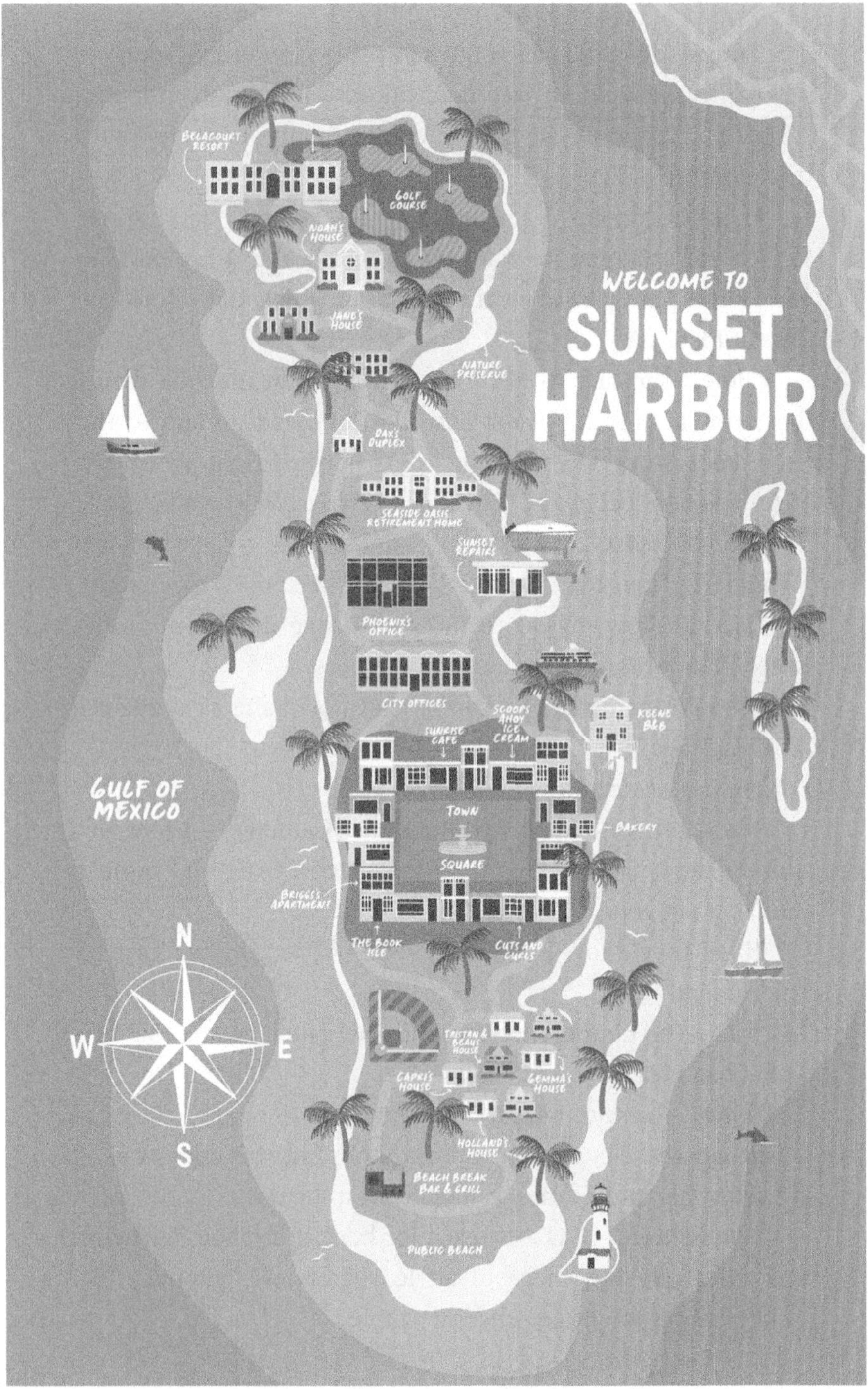

CHAPTER 27

Phoenix

MY GRANDMOTHER OVERSEES her empire from a massive corner office, one with floor-to-ceiling windows, two large couches, and a wet bar.

Clarence's office is right next to hers, and on the other side of his is Lawrence's, even though Lawrence doesn't technically hold an executive position—yet. Their offices aren't on the same level as Mavis's, but they're still nice; so was mine when I worked in this building.

Holland and I pass my cousin's and my uncle's offices on our way to Mavis's, and both of them notice through their windows; Lawrence gets to his feet immediately, looking interested, but Clarence just watches us with narrowed eyes.

I used to wonder why Mavis didn't care to leave the company to her son instead of her grandson, but I think Clarence himself would prefer Lawrence to receive the title. Lawrence would be easy to manipulate from behind the scenes, an easy puppet. Clarence and Mavis both like that.

When we reach the door to Mavis's suite, Wyatt is already there, waiting for us. He has his briefcase in one hand and his large leather folder tucked under the other arm, and the little nod he gives me assures me that everything is ready.

So I don't bother knocking. I'm not here to play nice, and I'm not here to ask permission. She asked to see me anyway;

she knows I'm coming. I simply walk in, Holland close behind me.

And like I thought, Mavis is waiting for me—waiting for us. There are no papers in front of her, and she's not looking at her computer. Her sharp eyes find mine the second we enter; she seems more foreboding when she's sitting behind her desk, and even though this room is full of bright natural light, she makes the whole place feel stifling and oppressive.

"Mavis," I say curtly. She's in a new chair, I notice with interest, one that looks more like a recliner than an actual office chair.

Maybe her health isn't so great after all.

"Hmm," she says, raising one penciled-in eyebrow at me and then turning her gaze on my wife. It's the only greeting we receive, and I don't expect anything else.

"You asked to see us," I say. I straighten my jacket and then approach the desk. "We're here."

Mavis doesn't look back at me, however. She's still examining Holland, her thin lips curled in displeasure, her features a haughty mask.

"Turn," she says in her thin voice, pointing one crooked finger at my wife.

Holland blinks at her. "What?"

"Turn," she says again. "Turn around. Let me look at the woman who sold herself to my grandson."

Holland's face turns red, not with embarrassment but with anger; that little jaw muscle is twitching on the left side, and her normally lively eyes have gone cold. She shoots me a glance and then rotates on the spot. When she's facing Mavis once again, she raises her brows expectantly at my grandmother.

She's cool and composed and Mavis will never, ever see the parts of her that make her who she is. *The woman who sold herself*—I try to swallow my fury, but it continues to rise in my throat, in my neck, spreading over my skin.

Mavis inspects her for several more seconds, but when she finally reacts, it's just to *harrumph*. Then she waves a dismissive hand and says, "You may see yourself out."

"Gladly," Holland mutters, but I grab her arm just as she's turning toward the door.

She does not appreciate this, judging by the glare she sends me.

I loosen my grip. "She stays or I go," I say.

Mavis shifts with irritation, the sun glinting in her iron curls. "Don't be dramatic," she says, her voice impatient. She waves her hand at Holland again. "Get out."

From over by the wet bar, a flash of movement catches my eye, and I realize that her secretary has been in here the whole time. I'm not worried about the secretary or the assistant—also tucked over by the wet bar, I see, and also completely silent. What I want to avoid is causing a scene that would attract the attention of security.

So although there are many, many things I'd like to say or do, I simply give a sardonic little bow. Then I turn away, and together Holland and I head toward the door, where Wyatt is stationed.

"Wait."

I freeze at the bark of Mavis's voice; Holland slows much more reluctantly.

When I look back at my grandmother, she speaks again. "This is hardly the hill to die on," she snaps as her body twitches with anger. "While I'm impressed by your dedication to the Butterfield legacy, you took this too far. I couldn't care less about the state of your supposed marriage, but the fact that you got caught is…sloppy. If I found out, others certainly will."

My fingers curl into fists, but she's not entirely wrong. It was my oversight; I should have expected one of the family would break in and steal the contract.

"I suppose it means nothing to you that our marriage has since become real in every sense of the word," I say. It's not a question, because I know the answer. But I still have to ask.

My grandmother just snorts. "So you slept with a pretty girl. That doesn't—"

"My wife," I spit out through gritted teeth. "She is my *wife*."

"At the moment, perhaps," Mavis says. Then she leans forward and presses a button on her landline. "Marshana, bring in your candidates, please." Then she turns her shrewd, pitiless eyes on Holland. "She's out," she says. "Certainly unfit for the position of partner to an executive, to say nothing of a CEO."

A small knock sounds at the door, and then my mother enters, hunched into a half-bow and followed by four young women.

"You seemed to prefer blonde," Mavis says as she waves in the women—yes, all blonde, all dressed immaculately, all objectively beautiful. "So that's what your mother looked for."

I don't prefer blondes. I prefer Holland.

"You," I say, jerking my chin at the woman nearest me. She has on a tailored tweed pantsuit and diamond earrings that are either wildly expensive or very fake. "What would you do if I put a dead fish in your mailbox?"

Her jaw drops; the other three look at each other, scandalized.

I nod. "And you," I say to the woman next to her, this one with her hair pulled into a sleek ponytail. "Would you ever replace the cream in my Oreos with toothpaste?"

From behind me, Holland snorts—like she's amused all over again by her own prank. But Ponytail's face just shifts from faintly scandalized to faintly disgusted.

"That's very childish," she says.

I nod again, because she's absolutely right. It's very childish. And then, for a moment, I stand perfectly still. I listen to my pulse pounding in my ears and I feel the sting of my fingernails digging into my palms. Then I glance around and catch Wyatt's questioning eye.

I duck my head, answering his silent inquiry.

"Is this your final decision?" I say to Mavis, pulling a still-grinning Holland closer to my side.

Mavis sniffs. "Of course."

I exhale as a surreal wave of relief crashes over me. "In that case," I say, and Wyatt hurries forward, presenting me with an envelope, "I'd like to formally tender my resignation. Consider this my two weeks' notice." I stride forward and drop the envelope on Mavis's desk.

And although she barely moves, for the first time, a crack appears in her facade; her ancient face twitches with something like disbelief and anger before returning to its cold mask.

"Don't be stupid," she says. She swipes at her desk, pushing the envelope off and sending it to the floor. "I'll pretend this lapse in judgment never happened."

"Pretend whatever you'd like," I say with a shrug as something jubilant and free rises in my chest. "I'm still resigning." I can feel the adrenaline racing through my veins, the twitch of nervous energy, my fight-or-flight preparing for the precarious, unprecedented situation I've put myself in.

"Listen here," Mavis snaps, and her mask disappears entirely, leaving open anger in its place. "You can't—"

"I think you'll find that I can," I cut her off. I vaguely

notice the feeling of Holland's arm looping through mine, an anchor I didn't realize I needed. "Feel free to email me with any further questions," I go on. "I'll swing by HR to start the paperwork."

When we turn our backs on Mavis, she's gaping, mouthing wordlessly. When we leave the office, I feel an immense burden falling away from my shoulders.

And when we pass Lawrence and Clarence in the hallway, I could swear I'm taller than I was when I went in.

"SO WHAT YOU'RE saying is that the qualifications for being your wife include a tolerance for dead fish and toothpaste-filled Oreos. Did I understand that correctly?" Holland says as soon as she and I and Wyatt enter the elevator.

I don't let myself smile. "Wouldn't you like to know?"

"And were you ever going to tell me you were quitting?" she goes on, more serious now.

"I was," I say, looking over at her. "I just wasn't sure when it would happen, so I held off." Then, turning to Wyatt, I add, "We'll look through the house's security footage tonight."

"Is there anything else you need to do over here before we go back to Sunset Harbor?" Holland asks after an odd moment of hesitation.

"No," I say. Then, frowning at the way she's playing with the ends of her hair, I ask, "Do you?"

"Yeah, actually," she says. "If we have time."

I'm about to ask her what she wants to do, but Wyatt speaks first. "Why don't you two take the car, then, and I'll handle the paperwork here? I need to gather some things from my office as well, so I'll get a ride back to the ferry later."

"That's fine," I say vaguely, my gaze still on Holland. Her face is pale, but her eyes are determined, and her lips are set in a stubborn line. I want to ask what's going on, but I force myself to wait; something tells me she might not want to explain while Wyatt is present.

The second we get in the car, though, I speak.

"Where are we going?" I say.

"Before I tell you," she says, shooting me a stern glance, "you have to be nice."

My instinct is to protest that I'm always nice, but then I look more closely at her; she's wearing a bossy, severe expression, but it doesn't reach her eyes. In her eyes I find anxiety or maybe even fear—a level of hesitance and vulnerability that have me agreeing before I even realize it.

"Yeah," I say in a hoarse voice. "I'll be nice."

Her shoulders rise and fall as she takes a deep breath. "I think..." she says, trailing off. She wears a faraway look for just a moment, but when she turns her gaze back to me, her expression is clear once more. "Yes. I think I want to go to the river."

"The river?" I say.

She nods. "The river. The one where—" She breaks off, swallows, and then speaks again. "The one where we crashed." She pauses as my heart begins to beat faster. "The one where Trev died. I want to go there."

CHAPTER 28

Holland

PHOENIX LOOKS PRETTY MUCH as dumbfounded as I expected. To his credit, though, nothing like pity or sympathy enters his eyes; he doesn't patronize me or discourage me. All he says is "Right now?"

"Yeah," I say. "Right now." Because honestly, I don't know when I'll be able to work up the nerve again. It's easy to tell myself *Now isn't a good time* when I'm over on the island. But I'm here right now, I have time, I have a car—and, maybe the most motivating factor, I just watched Phoenix quit his job with his psycho family.

It was strangely empowering. If he could do that, I can visit a body of water that just happens to hold bad memories.

"All right," he says, nodding slowly. Then he pulls his seatbelt on and starts the car. "But Wyatt will kill me if I let you go swimming in the clothing he painstakingly picked out."

"I don't even know if I want to get in the water yet," I say with a scoff. "I just want to go see it for now. I'll decide the rest when I get there." I pause and then ask, "Do you not think I can handle it?"

"Of course you can," he says immediately. "I'm just surprised." His eyes flit over my face. "Are you sure you want me to come?"

"I don't mind," I say with a little shrug. I wouldn't want anyone else to be there, definitely, but… "If it's you, I'm not opposed."

He was there. He understands. And he won't judge me for however I react to being back in that place—a place I haven't been since the crash.

"Have you gone at all?" I say. "Since then?"

He nods again. "I have. A few times."

"How was it?" I say, swallowing.

"The first time was a little rough," he admits, "but after that it was fine. I go once a year."

On the anniversary of the crash, probably, but I don't ask. I'm too nervous, too on edge.

And he seems to be aware of how I'm feeling, because he doesn't ask any more questions or say anything else. He just eyes me carefully and then looks forward again, and I'm grateful.

I want to do this before I change my mind.

We drive in silence, and I can't stop fidgeting; I'm twirling my hair and bouncing my leg and still the restless energy inside me builds. Slowly the scenery out the window grows more and more familiar, and it's both strange and sad to be back in a place that used to feel like home but has since become the literal stuff of nightmares. I flex my hands and force my legs to still as I try to regulate my breathing, but it's no good; my heart beats faster and faster and faster, and there's nothing I can do to stop it.

Phoenix, on the other hand, seems fine. I take a second to look more closely at him, but even his more hidden tells are absent; there's no muscle twitching in his jaw, no furrow in his brow. His hand is casual on the steering wheel, and he looks for all the world like we're just out for a summer drive. He doesn't have to search for directions, either; it's clear he knows exactly where we're going, because he finds the turnoff with ease and proceeds confidently down a road I've never taken.

The car dips and bumps over the packed earth as we drive, maybe half a mile, until we reach a gravel lot. The wheels crunch as we enter and find a spot among the smattering of cars already here; a gaggle of teenagers spill out of an SUV, all of them in their swimsuits, laughing and shouting.

Part of me is envious of them, so rowdy and carefree. I would have loved to come to a river like this one in high school. I liked swimming, I liked boating, I liked hanging out with my friends. But the other part of me wants to shout at them to be respectful, to scream *This river stole my brother's life and never gave it back.* I want to ask them how on earth they can play when something so horrible happened here.

I don't get out of the car immediately, even after Phoenix has parked and killed the engine. I stare around the parking lot instead, although I don't know why or what I'm looking for. I'm stalling, I guess. I let myself linger for a minute or two, and then I get out. Phoenix follows suit.

He walks behind me as we cross the parking lot. These heels were not made for gravel, so every step I take is wobbly, and I have no doubt we look like idiots. We've rolled up to a river in skirts and suits and ties. But I press on anyway, and Phoenix follows, not saying a word. We walk until gravel turns to dirt and sand and the river sprawls into view.

I come to a stop without thinking. It's a beautiful place, really, one that looks deceptively harmless. This is no raging river with angry undercurrents and fierce tides; it's medium-sized at most, meandering and lazy rather than swift. This is the kind of place people bring rafts on sun-drenched summer afternoons. I can see the bridge, too, not here but a ways down; I turn and begin the trek down the trail that runs parallel to the banks, my steps heavy but my heart frantic. I feel like pure chaos inside, spinning and whirling and too big for my skin—cut my palm and not blood but a tornado would leak out.

A tornado that could whisk me away to a place where Trev isn't dead, maybe—an alternate dimension—a place where he's alive and happy and he and I and Phoenix are at this same river together, laughing and splashing each other and being stupid.

But there is no such place.

I swallow thickly and walk a little faster, further and further until at last we reach the section of river with the bridge. My heart is a piece of whirring machinery, automatic and impossibly active even though it feels so broken. It beats and beats and beats as I turn toward Phoenix and hold onto his arm, lifting each foot in turn and removing my shoes. He stands steady until I'm done, at which point he holds out his hands wordlessly. I pass him the heels with a nod of thanks; he nods back, and then we make our way toward the water.

The breeze is warm and pleasant; from down the river I can hear faint laughter. But all I can really focus on is the water.

Why does it look the same? How is that possible?

How is it possible that the water beneath the bridge looks the same as the rest of the river? The place where Trev died isn't the same as everywhere else. It's tainted, foul. But the river flows cheerfully on, going about its business, Trev's memory swept away long ago like driftwood in a current.

It isn't until I look around that I realize I'm still approaching the water. And even though I wasn't sure if I'd want to get in, I suddenly know that I have to. I have to, and I won't be able to stop myself even if I try. So I step gingerly down the bank, footprints in the dirt and sand, until I reach the river.

Just my toes, at first. I can feel Phoenix behind me more than I can see him or hear him, but he doesn't speak or try to stop me. I take one step in, and then another, the water chilly against my ankles and then my calves and then my knees. The sandy bottom is sharp with pebbles and bits of rock and debris, but I barely notice.

When the river hits the hem of my skirt, I stop.

I look down at my clothes. I hate them. I mean, they're pretty enough. But they're not me, and they're not comfortable, and they belong to the world of Phoenix's family. They don't belong to my world or to this river. So I reach down and unbutton my shirt; from behind me I hear a noise of surprise from Phoenix, but I ignore it. I pull off the silk blouse and pass it back to Phoenix; he takes it without a word. Then I reach around for the zipper of my skirt, finagling it down until I can step out of that too, and then the pantyhose.

I take off everything until I'm left in nothing but my underwear and camisole.

When I turn to Phoenix, his eyebrows are up in surprise, but he still doesn't say anything; he just holds out his hand for the skirt and tights, his gaze darting up and down the riverbank, probably to check if anyone can see. When I've passed him the clothes, he steps around me, placing himself between me and the sight of anyone who drives across the bridge.

"That's looking better," he says quietly, his eyes on my now-bare knee. The bruising has gone down significantly.

"It is," I say. Then I continue on in my underthings, well aware that this is a weird thing to do.

I do it anyway.

My emotions rise with the water as I continue—a knotted jumble of fear and guilt and anticipation and grief up to my knees, up to my waist, up to my ribcage. When I'm about to go even further, I feel Phoenix's gentle tug on the back of my camisole, and I look over my shoulder at him.

"I'm not sure how deep this goes or if there are any drop offs," he says, his voice still soft. "It was pretty deep back then."

I stay where I am, looking around at the water surrounding me, because he's right. "Do you want to know a secret?" I say softly.

"Mmm." A low hum of assent.

"I'm not actually afraid of the water."

When I look at him, his dark brows are raised.

I nod. "The water itself doesn't bother me. What I'm scared of..." I inhale deeply and then let the breath out. "Is all the things the water makes me feel. The things it makes me remember."

Phoenix inclines his head slowly. "I understand that."

I know he does.

I've been running from those feelings and those memories for years, searching for something I'll never find because it doesn't exist.

There is no place on earth where Trev is still alive. He's gone. He's gone, but I'm not. That's the world I live in. And the emotions that have been chasing me, haunting me in my dreams—ignoring them won't change anything.

So I take another deep breath, hold it in my lungs, pinch my nose shut.

Then I crouch down and submerge myself completely, the kiss of chilled water on my lips and in my hair. I know a brief moment of panic, mind-numbing and all-consuming. But I force myself to wait one more second.

Then I rise—and I am reborn.

"YOU'RE ALL WET."

"Yes." Phoenix's dry voice sounds in my ear, his arms wrapped around my waist from behind, his chin resting on my shoulder as the water laps at our legs. "Water has that effect."

"You're so hilarious," I say, rolling my eyes and folding my arms over his clasped hands. "How did I ever live without your wit?"

"I've always lived without yours," he says, and I can hear his smirk. "You've never been funny."

I gasp and spin around to face him. "I am literally the funniest person you know"—he presses a quick kiss to my lips—"with an incredible personality"—he sneaks another kiss as his smirk morphs into something more real—"and a real winning attitude."

"Are you cold, sweetheart?" he murmurs, pulling me closer. "Are you cold, funniest person I know?"

"Yes," I admit, and he lets go of me immediately. He takes my hand and turns toward the shore, and I follow, wading through the water until we've reached the shallows. Then he lets go and emerges from the river in a few strides, leaning down to grab his suit coat from where it rests on the bank.

When he reaches me again, he drapes the jacket over my shoulders.

"There," he says as I burrow into the coat. He looks down at me for a moment, his gaze warm as it flits over my face. Then he adds, "I'm proud of you."

"Thank you," I say, shuffling closer to him, and he wraps his arms around me once more. "I'm proud of me too."

"You should be." I watch his throat bob as he swallows. "Hey," he says suddenly, his voice hoarse. "Should we get married?"

I blink up at him. "I don't know how to tell you this, but...we're already married. You must have missed it."

"I *meant*," he says as I snicker like an immature child, "should we—you know—" He swallows again. "Should we have a real wedding?"

Oh. My eyes widen as the idea sinks in, and I reach up, cradling his face—with its hesitant, unsure expression—in my palms.

"Do you *want* a real wedding?" I say.

"I want you," he answers frankly. "And...I guess I want the world to know you're mine."

"Ah," I say. "So it's a caveman ownership possession thing."

"No," he says, looking frustrated now. "I'm not a caveman."

"You've thrown me over your shoulder, dragged me along behind you, and called me *yours*. Sounds like—"

"You *are* mine," he says as his arms tighten around my waist, his eyes glinting. "And I regret none of the other stuff."

"Exactly," I say. "Which makes you a caveman. Because look, Husband"—his gaze heats—"I'm not yours. Okay? I'm mine. I belong to me. If I choose to give myself to you, fine," I go on, "but I do not *belong* to anyone."

"Wrong," he breathes. He lifts one hand and runs his thumb slowly over my bottom lip, and I shiver despite my jacket. "These are mine," he says. Then he trails one finger down my jaw. "This is mine. This" —he wraps his arm tighter around my waist, pressing my body against his—"is mine. And this…" Last of all he moves his hand and touches my chest, just over my heart. "This is mine too. Your heart is mine."

"Only if I give it to you," I insist.

He dips his head. "Then give it to me," he whispers against my lips. "All of it—all of you. I want all of you."

But I know, deep down, that all of me is already his.

"Let's get married," I say, kissing him lightly. "Again."

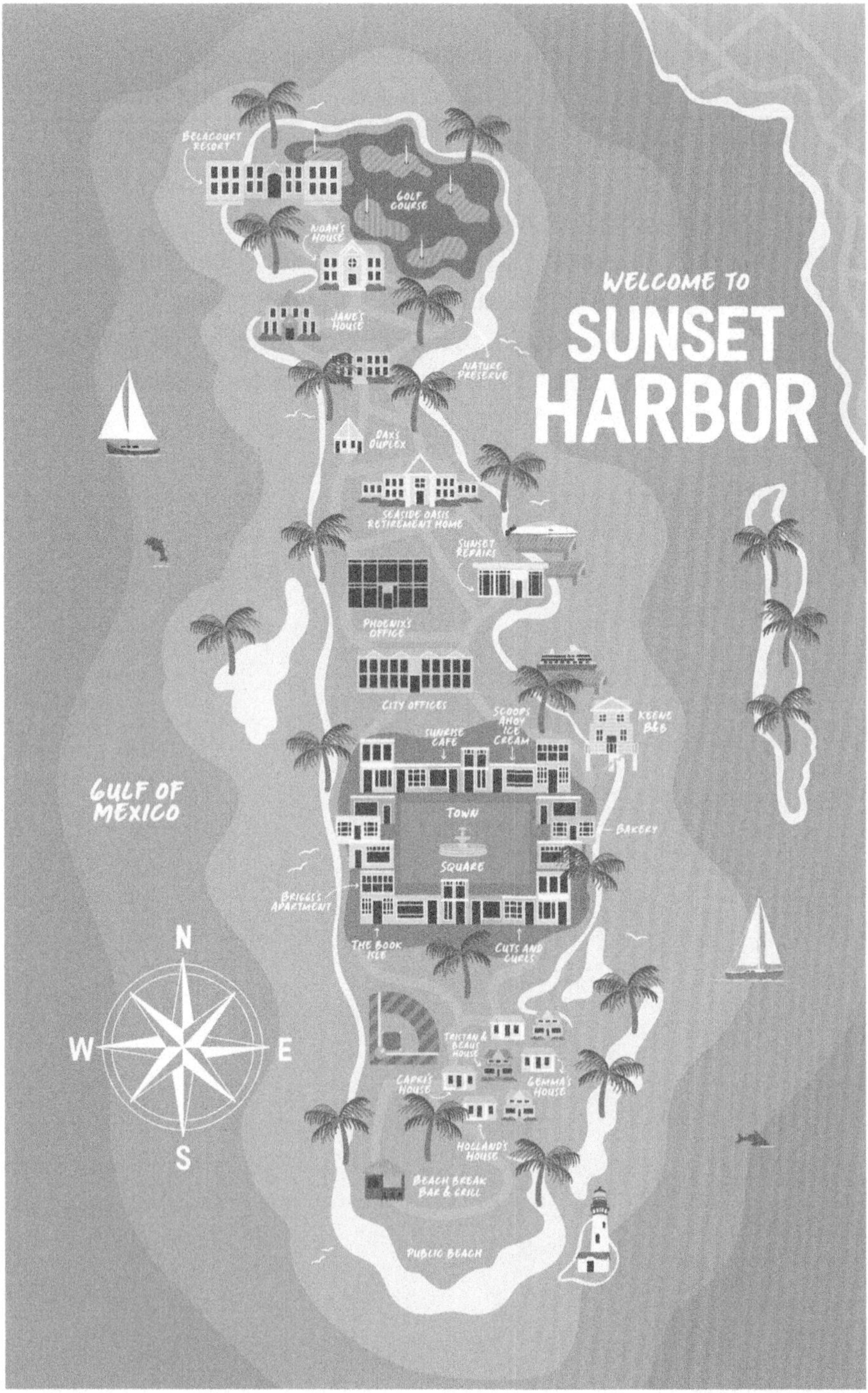

CHAPTER 29

Phoenix

MY SECOND WEDDING to Holland Park takes place on a hot day in August, and the entire town is there.

This was not my idea, for the record. I was given very little say; all I really got to choose was my suit and my groomsmen.

Maggie is Holland's maid of honor, and she looks supremely pleased with herself the whole day; she keeps saying she knew this was going to happen. Nana Lu sits in the front row along with Holland's mom, and although her mom is smiling, Nana is absolutely beaming.

Wyatt is my best man. The Butterfields were invited after significant debate, but my mother is the only one who came —my mother and, shockingly, Lawrence. He's jovial but smug, while Marshana Butterfield-Park pretends to dab nonexistent tears out of her eyes so that she can appear as the quintessential loving mother.

I don't know how accurate that is, since she turned out to be the one who stole the marriage contract from my home study and passed it to Mavis. She overheard my conversation with Holland while we were leaving the family dinner we attended, when I mentioned the contract.

So in a twisted way, I'm glad she's here. I'm glad she sees

Holland and I together. As Holland said—*"I sort of want to rub it in her face."*

I don't miss Butterfield at all. What I miss is the feeling of working hard, achieving goals, and sinking my teeth into problems until I solve them. Which is why, as of a few weeks ago, my new business is officially up and running: Park Logistics and Fulfillment. Wyatt and I have been working round the clock to make it happen, following the plan we laid out shortly after Mavis released her will to the family. I knew even then that I needed to be prepared for things to go belly-up in Butterfield.

Mavis had some scathing words to say about my new business venture and even tried to sue, citing breach of contract, but the company's lawyer went through my non-compete and pointed out that I was only forbidden from starting another sanitary or paper goods company. My logistics company is perfectly allowed.

That lawyer works for me now, and I'm happy to say that while his benefits package allows him to see a therapist as often as he needs, he's not nearly as miserable working with me as he was working with Mavis.

We're a small business still, and it will take time for us to grow—especially enough that I can start down the humanitarian road I'd like to take. But we'll do it.

Most of my new employees are here today, sitting in the chairs lined up on the beach—along with everyone else we know and then some. Wyatt, Beau, and Dax stand next to me, and waiting for Holland on the other side are Maggie, Cat, and Jane. Wyatt's gaze follows Marlyss Gapmeyer, the owner of Beach Break Bar and Grill—something I've noticed happening a lot recently. Beau is waving to Gemma Sawyer, and although Dax isn't a big waver, his eyes are on Ivy Brooks. Beau's brother, Tristan, lives on the island too, and he's here with Capri Collins. I see Briggs Dalton keeping a low profile in the back row, and next to him is the actress Presley James.

Yep. Everyone on earth is at this wedding. But I only have eyes for one: the woman who appears as if by magic and begins walking down the sandy aisle toward me, her arm linked through her father's.

And she's gorgeous. Breathtaking. Wearing the same dress she wore for our pictures, but it looks different today, and I know why—because she's so radiantly happy.

She's *that* happy—to be marrying *me.*

Hey, Trev, I tell my best friend. *I'm marrying your sister. I never told you this, but we made out in a closet once. It was an accident.* I let my eyes flick briefly to the cloudless blue sky, and then they're pulled back to Holland. *She makes me crazy, but I can't imagine not having her in my life. So we're brother-in-laws now.*

And I swear I can almost feel him by my side, another groomsman.

"Hi, Husband," Holland whispers when she reaches me.

I smile, taking her hands in mine as we stand beneath the white trellis. "Hi, Wife."

We look in unison at the same officiant who married us at City Hall; he looks much happier today than he did then, possibly because Holland isn't wearing black mourning clothes.

"We've gathered here today to celebrate again the union of Holland Park and Phoenix Park..." he begins.

Holland and I look at each other, and then we smile.

"FAVORITE ANIMAL."

"Hmm," Holland says from where she lies next to me. My arm is around her, and half her body is draped over mine, her head on my shoulder, her arm flung over my chest, our legs tangled together. "I think...penguin."

I tilt my chin, tracing my fingers up and down her side. "I think mine is probably a tiger."

"Favorite movie?" she says.

"*Matrix*," I say. My eyes drift absently over the ceiling of our hotel room as I think. "Or—no. *Raiders of the Lost Ark*."

"I'm a big Harrison Ford fan," she says.

"What would your movie be?"

"Probably *Father of the Bride*." Her breath ghosts over my skin as she speaks. "Or *Clueless*."

"I've never seen either of those," I say reluctantly.

"You will," she says, turning her head to grin up at me. "We'll watch them both. Many, many times."

Even though we were already married, we never had a proper honeymoon. Neither of us wanted to go back to the honeymoon suite at the Vida Grande, so we picked a different hotel on the mainland instead. We'll head home in the morning, and then it's back to the grind—my job, Holland's, our life.

I smile into her hair, inhaling deeply. "You always smell like peppermint and vanilla," I say.

"It's because I stock up on my favorite scent every winter," she says with a laugh. "I get enough of the soap and the lotion and the body spray to last the whole year."

"I like it." I pause and then go on. "By the way—I got you a wedding present."

"Did you?" she says, pulling away so she can look at me better. "I didn't get you anything."

"I did," I say with a nod. "It should be at home when we get back."

"What is it?" she says, and I grin at the excited look on her face.

"I'm not telling," I say. "It's a surprise. But you'll like it."

She's not convinced. But when we get home the next day and she sees what's in our living room—I had Wyatt set it up —her eyes go wide.

"It's a dog bed," she says faintly.

"Not just that," I say with a smirk. "It's a *human-sized* dog bed."

She stares at the large plushy bed; she looks at me. Then she laughs, and it's the best sound I've ever heard.

"What's the verdict?" I say, flopping down on the giant plushy pillow and pulling her with me.

"Good," she says, her voice still breathless with laughter. "Great. I love it." She kisses me. "I love *you*."

I kiss her back, sliding my hands into her hair and relishing the feeling of her lips against mine. "I'd hope so," I murmur as my lips move to her jaw. "Because you're mine, sweetheart."

"And?" she says, gasping as I reach her neck.

I smile. "And I'm yours."

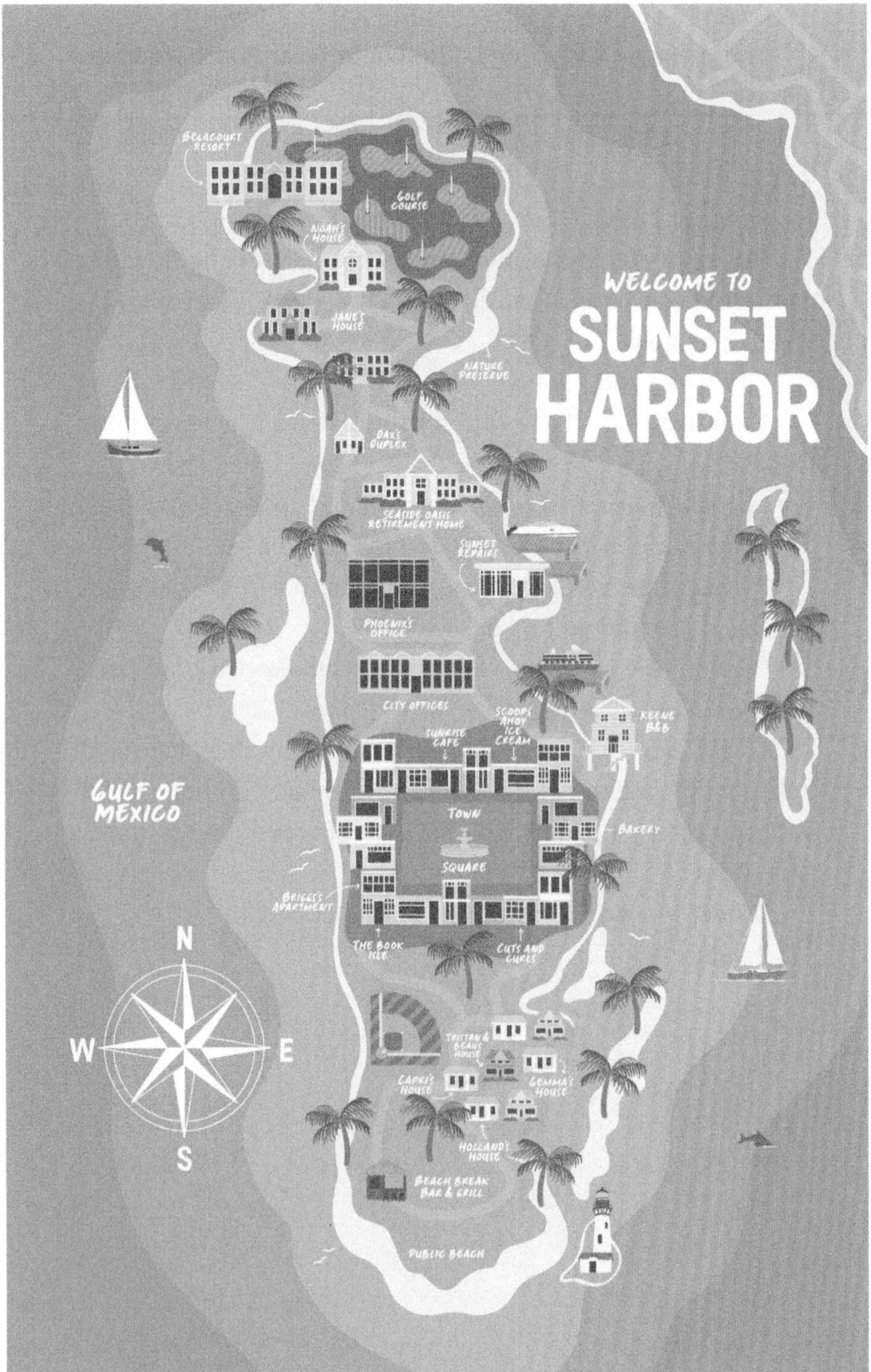

EPILOGUE

Ten Years Later

Holland

THE WATER IS A LITTLE CHILLY, but we all get in anyway.

Aeri's long, dark hair is pulled into two braids that drip water down her back, and even though I've told her twice now to stop splashing her brother, she keeps going. Trevor doesn't seem to mind, so I guess I shouldn't either; he just giggles from his perch in Phoenix's arms.

"Why are your kids so much better behaved than mine?" I say to Cat as we sit on the shallow bank of the river, water lapping at our legs.

Cat snorts and glances at where her husband, Noah, is chasing their kids through the knee-high water. "You should see them at bedtime," she says. "Noah included."

I look over at Phoenix, staring unashamedly as he lifts Trevor over his head, pretending to toss him. Trevor shrieks with laughter, his chubby toddler cheeks so perfectly squishy, and from below Aeri grabs at Phoenix's legs, begging for her turn.

"Hold on, hold on," he says, grinning down at her. He looks over his shoulder at me, and I stand up, wading over to take Trevor.

"Come here, sweet boy," I say, scooping him out of Phoenix's hands and into my arms.

"Yes," Cat says from behind me. "Come to Aunt Cat."

I laugh and pass Trevor to her.

"You're such a handsome boy!" she coos, tickling Trevor's belly. "You're so handsome!"

"What about me?" Noah says, slowing down as he passes us.

"You're so handsome too," she says to him, still cooing in that same high-pitched voice. "Such a big handsome boy, running all by himself—"

"Yeah, yeah," he says with a grin, and then he's off again, chasing after the kids. Cat trails after him, still making faces at Trevor.

"Hey," Phoenix says to me, approaching me with Aeri in his arms. She's four now, old enough to push for experience and independence but young enough that she still loves being held and carried. "Why aren't you calling me handsome?"

"Because your ego already knows no bounds," I say dryly. "You've never once doubted your own attractiveness, Pelican."

His jaw drops as he wades closer. "What did you just call me?"

"*Pelican*," I say, enunciating the word. "A giant water bird."

He comes to a stop next to me, his eyes sparkling. "I

don't remember the last time you gave me a bird name, Amsterdam."

"It seemed fitting today," I say as my pulse picks up speed.

One dark brow quirks at me. "Want to explain?"

"Because today I'm a bird too," I say. I swallow and then go on. "I'm a stork. Carrying your baby."

The emotions that flit over his face are priceless—he's dumbfounded for a full second, his jaw hanging open. Then he throws back his head and laughs, setting Aeri down; she runs off to play with Cat and Noah and their kids.

"That's the cheesiest thing you've ever said," Phoenix says, still laughing as he steps closer and puts his arms around me. "Are you sure? Did you take a test?"

I make a face at him.

"You took *two* tests," he corrects himself, his smile widening. "Got it." He presses a kiss to my lips, to my nose, to my forehead. "Another little person," he whispers.

I nod. "Due late March."

"Amazing," he says, glancing down at my stomach. "Congratulations, Stork."

"Congratulations, Pelican," I say, smiling. "Want to be iffy parents and feed our kids ice cream on the way home?" I pause and then go on, "Because I've been craving ice cream lately."

"And the truth comes out," he says as something playful enters his eyes. "All right. Ice cream."

When we leave an hour or so later, we go with Trevor and Aeri in our arms. We walk slowly out of the water, our eyes on the path we're about to walk, sand and dirt sticking to our wet feet.

We move forward together, our babies held close, our friends at our sides—

And we don't look back.

THANK you for reading *Beauty and the Beach!* If you loved this book and want to see what Holland and Phoenix are up to in the future (hint: there are pranks involved), click here! Please also consider leaving a review; it helps more than you know! If you want to return to Sunset Harbor (you totally do!), you can read about actress Presley James and Briggs Dalton, the sexy nerd she falls for, in *One Happy Summer*—coming July 24, 2024!

FALLING FOR SUMMER

Summer Ever After by Kortney Keisel

Walker + Jane

Beachy Keen by Kasey Stockton

Noah + Cat

Plotting Summer by Jess Heileman

Tristan + Capri

Summer Tease by Martha Keyes

Beau + Gemma

Beauty and the Beach by Gracie Ruth Mitchell

Phoenix + Holland

One Happy Summer by Becky Monson

Briggs + Presley

Rebel Summer by Cindy Steel

Dax + Ivy

ALSO BY GRACIE RUTH MITCHELL

City of Love (#2)

STANDALONES

No Room in the Inn

ACKNOWLEDGMENTS

This entire series would not have been possible without the dedication and hard work of my fellow authors: Martha Keyes, Kasey Stockton, Jess Heileman, Kortney Keisel, Cindy Steel, and Becky Monson. I lucked out big time, getting to work with them. They're phenomenal authors and amazing at their craft!

The lads of Scribere Ferro (Latin, the meaning of which I'm still unclear on) are my cheerleaders and the ones who tell me I'm allowed to take a break. They're also the ones I discuss K-dramas with in the middle of the night; aka they are irreplaceable. My early readers and author/Bookstagram friends pumped me up to keep going when I felt like giving up.

I'm hugely grateful for my readers. I am literally living my dream with this job, and it wouldn't be possible without everyone who picks my books up. It also wouldn't be possible without my family. They are everything.

And to my God, my eternal thanks—He has always heard the songs I cannot sing.

ABOUT THE AUTHOR

Gracie Ruth Mitchell lives in a little Idaho town with her family, her dog, and the characters in her head. She loves that her job involves playing make believe—and working in her pajamas. When she's not writing, you can find her hanging out with her people, bingeing Asian dramas, and daydreaming about all the stories she wants to tell.